Isosceles Triangle

Robert L Mason

authorHOUSE®

AuthorHouse™ UK Ltd.
500 Avebury Boulevard
Central Milton Keynes, MK9 2BE
www.authorhouse.co.uk
Phone: 08001974150

First published by AuthorHouse 9/21/2009

ISBN: 978-1-4389-9998-2 (sc)

To Mary

This is a second book of a trilogy. The first, "The Black Diamond" tells of Charlie Forbes' adventures during the Second World War and how he came to meet and fall in love with the Robinson Twins, Susan and Lucy. I hope that you will read and enjoy it before you read this book.

The Isosceles Triangle, continues the story after Charlie's Prologue.

Contents

Illustrations

Maps

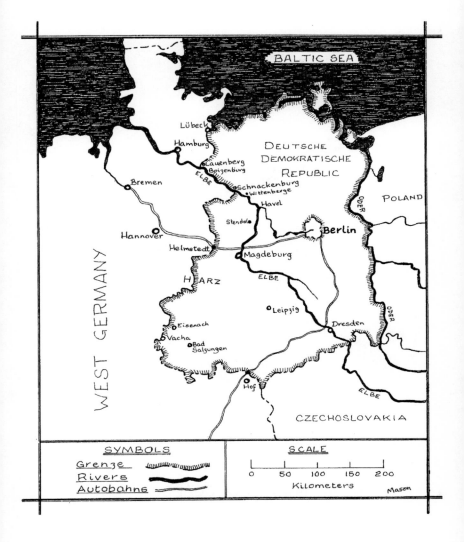

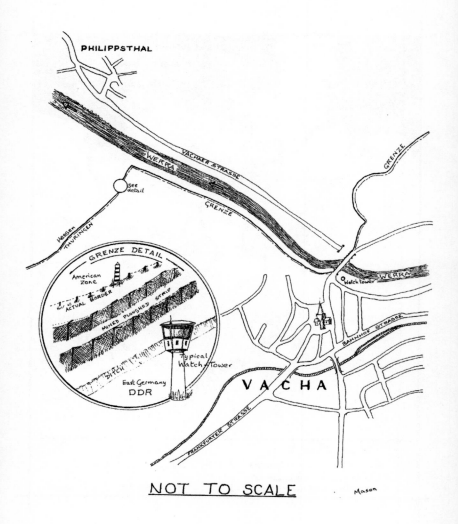

PHILIPPSTHAL

WERRA

VACHER STRASSE

GRENZE

See detail

Hessen
THÜRINGEN

GRENZE

GRENZE DETAIL

American
Zone

ACTUAL BORDER

MINED PLOUGHED STRIP

DITCH

East Germany
DDR

Typical
Watch-Tower

Watch tower

WERRA

BAHNHOF STRASSE

VACHA

FRANKFURTER STRASSE

NOT TO SCALE

Mason

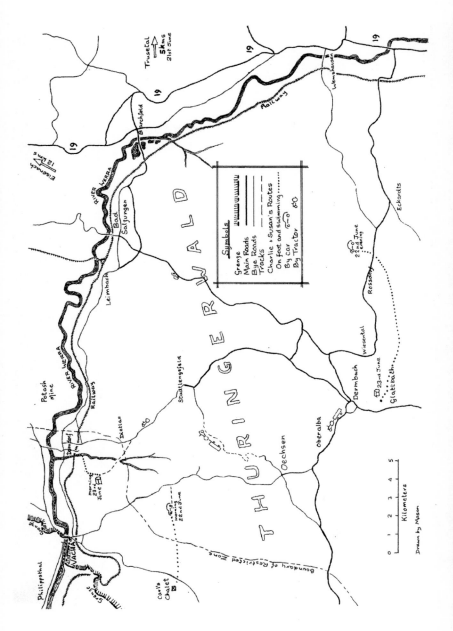

ix

Prologue by Charlie Forbes

Since the publication of the book by Robert Mason called 'The Black Diamond', my son, Charles, has persuaded me to write some explanation of my early life. I have had occasion to correct some of the detail and impressions in this book and now that his second book, The Isosceles Triangle, has been published Charles wants me to point out how the second book is affected by the first.

It is true that, by a wild coincidence, I met the Robinson twins again at Blackpool in 1937. We had met the previous year in Cleethorpes, my aunt's home town. I loved my aunt, Peggy, and used to spend two weeks of the summer staying with her. When our home was bombed later in the war, my mother went to live there.

The meeting in Blackpool changed my life and that of the twins also. The description of the meeting in the gardener's shed at their boarding school has been exaggerated by Mason. I suspect, to sell his book. However Susan and Lucy's father, Sir Hugo, blamed me for their expulsion from St. Hilda's school, despite their headmistress finding them unmanageable.

I should explain that the twins are identical. They have always had fun causing confusion and some people think that it is impossible, after close acquaintance, to mistake their identities but I know otherwise.

In 1938 Hugo, more in desperation than love, and on his brother, Frank's, advice sent his daughters to a Swiss finishing school. When the frontiers were closed a year later, they were forced to remain there until the end of the war in 1945. Their mother, Violet, was killed and Hugo sustained injuries in the Manchester blitz when their home was bombed.

I am the son of Jack and Eliza Forbes. I was brought up in Grimsby. Until he was killed at Dunkirk in 1940 my father owned three steam drifters. Two of his vessels were sunk in the battle. I was skipper of the King of Diamonds and my Dad had The Ace. My boat was hit and the boiler blew up. Both my mates were killed but I survived and managed to get to Antwerp in the small dinghy. Here I was befriended by the owner of a Rhine barge, Hans Zanten, and also by 'Abe', Abraham Goldstein, who with his wife, granddaughter and two teenaged daughters of a friend who had been interned, were secretly travelling on the barge, La Tulipe, to Basel in Switzerland. I joined them as a crew member. Hans and I became good friends.

Knowing the twins were at a Swiss school near Basel, and hoping they had not been sent home before the outbreak of war, I set out to walk from Strasbourg, where I left the barge, to the small town of Breiten. It was a perilous journey. At the Swiss border I had to teach myself to breach the German mine - field. My luck was in and I found the school and was delighted to discover the twins were still there.

The school was in a beautiful mansion owned and run by Marlene Lescault, assisted by Ursula Koch – always known as Koch. I was given accommodation above the old stables on the estate. Because the building was a distance from the mansion, I knew nothing of the problems the school was going through. Due to lack of fees coming in from the remaining girls, Marlene was persuaded by Emil Kramer, her banker-friend, to stage elaborate cabarets. These were a big success and some of the German officers attending these parties became involved with the young ladies at the school.

An expedition was arranged by Emil to Lake Constance which was greeted with great enthusiasm by the girls. I was persuaded to go too. The captain of the boat, waiting for us at the quay, was Carl Wogart. He had met and fallen in love with Lucy at one of the parties. None of us realised that the outing had been arranged to kidnap the eight girls and take them to Germany. When Carl realised that Lucy was one of the party, he thwarted Emil's plan. Emil and Marlene were imprisoned.

With the help of Abe, who was a very rich man, the school became a home for young girl refugees until the end of the war. Later I became involved in MI6 working for David Brown, who was in charge of the operation to set up a life-line for airmen shot down over Germany. It was dangerous work. The slow trickle of men needing help became a flood. My job was to get them across the border into France. Susan often helped me and one night we were captured by a German patrol. We owe everything to Carl who smuggled us back across the border into Switzerland.

As the war drew to a close we made our way back to 'Blighty' but not before I had married Susan. A short holiday in Cannes did nothing to allay Lucy's misery. When they were girls they had always vowed they would never marry but that is another story. Needless to say Lucy became jealous to the point of insanity. You may think me naïve but I only found out much later that she had deep feelings for me.

The Robinson home, still in ruins after the blitz, had been abandoned by Hugo who had taken up residence in a nearby hotel. To my shame, Hugo and I quarrelled soon after Susan, Lucy and I had moved in with him. The atmosphere in the hotel was poisonous, so I decided to spend some time in Cleethorpes with my Mum and Aunt.

No sooner had I reached there, than a letter from Susan informed me that Hugo had had a stroke. Naturally I returned to Manchester as quickly as possible, which is where Mason takes up the story again.

1 Manchester and Cleethorpes

His train was late, very late. "Would they still be waiting? He must meet the new man in his mother's life." With these thoughts Charlie leant from the carriage window, his eyes watering, as it drew alongside the platform. The sharp breeze from the North Sea had turned the recent April shower to sleet. In the gloom of evening it was almost impossible to see through the locomotive's steam.

"Mum", Charlie shouted as he stepped out of the coach. "Hello Mum, Aunt," giving both of them a kiss and a hug. Next Charlie found himself looking down on the man. He remembered his Mum telling him that she and Bert were the same age..

"A bit of an uncut diamond," she had explained.

"Not like Dad," Charlie thought. He hoped that she knew what she was doing but who was he to judge? She deserved some happiness. He moved forwards.

"This is Bert, Bert Higgins," his mother said.

"Hello Bert, I'm Charlie," shaking his hand. Bert's grip was as strong as his own.

"Bert helped me a lot when I was trying to get news of you dear. I'll tell you all about it later. Let's go to the new chippy. It's here, just across the road," Eliza said.

"OK Mum, suits me."

Back at his Aunt Peggy's home, which Charlie remembered so well as a boy, the four of them had a good-night drink of hot whisky and water. Charlie was amused to see Bert and his mother sharing the best room. His aunt was in his old room. He wondered if Peggy still had the old picture of 'Stags at Dawn' over the chest. He was to sleep in the tiny attic. In the darkness he could just make out the black shadow of the pier where he had first met the twins and where it all began so long ago. He went to sleep thinking about all the things that had happened to him in the last few days, from Paris to Cleethorpes, the one still in turmoil after the chaos of war and the liberation and the other undamaged and placid; it was almost a dream.

On the following day Charlie went to the Admiralty office in Kingston. They turned up the records of the losses sustained at Dunkirk by the boats from the Humber. They were considerable. Of all the small vessels which had gone from the ports of England, half had never returned but in spite of that over three hundred thousand men were rescued. It was a miracle. Charlie filled in a large form, with help from an officer, and signed it as a claim on the government for their losses. There was also compensation for the subsequent loss of the 'Queen of Diamonds' which sank at her mooring after an air raid in 1941.

"Where were you throughout the war?" queried the officer. "Did you finish up in a concentration camp? Because if you did you will be due a lot of back-pay."

"I escaped to Switzerland."

"Indeed, then the war passed you by."

"Not exactly." Charlie then went on to explain what had happened to him and what he intended to do next. "If I get called up for National Service I shall apply for deferment. I'm entitled to that and maybe when I'm qualified I can join the RAMC."

"Good idea," said the officer. "Or maybe as a ship's doctor."

"Food for thought." Charlie smiled as he left.

At Peggy's again he joined his mother and aunt in the front parlour for tea, round a lovely coal fire.

"We're going to be rich," he announced. "I told the officer that we were 'skint' and he promised that we would have some money in a day or two. What's more, we'll get paid for the 'Queen' as well."

Bert had a little Scotty, a thoroughbred black terrier called Soot. Each evening Bert walked him on the beach and then called in at the Coach and Horses for a pint before bed-time. One evening Charlie said he would like to go along for a chat. As they reached the sand, Soot scampered away, chasing the gulls that waited until the dog was within a few feet and then lazily taking to the air, calling loudly as if mocking him. Meanwhile the two men strode along further than Bert had ever been before but he was determined not to be outpaced by the younger man. Charlie's six foot two frame, he knew, made his five foot six inches look even smaller but he wanted to prove there was still plenty of spirit left in him.

Presently Charlie said, "I expect Mum has told you all about me. Would you like to tell me about yourself, Bert?"

"I'm a Hull man, born and bred," Bert replied. He was beginning to sweat now and panting to keep up with Charlie's long strides.

"Hey-up a touch, lad. What with the wind an' all I can hardly think. I've not much to tell really." Charlie slowed his pace and then said,

"Shall we turn round? We'll have the wind on our backs."

"Suits me lad."

Charlie interrupted,

"Bert, do you mind dropping the 'lad'? I get 'my boy' from my father-in-law and I used to get 'lad' from Tim, our engineer, but that was nearly six years ago now. Poor Tim fell at Dunkirk. So did I, very nearly. But for him I think I would have done. I really liked Tim. He was nearly old enough to be my grandfather. I didn't mind him calling me 'lad'."

"Sorry Charlie. I'll remember. Anyway, like I said, I've not much history. Left school at twelve and joined the merchant navy as an apprentice. Got to be Bosun on the Melrose eventually. We were at Dunkirk too you know. Got a direct hit from a bloody Stuka on the foredeck. Blew most of the bow off. Poor old Melrose was repaired and then got sunk two years later, torpedoed. Part of ON 154, outward bound from Liverpool, round about Christmas in 1942....... I could have been there."

"Why weren't you?"

"I spent three months in hospital and then got a job on the docks as a crane man and then a foreman in charge of the stevedores. Rotten job, really, but it paid well enough. I've never been married. Never seem to 'ave 'ad the time for courting proper. That's not to say that I don't know what life's all about like. Me and the barmaid, Annie, at the Coach, used to go out together."

"Why didn't you marry her then?"

"She was ten years older than me. I did propose once and she just laughed. Said she didn't marry school-leavers."

"And?"

"So 'ere I am."

"Do you love my Mum?"

"She's a good old stick. Art's in the right place and we're about the same age. She's knocked about a bit. Knows what's what an' all that. She's lucky to 'ave a lad like you to look after 'er."

"Is that it then?"

"That's it."

"So you're not thinking of proposing marriage?

"Lord no. See here Charlie, I've nothing. Everything I earned I spent."

"Where do, did you live then?"

"I lived with my Mum. She died in thirty-six. My house was bombed like yours."

"Good Lord, Bert, haven't you done anything about that? The Government should be paying you War Damages. We'll have to have a chat about that. Here we are. Where's Soot."

Bert raised his voice and called. The little Scotty came and sat beside the pub entrance as the two men entered for their 'wet'.

"What's it to be then Charlie?"

"No, let me."

"I insist."

"OK then. Pint of bitter. Thanks a lot." They sipped their beer in silence then some time later Charlie said,

"Tell me Bert. I'm dying to know. What did Mum say about me?"

"Sounds as though you had a cushy little number then?"

"She would say that. They don't give away the George Cross for cushy numbers, do they? But that's like Mum. It was the same with Dad. She'd say, 'Have a nice cruise then?' as Dad came in after three sleepless nights turning arse over tit in a northerly gale."

"Typical. They're all the same. That's why I never married, see. Couldn't be bossed about."

"Don't get me wrong Bert. Mum's a star. Best Mum in the world. It was just her way, that's all. Dad used to take it all in his stride, just a joke to him it were."

"I like 'er, and that's a fact. I hope you don't mind me, that's all."

"Why should I mind you Bert?"

"Well, carrying on an' all like."

"I don't mind you carrying on, Bert. Carry on carrying on. I'm not one to preach."

"But?"

"No buts. Is that what they say then? I've had an easy time?"

"I don't know much about you Charlie. Your Mum says you've grown up in nearly six years. Been through a lot and now you're to be a father."

"Yes. It's not going to be easy. Hugo hates me."

"Who's Hugo?"

"Susan's father, Sir Hugo Robinson JP. FRCP. Fellow of the University and Trustee of the Hospital, SOB."

"What does that mean?"

"Senile Old Bastard."

"Sounds as though you 'ate him too."

"No I don't hate him, not really. I knew all about hate in the war. People like Hugo are on our side. I know that. It's just."

"That you can't stand the man."

"OK. You've said it. I just don't like the way he tries to wreck our marriage. Runs me down. Though I never met her, Susan tells me her Mum was worse. Susan says her parents didn't know how to love, how to love each other or how to love them. Susan says that she and Lucy clung to each other. 'We had no one else to love, until you came along Charlie, she would say."

"Do you love them?"

"Of course I do Bert. I'd die for them."

"But you married Susan."

"I'm passionate about her."

"But not 'bout Lucy."

"Lucy's lovely, gentle, vulnerable. Lucy needs more love than Susan, more than I can give. Lucy will smother someone with love one day but."

"What?"

"She has a problem."

"Problem? Tell me."

"I may be wrong, so I don't talk about it."

"You must have an idea."

"Idea! I'm full of ideas. She's heartbroken. The trouble is she was my first love. I was only a boy. We met, all three of us. It was only a small thing really. She wiped seagull shit off my head. Just like a mother would've. Susan laughed. To her it was a joke. Then Lucy said she would come to me in the night, outside the school but Susan came, pretending to be her. I was horrible. I don't like to talk about it now. I was just a kid. I didn't know much."

"And?"

"Nothing."

Bert persisted.

"But you married Susan. Why the switch? Lucy's the loving one."

"Yes, I suppose so but Susan's exciting, lives, lives for everything. She wanted me and she wanted a baby. She cheated on us all."

"How....why did she do that?"

"I knew she was cheating. That's the funny part about it. She told us she was expecting when she wasn't. I went along with it because I was flattered. She wanted me or, to put it another way, she would have been very jealous if I'd married Lucy."

"That's madness Charlie."

"Oh, I know, I know all that. Haven't I agonised about it? Sex is sex, Bert, you can't gainsay that and I wanted a baby too. I don't think Lucy did. I do love Susan. All the more, I think, because she did cheat. Of course it came out in the end. That was why Lucy reacted so badly. She had a breakdown. That's why we had a holiday in France. By the time we got to Paris she was much better.

"Well, I hope you know what you're doing, Charlie."

"Everyone thought we had to get married and, when they found the truth, I was a laughing stock but I didn't care about that. I knew I'd married a girl after my own heart. She wanted me and she got me. Now I have to justify her faith by getting through University. With Abe's help I will. I'm going to do well."

"Whose Abe then?"

"That's a long story. I'll tell you all about it one day. He's rich and he's promised to get me through. Lives in Switzerland."

"Lucky boy. I bet there's a real story there. You should write it down."

"I may do one day. I helped to save his life and his family. He treats me like a son."

Both men sat looking into the remains of their almost forgotten beer.

"Want another?" said Charlie eventually.

"No thanks lad, oops sorry. No thanks Charlie."

"A chaser then? Have a whisky."

"Not me. Rarely touch it. Come on. Let's be off."

When the men reached the house, all was quiet. Eliza and Peggy had gone to bed. Charlie lay awake thinking about his studies and the future.

The following morning his aunt came up to his room with a mug of tea and a letter. It was from Susan.

Darling,

Terrible news, Daddy has had a stroke. He is in the hospital under Doctor Prendergast. He is having every care and round the clock attention. Lucy and I are at our wits end. We shall visit him every day of course. I am sure he knows us but he cannot get out of bed. We think that his left side is paralysed.

Uncle Frank is being marvellous and when Daddy is a bit better we may persuade him to hand over his affairs to Uncle for the time being. There will be bills to pay and of course the house.

Please come back as soon as you can. It would be lovely to hear your voice on the phone if you can get through. I know it's difficult. Lucy sends love and so do I darling.

Love also to your Mum and Aunt,
Susan.

At breakfast the four of them were seated at the table.

"God Mum. What should I do now?"

"You know what to do better than me, dear. Your first duty is to your wife. If she wants you back then you'd better go."

"Do you think I'm to blame?"

"Goodness me, of course not. How could you be to blame? You were here."

"I know. But Hugo hates me. Just before I left we had a bit of an argument. He was very upset. If I go back it could make him worse."

9

"Well, I don't believe that for a minute. You go. At least you will be a comfort to Susan and Lucy and you can keep out of the way of Hugo."

"Then there's Uncle Frank. I hardly know him and I don't know how he regards me."

"Well in that case you'd better be away and find out."

"Will you and auntie be OK?"

"Of course we will. We've managed all through the war haven't we? And we've got Bert now."

"Anyway, the Town Hall and the Navy owe you a lot of money. Don't forget that."

"Be off with you and don't forget to write. I shall be anxious."

****

"Darling." With a shriek of joy Susan ran into Charlie's arms as he jumped off the train at London Road Station. "Let's get a taxi home," she said.

"How's your Dad?"

"He's ill Charlie, very ill. Oh dear. I'm going to cry again."

She pulled on his arm. They stopped. She buried her face in his rough coat. Convulsed with grief, they stood like this for several minutes while the passing soldiers gave them both friendly wolf-whistles.

"He's not going to get better Charlie," she said through her tears.

"How's the house, coming on?" asked Charlie gently, hoping that his question would help Susan overcome her emotion.

"It's OK. The builders are very slow. Let's not talk about it now."

Susan was still sobbing as they climbed into the taxi.

"She all right then, Boss?" the driver asked.

"We've had some bad news. We'd like to go to Manchester Royal please"

Susan dried her eyes and tried to resume normal conversation.

"No, let's go home Charlie. We can't get to see him until visiting time anyway."

"How's Lucy taking it?"

"Better than me actually. Surprisingly calm. She's pinning her faith on a recovery. I can't do that. I've got this feeling of guilt."

"What guilt?"

"Well I've never been kind enough to Dad. I blamed him for us being sent away and said some horrible things. Lucy never did that. She's always been the loving one."

"Your Dad loves you. He can't wait to see your baby. I hope he does."

"By the way, Lucy had a surprise this morning. Guess."

"I haven't a clue."

"It's a letter."

"From?"

"Guess."

"I don't know any of Lucy's friends."

"You know this one."

"Is it from Germany?"

"Warmer."

"Carl."

"Right. Clever you. It is Carl. He's in Switzerland. He's had the promise of a job from David."

"Has he indeed. Why did he write to Lucy?"

"He wants to come over, before this job starts, whatever it is."

"He does, does he? I'm not sure I want to meet him again after he added to the terrible things Marlene wrote about me to Hugo. What do you think about that?"

"Not much. We know he wants to marry Lucy. If she says 'yes', she'll be going back to Germany."

"You don't know that. If he finds work here he may stay. Don't, whatever you do, try to influence the outcome. You might make it worse."

"I don't want her to go away."

The following day Susan arrived back from visiting Hugo. Charlie was waiting outside their hotel.

"How was he?"

"Much improved. He knew us. We shared a joke even. The doctor may let him come home in a week or so. Uncle Frank has been wonderful."

"Oh. Home?"

"To the hotel, Uncle's organising everything, wheelchair, full time nurse and a daily visit from a physiotherapist."

"What's that? A physio-something."

"Therapist. They're trying exercise to get his muscles going"

"Let's hope it works, but what about me?"

"What about you?"

"I'm not going to be the one to upset him again. You know he can't stand the sight of me. I'm going to move into Farmleigh."

"You can't do that."

"Why not?"

"The bomb did more damage than you might imagine. It's in a hell of a state inside. The whole house may be condemned. We may be lucky but it's too early to say definitely. No wonder Mother was killed. It's going to be awful having to live there again. The surveyor spent most of the day looking round and taking measurements. The local builders are working according to his directions. We'll have to pay about half."

"I thought the Rep. Com - that's the Reparation Committee - are supposed to pay it all."

"Only up to a fixed maximum. In about three months we'll have a house, at least the shell of a house. I suppose you'll want me to move in too?"

"Not in your state darling. Charles is due in six months."

"It might not be Charles."

"Well then, how about Charlene? I think it will be Charles."

2 The Forest

"British Embassy."

Hallo. This is Carl Wogart speaking. Captain Wogart. Please may I speak to Mr David Brown? He knows me."

"Certainly Sir. I'll have to check if he's available. Please hold the line." There was a delay which seemed like an age to Carl.

"Herr Wogart? Brown here."

"Call me Carl, Mr Brown, you always used to."

"I remember. Where are you speaking from now Carl?"

"I'm still at the Lescault Mansion in Breiten. Used to be the Finishing School."

"Ah yes. What can I do for you?"

"I'm getting nervous Mr Brown. It is only a matter of time before the authorities repatriate me. Before that happens I had hoped you would call me. I am engaged to be married to the English girl, Miss Lucy Robinson. Do you think you can help?"

"I've been reviewing your case Carl. I'm sorry it takes so long to get answers. I'll ring you back to-morrow."

"This is a call box I'm afraid. I'll have to call you. Will that be all right?"

"Very good. If you can't get through then please leave a message with my secretary, Miss Gray."

"Thank you Sir, a million thanks. Danke schön." The line went dead.

Deserters from the German army were being repatriated from Switzerland. Many German officers, such as Carl, made their escape into neighbouring countries, some claimed asylum but the majority were sent to internment camps in the American Sector of southern Germany. Carl was a worried man. He knew that he would not be welcome back home. For several days he had been trying to 'phone David. The following day he managed to speak to him again.

"What have you arranged, Mr Brown?"

"I've fixed you up with a temporary room here at the embassy. If it's all right with you, I'll drive over to collect you tomorrow or the day after. I can't go into details now."

"Yes, yes of course, Sir. Tomorrow will be fine. I'll be ready and waiting. Auf Wiedersehen und vielen Dank auch."

During the journey to Bern, Carl asked what would happen on his arrival.

"You'll have to wait for a detailed answer to that question Carl," David said. "Meanwhile you will be confined to the embassy grounds for a while. If you venture out you may be picked up by the police and that will be very embarrassing for both of us……. understood? There is no possibility of travelling to England yet but I have it very much in mind. Trust me."

"Yes Sir."

"The embassy staff will know of your existence of course and they will be informed that you are displaced from Polish occupied Germany and that you have sought political asylum. We have done this before, so they will not be suspicious. In fact we have another family from Sudetenland with us at the moment. We are negotiating a safe passage for them."

"I'm very grateful for the trouble you are taking with me Sir."

"Well," replied David, "I think you may be able to help us in return. For one thing we need a good interpreter and we also need local knowledge of the position in Germany during the reconstruction period. We may be able to offer you a more permanent post in Berlin, in due course, but there is no embassy there at the moment. The whole of Germany has been occupied by the Allies and is still under martial law."

Three months later David drove with Carl to the Headquarters of the British Army of the Rhine (B.A.O.R.) in Western Germany. On his second day there he was asked to attend a briefing with a special unit which had been formed, consisting of ex-officers of the Wehrmacht.

A British Brigadier talked to them for about half an hour.

"I am Brigadier Morris, Jim Morris to my friends. My task is to form a new unit of soldiers who are all ex-members of the German forces. You men have been selected from several hundred officers and N.C.O.'s because you fulfil the criteria that we are looking for. That is to say you are fluent in English and German and preferably Russian also. We would be delighted to find an officer who had French as well, although in this sector this is not essential. We have no evidence that any of you are, or were, members of the Nazi Party. On the other hand we know that you have, on occasions, taken overt action to foil German war crimes. We require men who are brave, resourceful and able to remain calm in a crisis. If you consider that you are able to fulfil our requirements then we will offer you training. If you pass our tests you will be assigned to this unit. Needless to say, your membership here is entirely voluntary and you will be financially well rewarded. Although we have only recruited twenty so far, others will follow. You are a very select bunch. Have you any questions?"

During the weeks that followed Carl was billeted in the town, with instructions to report the HQ's guard house each day. He longed to visit Lucy in England. David Brown assured him that he would arrange this, while dealing with his application to become a British citizen.

At the beginning of the second month there were thirty-nine members of the special group. They were waiting in the lecture room for another briefing by the Brigadier.

"Everybody stand," shouted the Sergeant Major. There was a scraping of chairs on the concrete floor as the company rose to their feet   After a few minutes silence three officers entered and took up positions on a small dais.

"Guten Morgen meine Herren, bitte setzen Sie sich," said the Brigadier. He continued,

"Today it is my task to explain the purpose of this new unit. Firstly, as to a name - You are MISU, which stands for Ministry of Intelligence, Special Unit. We shall no doubt be called 'Miss You' before long. (laughter). I will now describe the background and reason for our existence. It became apparent at the Yalta conference that the Russian Government intends to pursue political as well as military domination of Poland, the Baltic States, Czechoslovakia, Hungary, Bulgaria, Rumania, Yugoslavia and Austria as well as a large area of Eastern Germany. We, that is to say the British and American forces, have agreed to withdraw from large areas of Germany. These areas will be occupied by the Russian Military and will be administered by them. For the future protection of Western Europe the decision was taken in London to establish listening posts along what will become, in the very near future, a new international frontier. For their part the Americans have also made a similar decision, although the details are not yet known to us. Our agents from London have been operating along this new border for several months, even before hostilities ceased. They were unarmed in the conventional sense, their only armaments being very large chequebooks; I speak metaphorically. Consequently this unit is now the proud owner of a chain of farms, some small, little more than smallholdings, and some extending to several hectares. There are woodlands and fields, all on the eastern side of this new border. Your task gentlemen will be to inhabit these farms and to carry on business there to the general profit not only of yourselves but to the benefit of villages in your area. We shall maintain contact with you in several different ways, for example, by radio or mail, by telephone wherever possible and by direct contact. We shall expect you to maintain contact with each other. Your overriding task, therefore, will be to report military movements by the Red Army, the names of their regiments, their strength and armaments, permanent fortresses under construction etc. and the locations of all these activities. We consider this information is vital to the safety of the West and will enable us to deploy forces on our side of the border according to need. Now gentlemen, you have spent the last month learning the techniques of communication employed by us, letter boxes, radio codes et cetera. In six months time we expect to be placing you on station, meanwhile agricultural experts will be teaching you about farming et cetera. Several of you have considerable farming experience already. We shall expect you to help with the instruction of your fellows. Have you any questions?"

Carl stood up immediately.

"Yes Carl," said Morris.

"Sir, will not the Russian authority check up on everybody owning property along this proposed border and how can we be reassured that we will be left to farm in peace. The Russians normally collect all farms into a common ownership?"

"Good question Carl. I will answer it in the best way I can. Firstly, no one can know the future intentions of the Russian civil authority but we do know that they will rule the countries they have overrun through puppet governments and it is unlikely that they will impose collective ownership of farms in the satellite countries. There will however be severe inspection of border activities in the towns and in the countryside. You will have to be prepared for this and you must also be aware that there will be an element of risk involved. During the next few months you will get the opportunity to rehearse methods of clandestine concealment and communications in the field. Needless to say, all your day-to-day activities must be open and innocent. You will be unarmed except for shotguns, which may be permitted by the authorities for shooting pests or game. It will be up to each of you to apply for a gun licence. Do I make myself clear?"

From this point on the discussion proceeded, covering many subjects. Another question took some time to answer in detail.

"Sir, the Russians and our countrymen in the east, who sympathise with Communist ideals, will be checking up on recent acquisitions of land and property. How can we be sure that the ownership of these farms will not be scrutinised?" Jim Morris turned to a colleague.

"Captain Jack, will you answer that?"

"Yes Sir. I would like to re-assure you all. We in MISU are very thorough. We have been operating in the new frontier area for over a year and have well tried and established links with many officials who were working, still are working, for local and state bureaucracies. Many old records have been destroyed in the bombing and fighting. Furthermore we have established identities for you all and property deeds lodged in appropriate archives. With a few exceptions we have linked you back to your real families, who are aware of your future activities."

"Not mine I hope, protested Carl."

"You, Herr Wogart, are one of our exceptions. As far as your family are concerned at the present time, you were shot while deserting your post in Belfort." This provoked general laughter and the end of the briefing.

In the summer of 1946 Carl found himself managing part of the forest in northern Thuringia.

****

The dark trees seemed endless. Carl had spent the first month of his posting exploring the area. His home was a log cabin on the northern fringe. Now, over two years after moving in he knew the area well and had made friends with some of the neighbours and shopkeepers in the nearby small town of Vacha. He tended a small holding of 10 Hectares but his work, of tree husbandry, extended far outside his own boundaries. He cycled into Vacha each week for provisions. Across the river Werra he could see Philippsthal in the American Zone.

It was almost silent in the depths of the forest. There were no birds and no animals except wild boar. In the first few months he had seen several and shot two for food. Since then they seemed to be keeping well away from his home. The stands of tall firs were like sentinels. Their lower branches, almost touching, made progress difficult and tiring. Now the summer was over and the winter rains were setting in. He had used the months well, creating a network of paths across the wood from one side to the other. Everyday a new batch of refugees would thread their way through the Thuringerwald and then cross the ploughed strip into the west. Normally he did nothing to interrupt their progress but sometimes he would turn them back. He had no wish for them to be discovered in his area.

They came in groups of six or so, never more than ten, carrying what few possessions they could. Some pushed loaded bicycles. Many pushed prams, with or without a tiny child, but nevertheless loaded with essentials for living in the open air for a few days. Many came from the east, from Prussia, now part of Poland. From time to time they would pause by his cabin and ask for water, never food. Occasionally they would camp nearby.

He was concerned that he would be implicated in this illegal traffic. For the present, crossing the border was easy enough. There were no obstacles, only the ploughed strip ten meters wide and the constant patrols by the German Border

Police. But he knew that in a matter of months the situation would change. Already fences were under construction around villages in the North, the British Zone. When they were in position then mines would be laid. By the end of 1952 he expected the fence to be complete from the Baltic to the Czech border.

Meanwhile, working with a contingent of the Peoples' Army, he had been given the job of clearing the forest along part of the frontier. On two separate occasions in the last nine months he had blown his whistle to alert the Border Patrol when members of his team tried to dash for the west. He shed no tears for their deaths. They knew the risk and it was more important for him to preserve his reputation for reliability.

Fifty kilometres to the north and south of his small farm other members of MISU were tending their land. Slowly but relentlessly the border barrier took shape. The ploughed ten meter strip was abandoned. Nearly all the roads and tracks which bisected the frontier were ruthlessly barricaded with logs or rocks. Villages were cut in halves, relatives separated from their next of kin. The Peoples' Army Pioneers erected the high mesh fence. In many areas another parallel fence was put up and, between the two, mines were laid close to towns and villages. Again, on the DDR, there was a new ploughed strip and a ditch, a sure obstacle for any vehicle attempting to force a way through to the west. The DDR or Deutsche Demokratischen Republik became the name for what was formerly the Russian Zone. Slowly it dawned on Carl and his few colleagues to the north and the south of his post that they would be in the front line of any attack by Russian Forces. By the end of 1952 the work was almost completed. The Iron Curtain forecast by Winston Churchill in 1946 was a fact. To the ill-equipped civilians the border defence was impregnable. Its presence justified by the desperate need of the DDR to retain its skilled manpower and professional workers.

3 Proposition

The assembled throng rose and stood in silence as the platform party entered the Great Hall of Manchester University. In 1951 this was the first graduation ceremony since the war that had involved many who had fought. With due solemnity the Vice-Chancellor called out the name of each graduate who then ascended the short flight, bowed to the Chancellor and then received his or her degree scroll neatly tied with pink tape. This short citation was the reward for six years of unremitting toil.

Academic study did not come easily to Charlie but his efforts had been repaid. He worried about how he could complete his medical training. Charlie's open and cheerful disposition, combined with an aptitude for hard work, had done much to heal the breach with his father-in-law but he knew, in his heart, that Hugo would do his best to obstruct his ambition because of the lies Marlene had told about him.

Much had happened in the years since Charlie had got to know and like Bert Higgins. For one thing his mother had married Bert and they had bought a house in Cleethorpes not far from Peggy. Charlie still went to stay with his aunt when it suited him. Every time he went he saluted the stag over his bed. Sometimes Susan came too and looked down from the window at the view Charlie had had when she and Lucy had picked flowers from the garden below twelve years ago. It seemed like a whole lifetime.

Little Charles was nearly six years old. Eliza and Peggy adored him and spoilt him just as they had spoilt his father.

In Manchester, 'Farmleigh', the old home in Barlow Moor Road, had been fully restored and Hugo, who had made a partial recovery, had moved in with his daughters, the toddler and Charlie. He and Hugo had reached an uneasy truce. Hugo had no desire to lose his daughter and his grandson and so he made Charlie welcome at home but unwelcome at the hospital. With this uncomfortable arrangement in place, Charlie knew that, after he had graduated, his days at Farmleigh would be numbered.

Susan and he had taken Charles to Bern to see Abraham Goldstein. Since Abe had paid for so much, they felt that was the least they could do. They found him in good health but noticeably older and more frail, spending most of his time trying to trace his family throughout the length and breadth of Germany. Abe was delighted at Charlie's success and wished him well in his future career. They arrived home three weeks later to find an official letter from the Foreign Office awaiting them. The contents filled Charlie with excitement.

"I can hardly believe it, after all this time," he said to Susan.

"He hasn't changed. He always was a canny bastard," she replied.

He turned it over and over in his fingers trying to decide if it was an elaborate hoax or genuine. Susan pronounced it genuine. He decided to draft a reply.

24th September 1951
David Brown Esq,
The Foreign Office,
Whitehall,
London.

Dear David,

Thank you for your letter. Your proposition sounds very interesting and intriguing. I shall come next Thursday, as you have suggested. Thank you for your kind offer of lunch at the Red Lion. I shall be there at about eleven-thirty - looking forward to it. As I think you must know already, I graduated in medicine last June. I am now seeking a post where I can complete my training.

Yours sincerely,

Charles Forbes.

That night Charlie dreamt of the past. Of the suave young diplomat who had entered their lives in Switzerland. How he had co-opted him, Susan and Lucy in the escape 'pipeline' which stretched from the German border to Spain. How they had gone in fear of their lives and had a brush with the Gestapo in France. Charlie thought that he owed nothing to Mr David Brown but he was curious.

"What is he up to this time?" he asked himself.

The following week Charlie met him, at the Red Lion in Whitehall, opposite the Foreign Office.

"David, how nice to see you again."

"Hello Charlie, it's been a long time. Let's sit over there, in the corner. My boss may be joining us later."

"Oh, really, who is that?"

"You'll find out soon enough. He's the head of my section. We just call him JB." Charlie took a long hard look at David. The years had not treated him kindly. He had a paunch and his face bore the marks of strain. His hair was turning grey and he had developed a slight stoop.

"Fancy a drink?"

"A pint of bitter please, if it doesn't break the bank."

"Now then, no need for sarcasm," said David with a smile.

"How are things with you then? Married yet?"

"Well and truly."

"I always knew you were a busy fellow. Swiss?"

"Not a chance. She's Mary Gray-as-was. A thoroughly nice girl. We fell for each other almost from the day we met in '46. Used to be my secretary."

"Kids?"

"A toddler. Boy, aged two."

A waitress appeared to take their order.

"Hello Mr Brown," she said with a cheeky smile. "Another recruit?"

"Enough of that Clare. Mine's a steak pie".

"Same for me," said Charlie as he turned back to face his future tormenter.

"Now to business. How would you like to be working for me again?" said David.

"I thought you would be saying something like that," replied Charlie. "I'd like it very much if you make it possible. The fact is, at the moment I can't earn enough. Susan and I are living with her Dad. It's not a good idea. The old man hates me although he dotes on Susan and little Charles."

"Well, we've worked together in the past, very successfully," said David. "I can meet all your needs. I'm offering you a permanent position on a salary of £5,000 per year." Charlie whistled softly.

"This has got to be something special."

"It is. You will be commissioned into the Army Medics and for the next five years you will work at the Army Hospital in Osnabruck, Germany. The high salary is to cover the work you will be trained to do in my outfit - secret work, something like you did before.

"You seem to have done your homework well, David. Do you know what I had for breakfast?"

"Almost."

"I didn't think I could work abroad at this stage of my career."

"Under normal circumstances you couldn't".

"So the circumstances are not normal?"

"Let's just say that if you work for me I can make special arrangements."

"I'll have to talk to Susan. I want her and Charles to be with me."

"That goes without saying. You'll be living in the married quarters of HQ. BAOR. Very comfortable they are too and, in due course, Charles will start at the school we have out there."

"Is that it then?" asked Charlie.

"Ask anything you like."

"What do you mean, a bit like I did before?"

"Come back to my office now and I can explain with maps and things."

"No, it's all right. I've got to be on the 3.30 train. I'll clear it with Susan first. Can I tell her the whole story?"

"Tell her you are doing your National Service in Germany as an officer in the RAMC. That should be enough for now. Later on we could sign you on for a short service commission, seven years."

"That's not all is it?"

"No it isn't. All I can tell you, at the moment, is that the East Germans, supported by the Russian occupation, are determined to seal their western border. Over three million Germans have crossed into the west since 1945. The DDR, as they now call themselves, has to stop this traffic for its own survival."

"And I'm supposed to help in this then?"

"Not at all. Quite the reverse. I'm forming a team to help important men come to the west if they want to."

"Men? What about women?"

"Them too, if the occasion should arise, but the sort of people we need are those who can tell us about the Red Army's capability."

"So I'm to be a sort of spy then?"

"Not really, but we think that there will be a role for someone with your experience of crossing borders, sealed borders, that is. More like a courier."

"OK. I get the picture but, like I said, I'll have to talk it over with Susan. I'm going to have to move to get that train."

"Yes you will. There's always a taxi about. I'll say goodbye."

"What happened to the boss then?"

"No need for him now. You accepted."

"How did you find my address?"

"Not difficult. It's my business to find addresses."

"See you soon David." Charlie shouted as he ran for the taxi.

Back at home Susan and Charlie talked long into the night.

"She will have to come too, Charlie."

"Out of the question Susan. We can't trail your lame duck of a sister round with us all our lives."

"Then I'm not coming either."

"You must."

"There's no must about it. You'll just have to lay it on the line with David. Anyway…." Susan gave him an enigmatic smile. "She might meet someone out there."

"OK. You win…as usual. I'll ask David. It'll stir things up in the Officers' Mess if nothing else. Just so long as you don't expect me to take Hugo as well and talking of the Officers' Mess, there'll be no more cabarets. Understood?"

"As if …. What with my stretch marks! Dream on lover boy."

A few days later Charlie got a phone call from David.

"It's all fixed. I've got you a flat in the mess with three bedrooms and a job for Lucy too. They need another pair of hands in the Ops. Room. She'll be ideal. No problems signing the OS, I suppose."

"OS, what's that?"

"Official Secrets old boy. It's routine for you and all the staff at HQ."

No probs. David. When do we start?"

"The sooner the better. Have you broken the news to the old man yet?"

"Susan has. He's pretty upset. Wanted to know how much leave we would get."

"Well Susan can come and go as she pleases. Lucy can have a forty-eight every month and fourteen days every six months plus compassionate if necessary."

****

It was the anniversary of the Manchester Blitz in 1941.

"Come on Susan, Dad's waiting."

"I'm not coming. You two go. I can't see the sense in it."

"Susan, you promised. Come on."

"When did I promise?"

"You said you would come. Only yesterday you said you would come."

"Alright then I will come but not if it's going to take all day. Where's Dad?"

"I've wheeled him into the lounge. That's where he likes to be in the morning."

"Well I'm ready if he is."

"You can't go like that."

"Like what?"

"Dressed like that."

"Have you two finished arguing yet, on this day of all days? Your Mother will be wondering what's gone wrong."

"Oh Daddy, she's not a real person any more. It's weird. You can't talk about a dead person like that."

"I can and I shall. I'll do it just as long as I'm alive which won't be much longer and then you'll be free of me and my idiosyncratic ways."

"Susan, are you going to change or not?

"Daddy, do I have to change?"

"Have you no respect? You will soon be going away. This is the last chance you will have for a long time to pay your respects to your mother."

"How can I respect a corpse, a rotting body. It's not real. Mother's remains are just chemicals now."

"I won't have it Susan. Have some regard for me and for the memory of mother."

"I do respect her memory. I'm not arguing Daddy. I'm going to change like you asked." As Susan slowly climbed the stairs to their room, Lucy said,

"Oh Dad. How can she be like that? Sometimes she is so nice and loving and at other times she's horrid."

"I've learnt to live with it. She's just like your mother was, headstrong, wilful, obstinate."

"She's not all that bad. I love, we love her. I sometimes wonder if she loves me as much as I love her."

"You make too many allowances, excuses. When she's the 'wrong way out' I wonder why you don't give her a piece of your mind." Hugo retorted.

"You can't put out a fire by pouring petrol on it Dad. Today's going to be a nice day, sad but nice. The taxi will be here in ten minutes and when we get to the cemetery the lady will be there with the flowers. We'll push you to Mother and say a little prayer. The gardener promised to cut the grass and polish the stone."

"That's where I shall be one day soon. Will you come…."

Descending the stairs, Susan interrupted. "Here I am. All ready. Just like you Lucy. The pink. We're in the pink. Come on let's go. The taxi's here."

A month later Uncle Frank and Hugo saw the quartet onto the London train. Susan and Lucy hung on their father's neck until the last moment. Hugo turned to Charlie as they parted and took his hand in his.

"Well my boy, I'll wish you the very best of luck and I hope all goes well for you. One last request, look after my daughters and Charles." Susan put Charles onto Hugo's lap as he sat in his wheelchair. In uncharacteristic mode, Hugo wiped a tear from his eye with the sleeve of his right arm. The twins kissed Uncle Frank and then leaned from the window as the train slowly gathered way. As the carriages hit the gentle bend at the end of the Platform One, Frank and Hugo passed out of sight.

Susan said,

"That was a breakthrough."

"First time we've ever shaken hands. Trust him to make a show of it now we're leaving and in front of Uncle too."

"Never mind dear. Don't make a big thing of it. I knew he would thaw one day. We must write once we are installed."

****

The headquarter complex at Osnabruck had been built for the Wehrmacht in 1937. It included a large hospital as well as offices, living accommodation for the staff and their families, assembly halls, two chapels, workshops and many sporting activities. The whole was surrounded by extensive park-land in which the British had constructed numerous Nissan Huts for army units, more workshops and classrooms. In one of these Charlie was interviewed by Brigadier Morris soon after his arrival in October.

"Are you settled in then?"

"Yes thanks Brigadier."

"Digs OK and what about the job?"

"Fine thanks. I'm doing a ward tour for the first month and then they'll give me a junior post."

"Good. Let me know if you have problems, problems of any sort. Now to business. We, that is my intelligence team, estimate that the Iron Curtain will be solid by the beginning of 1952. At the moment it hardly exists."

"It exists round here," said Charlie. "The perimeter fence is impregnable. It's a bit like being in prison. My wife is grumbling already."

"Civilians living on the station have every facility here and they can go out whenever they like. All they have to do is to remember to take their ID card and sign out at the guard room."

"Oh yes. I know all that. It's just that they feel a bit shut in, claustrophobic."

"They?"

"My sister-in-law, Lucy and my wife, Susan."

"Yes, of course. They'll get used to living here very quickly. I've heard that Lucy's living with you both. Is there a reason why she does not have a single person's flat? She's entitled to one and there is one vacant at the moment."

"Yes," said Charlie. "There is a reason but it's a private problem. Actually it's not a problem. We are one big happy family."

"It could be a problem to us."

"Why is that then?"

"Your wife and her sister are very alike. I didn't realise that when we got Lucy a job in the Ops room. Either one could easily pose as the other but they are going to work with different security clearance levels. That's all. Your sister-in-law has access to the Op's Room with all the military dispositions in Germany, including the Americans. They, the Yanks, might get a bit concerned if they knew about it."

"You don't have to worry about that but if you like you can raise my wife's level to be the same as Lucy's."

"I'll think about it. The problem is she's not employed here. Leave it with me. Now really…. to business. I've not a lot of time…"

"Yes Sir."

"Last year our reception centres processed over one hundred thousand refugees and the numbers are going up all the time. At the present rate of increase, unless the DDR does something dramatic, the number will top a quarter of a million per year by the end of 1952. That's not counting those who make their own way, living with relatives or emigrating elsewhere. It's difficult for us because of the housing problems. We can't keep them in camps for long but it's even more difficult for the East Germans. Their skilled men and women are haemorrhaging away and their economy is suffering. Whole towns have lost doctors, nurses, solicitors, teachers. Need I go on?"

"No need, but how does that affect us, BAOR?"

"Indirectly it affects us a lot. The DDR must stop all emigration and that will make life more and more difficult for us. We need to undermine their war effort and at the same time acquire techniques in the design and development of rocketry – the successors to Hitler's V2's. We've identified about a hundred scientists who used to work for the Nazi's and who are now working for the Russians. We want to get our hands on them, at least on a good number of the most important."

"Is that where I'm supposed to come in?" asked Charlie.

"Not to put too fine a point on it …. yes. That's what you're here for.

"I'm not sure I'm up to the mark."

"You will be. Take my word for it, but you'll need a lot of training."

"I'm here mainly as a doctor. I don't expect to have time for much extra training. What will be involved?"

"Believe me, your medical knowledge will be useful but the work you do in the hospital is your cover for something much more important and, dare I say it, secret. You'll have to brush up your German as well."

"Mr Brown said I could complete my training here."

"So you shall but it may take longer that's all."

"I really do want to get on with it though."

"Yes, we understand your feelings. We are making special arrangements. As I said, your work for me will take priority and the hospital authorities have agreed to co-operate."

"That's not what Brown said."

"Trust us Charlie. It may take a little time to organise something. Meantime you can concentrate on working for MISU."

"What?"

"MISU it's the abbreviation for the title we've adopted, Ministry of Intelligence Special Unit."

****

Susan and Lucy were chatting whilst unpacking another crate of belongings from England.

"How are we going to work things out Susan?"

"What do you mean?"

"Well it's not like the old times is it? Charlie's changed. We used to rotate, you know, bed-wise"

"We've all changed Lucy. You and I. We've just grown up that's all. Charlie's a busy man what with the hospital and his other work with Brigadier Morris."

"Must he work so hard? We never see him these days and he seems to be on call at the hospital, day and night."

"Isn't it time you and Carl got together? We all thought he would pop the question on his last leave, before he went?"

"Carl and I have an understanding. Now he's working behind the Iron Curtain we can't possibly contemplate marriage. I could go over too, legally, but there would be an ocean of red tape and it might, probably would, provoke a detailed investigation of Carl. He just wants to be left alone."

"What's he doing over there?"

"To be honest…. I don't really know. Something to do with reconnaissance I think.

"Good Lord. I wouldn't have thought he was used to that kind of work. What about his leg?"

"He manages. Doesn't get much pain these days. His other foot seems to give him more trouble than his wooden one."

"I'm going to see our Dad soon. He's asked me to stay over Christmas and New Year and I know Eliza will be glad if I take Charles over there. Can't you get away?"

"I'm not due for leave. Someone else has leave so they won't let me go, Sorry."

****

The early morning sun was trying hard to break up the thick mist which hung like a blanket over the headquarter buildings. A thin line of leave-takers straggled across the wet grass towards the waiting bus.

Come on Susan. Hurry, you're going to miss it."

"Charlie, don't nag. Here, you put Charles' coat on and walk him to the bus. I'll catch you up. I just want to say cheerio to Lucy."

With Charlie out of the way Susan went into Lucy's bedroom. She was awake but still in bed.

"Bye darling. We're packed and just off. Now behave yourselves," she said with a wink and a smile.

"Don't worry Sue. Charlie won't pester me. I can guarantee it. I wish I could have got leave. Perhaps the Ops Room will let me get away at Easter."

"That would be great."

"Good bye then. Give us a kiss......Now hurry up or you'll miss it."

Charlie, with his small son, walked briskly across the wet grass to the waiting bus. He said,

"Be good for Mummy Charles. You will have a lovely time and lots of Christmas presents."

Susan caught them up, running with the canvas bag. "Sure you've got everything darling?"

"I'm not taking much. What I haven't got we can buy."

Charlie put Charles down and turned to embrace his wife.

"Have a safe journey and a lovely time. I shall miss you every minute."

The bus drew away as those left behind stood and waved until it was lost in the mist.

Charlie walked back to the flat. The telephone bell was ringing. Lucy was in the hallway. She picked it up. A voice asked for Doctor Forbes. She passed it to Charlie. Her hand lingered for a moment on his sleeve.

"Yes, straight away. Give me five minutes to get ready. Send a car. That will save ten minutes."

He replaced the receiver.

"Lucy I've got to go. There's an emergency on."

"But you haven't had any breakfast."

"No time for that."

Charlie grabbed his bag and headed for the door.

"Sorry Lucy, no time to waste."

"A kiss then?"

"Quickly."   A cheek-peck.

The car dropped Charlie at the entrance to the emergency ward.

"What's going on?" he said to the sister in charge.

"Six men, sappers, badly burned, shocked. One dead."

"Where are they now?"

"In theatre. They need you Sir. Scrub up here and there's clean clothes in there."

Twelve hours later a weary Charlie struggled across the campus back to the flat. It had been a terrible day. One other man had died leaving four who were treated for their severe burns. The soldiers had been travelling on a low loader with a mobile crane. The rig had snarled and brought down the overhead tram wires in the main street of Wuppertal. The men had been electrocuted before the power went off automatically. Rescue workers had taken half an hour to get army ambulances to the scene. It was the worst experience Charlie had ever had.

Lucy had been waiting all day for his return. Charlie was touched by the effort she had obviously made to prepare a nice meal, not knowing when he would be back. He sat on the sofa and burst into tears. She came and put an arm round his shoulders. The sadness and futility of the deaths of those young men affected them both. Gradually Lucy's tenderness quietened his sobs.

They sat in this intimate way until his cries had subsided.

"I need a shower," he said getting up. "I'm sorry about the meal. I really am and you made such an effort. I've not had anything all day but those terrible wounds just turned me over. I'm not over it yet. If they live they'll be badly scarred for life and the pain. I can't think about it. A heavy meal would finish me off completely."

"I'll scramble you some egg." Lucy whispered.

"Thanks. I won't be long."

"Shall I scrub your back?" she said jokingly.

"That won't be necessary. Thanks all the same."

"I did it once before. Remember?"

"How can I forget but let me sort myself out and then I'll join you on the sofa and we can talk about old times. All I want to do is to blot today out of my memory completely."

"Have a sherry first?"

"More like a brandy and then I really will go for a shower."

Later on Lúcy called,

"Have you finished yet?"

"Nearly. Hey. You can't come in here yet."

"Just you try to stop me. I've only brought you a nice warm towel. Here swap."

"OK. Thanks. Catch."

"It's horrible. You couldn't get dry on a soggy thing like that anyway."

"Like I said. Thanks. Now you'd better go."

"Since when were you so coy?"

"Since I was married I suppose. Now buzz. I'll come in soon. The brandy was good. Just what I needed."

"Have another?"

"I will. A double."

"Eggs coming up. We'll have it in the comfy chairs by the fire. Pity it's not a real one. Be with you in a moment."

Charlie entered the kitchen.

"I hope you don't mind. I'm so tired I just want to hit the hay. No point in dressing up is there?"

"No point at all. Here you are, double Cognac. Link arms with me and toss it back."

"When was the last time we did that?" said Charlie.

"Don't you remember? It was when you and Susan got safely back from the grip of the Gestapo."

"Yes, we had Abe to thank for that and Carl. Did you ever hear the full story?"

"I think so. Susan told me. She said Carl had a crush on me so the last thing he wanted to do was to hand her over to them. Getting out of France without being caught must have been a bit hairy."

"Let's go into the lounge."

"OK. It'll be ready in five minutes. I'll follow."

But when Lucy entered the lounge with the tray of food, Charlie was asleep on the sofa. She went for a blanket and settled down on the floor beside him. In the early hours, drugged with sleep, he turned and slid off the sofa. The familiar scent seeped into his semi-consciousness. He thought he was with Susan and pulled her into his arms. It was impossible for Lucy not to yield to the touch of the man she so desperately loved.

****

"Hello you two," called Susan. They were waiting by the stop as the 'camp-bus' drew in. The passengers, returning from leave, unloaded their cases and melted away into the complex of buildings. Charles ran across the grass into Charlie's waiting arms. He swung him round with a cry of joy and the boy squealed with delight.

"Careful with our baby."   He placed him down and Lucy came forward to shower the boy with kisses. The two sisters kissed, and then Susan kissed Charlie.

"What's been happening in my absence?"

"Nothing much. Same old routine."

"What about you Lucy? Anything to report?"

"No, just work. A new press arrived so now we can print the maps in colour."

"Charles starts in the school next week," said Susan. "Maybe I'll be looking for work in a few weeks."

"Do you want to come into the Op's Room? I can't recommend it."

Later that evening Charlie read Charles a bedtime story. They all listened until he was asleep.

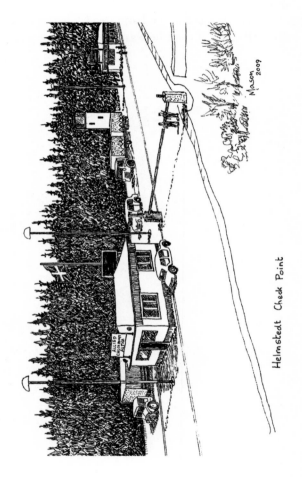

Helmstedt Check Point

4 Break Point

Lucy was sleeping. Susan had given Charlie and Charles their breakfast. Charlie said he would drop Charles at infant school on his way to the hospital, which was a long three story yellow brick building, holding five hundred beds and designed by Albert Speer in 1935 for the armed forces of the Reich. Charlie was working as a houseman in the Orthopaedic wards. The consultant knew that Charlie had other responsibilities and he had instructions to release him for other work when occasion demanded. Sometimes Charlie could be away from the Headquarters for several days at a time. What he did on those trips was always a secret but nevertheless sanctioned by the mysterious MISU. It was now five months since Susan's visit to their father.

The spring sunshine illuminated the spacious lounge of their flat. Lucy was still wearing her night dress as she drew back the curtains. At that moment Susan entered the room with a tray of tea and toast. She stopped suddenly, arrested by Lucy's silhouette against the light. Placing the tray carefully on the table she went to the window and stood in front of her sister. Taking her hand she said,

"Lucy dear, you're pregnant, aren't you?"

"So you noticed?"

"I know a bump when I see it. Who's the lucky father?"

"I didn't, I hoped it, Susan, I."

Lucy's flushing cheeks, her hesitation, her reluctance to make eye contact, sent a sudden shiver down Susan's spine, Softly she said,

"Lucy, look at me. Is it Charlie?"

Lucy turned and walked towards the door.

"Lucy, talk to me. It's got to be Charlie hasn't it?"

Lucy sat on a chair by the table and slumped her head onto her hands. Her shoulders shook.

"I didn't want to Susan," she cried. "I really didn't. Yes, it's Charlie. It was when you went away."

"You bitch."

"Susan. I didn't want it to happen.

"And you let him do it."

"It was an accident. Charlie had had a terrible day in the theatre. I tried to comfort him. He was in such distress. If you had been here Sue it would all have been different."

"I bet it would. Accidents like this don't happen. What do you take me for? Two whole weeks you had him. I bet you rolled everyday."

"No we didn't. All right then. It wasn't an accident. But Charlie said he loves me."

"Charlie loves everything in skirts. He's a bastard. I could kill him."

"Susan, please. It wasn't his fault. It really wasn't. If only you'd been here. He cried himself to sleep on my shoulder."

"And then?"

Lucy sunk her head and put her hands over her face as she cried while two minutes passed.

"No. Really." Susan resumed. "I don't want to know the sordid details."

"It wasn't sordid. It was the first time for me. You know that. I'm so so sorry Sue. I really am. Oh why can't we go back and be like we always were? We were happy then and now I'm just miserable and so are you Susan. Aren't you?"

"My feelings are mine."

"What's going to happen now Sue?" in a small voice.

"Nothing's going to happen. If you think I'm going to divorce him you're mistaken."

"You do love him don't you? You won't kill him, will you?"

"Don't ask me that now. It's not the right time to ask a question like that. No of course I couldn't really."

"I love him. I really do. I love him more than you. I couldn't live without him."

"Maybe, but I'm his wife and I'm going to stay his wife....... If you want to do something useful go and meet Charles from kindergarten and take him down to the NAAFI for the afternoon. I've got business with his father."

On the way to find her nephew Lucy met Brigadier Morris.

"Ah, Lucy.... Or is it Susan?"

"Lucy, Brigadier."

"I've bad news for you. I can't get security clearance for your sister Without it we can't be responsible for you or Susan. We shall have to find other work for you. The Op's room will be out."

"But."

"I'm sorry. The map room people said you are the best they've ever had. They'll be sorry to lose you."

"Why can't Susan get clearance for the map room too or maybe I could work for you?"

"The map room doesn't have a vacancy for Susan and I wouldn't be happy to see her work there anyway, too great a risk of cross fertilization between my department and Ops. If things change we may review it. For the moment I suggest you help out in the kindergarten. They're very short handed and the pay is quite good."

"I'll think about it Brigadier."

"Bye now."

Lucy turned on her heel and made her way to collect Charles as Susan had asked.

****

"So you couldn't keep your hands off her."

"Darling......."

"Don't darling me. You're a bastard.... A blaggard just like Dad said."

"I'm not a blaggard. I've made a terrible mistake. I know that, but."

"No buts."

"But I can't not love Lucy. That's all."

"That's not all. Far from it. Lucy's expecting your baby. How do you think that makes me feel?"

"Oh God, darling. What can I say? I love you, honestly, deeply, you and Charles."

"OK Charlie. I suppose you think that you can talk your way out of this. Just like you talk your way out of every bloody thing. I sometimes wish the Gestapo had got you."

"That's a terrible thing to say. Anyway if they had, they would have got you too. Luckily Carl took a liking to us, saved our lives."

"Well, come on then. Tell me. What's the great plan?"

"I haven't got a plan."

"Surprise, surprise. You must have known. Of course you've got a plan"

"I did know, months ago, but I was afraid to mention it. I saw her vomiting one morning. We could bring it up as our own, if only Lucy would agree."

At last the appalling consequences of the scandal hit Charlie. He felt sick at the thought of the damage he had done to his marriage. He subsided into a chair and covered his face with his hands.

Susan said,

"I'll think about it. It depends on Lucy. Meanwhile Charlie, keep away from her. You'll have to choose. You can't have both of us."

"Lucy's our sister. I can't keep away from her, from loving her. I know it shouldn't have happened. I'd had a hellish day and I drank too much brandy. I was comatose, asleep. I didn't realise until too late. I thought I was with you."

"I don't want to know the gory details."

"It's not like the life we led at the Mansion is it?"

"No, it certainly is not and never will be. That's well and truly in the past. We've grown up, that's all. You've grown up and it's time you realised it, your responsibilities."

"Really. Have you two grown up too, as you like to put it?"

"Mind your own business."

"I'll take that as a 'no'."

"You're impossible."

"I know. I am impossible but I do love you…. To distraction."

"Words, words, just words."

"Susan. I love you and I'll prove it. Just give me time."

"Leave my sister alone. That's all I ask. She doesn't really want a man. Not at heart. Don't you know that?"

"I don't believe that," he said. "Any of that. If you mean what I think you mean then."

"Believe it or not. I don't really care. By the way, there's a letter here for Lucy. It's got to be from Carl. I wish he wouldn't keep writing to her. This letter has been in the post for two weeks and it's been opened, not by me I hasten to say."

"It will be the censor."

They heard Lucy's key turning the latch. She came in with Charles. Charlie and Susan lowered their voices. Lucy pretended not to notice the tension.

"Lunchtime?" she asked breezily.

"Lucy, there's a letter for you from the east."

"From Carl? How nice. Let's see. Carl's wants to see me," Lucy exclaimed. "He wants to meet me at the Helmstedt check point."

"Why there?"

"It's the obvious place. He can't come here. He says he's got leave from the forest authority for a week. I'll have to get a temporary visa."

"Are you going to go then?" asked Charlie.

"Do you think I should?"

"Lucy, dear," said Susan. We can't run your life. Do you want Carl? If so then go. If not then apologise."

"He may not want me when he finds out I'm pregnant."

"That's your problem Lucy. For heavens sake, don't go unless you love him."

"I don't know whether I love him or not."

"Then you probably don't."

****

A week later Lucy caught the train from Osnabruck to Hannover. Then she caught the Berlin-bound train but alighted just before the DDR border at Helmstedt. She walked to meet Carl who arrived at the checkpoint on his old Lambretta. Lucy saw him across the barriers as he approached the eastern side. She jumped up and down with excitement and waved. Carl waved in return. When Lucy had completed the formalities she ran towards him across the border and they embraced.

Carl said, "I have a friend in Morsleben, Joachim Kuhne. He was in my group in the war. His wife is Helga. They said we can stay with them. He works on the railway."

"How far is it?"

"No distance. Get on behind me and we'll ride."

"What about my bag?"

"Leave it. They'll look after it. I'll come straight back."

In a side street near the main square they came to an apartment block. Joachim was there, having just arrived back home from his work. Introductions over, Carl fetched Lucy's bag from the station.

Helga soon came in. The Kuhnes were most hospitable. Lucy and Helga went to the kitchen whilst the men chatted in German about old times, the excitement of the panzer attacks and the horrors of the occupation. Helga knew little English so they had many laughs together. In the days which followed, Carl and Lucy explored the nearby 'Naturpark'.

"You know I'm pregnant, don't you."

"I knew the moment we met."

"Why didn't you mention it then?"

"I was waiting for you to tell me. Who's the father?"

"It's Charlie's."

"I might have guessed. You three have been living a strange life, haven't you?"

"It seemed all right at first. Dear Carl, I can't expect you to understand us. We used to get on so well. Susan and I always said we would never marry and, as children, we shared everything."

"Beds too?"

"Clothes, toys, friends, everything."

"Until Charlie."

"When we met him again in Breiten things started to get complicated. He came between Susan and me. I wanted us all to remain friends. We felt so sorry for him at first and then he seemed to take so many things over. It was almost as if he was running the place."

"But not the parties and the cabarets surely."

"No, not those. He never had anything to do with that side of our life."

"But you got involved with the airmen."

"Yes, that was David Brown's doing. He persuaded Charlie to recruit us. We just acted as couriers and guides, helping the airmen escape to France and Spain. We never entertained any of them in bed."

"And that's when my men captured him and Susan."

"You saved their lives. But for you they would have been shot. Carl, after I've had the baby in about four months, you won't want anything to do with me ever again will you?"

"Lucy, I want to marry you. I'll never give you up. Do you believe in 'love at first sight'?"

"No, not really."

"Well I do. I've loved you ever since I first saw you. Lucy, will you marry me?"

"Yes Carl. I want to say yes but......."

"But what?"

"I'm not going to give up my baby. Susan wants to adopt it as hers. I don't want that and where will we live?"

"Come with me, back to my forest. It's a good life. I will grow to love your baby. It will be ours. Come and see my place. I've got a log house. It stands in a clearing near the edge of the woods. Once a week I ride into Vacha for supplies. It takes a quarter of an hour. If you marry me we'll get a car. It will be wonderful. The DDR authorities make life impossible for those who want to cross the border into the west but it should be easy to get a permanent visa for you if we are going to marry and live together."

"I've never been separated from Susan. I don't know how it will be for us. I shall be dreadfully homesick."

"Your days will be full. I promise."

"Why don't you come back to the British Zone?"

"It's my life now. I am working for the British. It won't be for ever."

"You're a spy for us?"

"I work for Brigadier Morris, like Charlie."

"Charlie doesn't work for Brigadier Morris. He's a doctor at the hospital."

"That's his cover. I see Charlie from time to time. He's a courier. He gets people out of the DDR. He knows the paths and the safe ways through the mines."

"I can't believe that. It's incredible. Do you think Susan knows about it?"

"She must know about Charlie but she may not know about me."

"Isn't it terribly dangerous?"

"I hope not. I've been at it for almost six years and I'm accepted by the neighbours, not that there are many, and the border patrols all know me. I just mind my own plot. Occasionally I turn back refugees. The border police have been very lax until recently."

"What's the change?"

"I think the border will be made into a very formidable barrier. The fences and watch-towers are going up already. Progress is fast. Brigadier Morris thinks that by the end of the year or the beginning of 1953 at the latest, the cross border traffic will stop except for a few carefully controlled checkpoints. Anyone who tries to cross the border illegally will probably be shot or arrested and put in prison."

"There's no way I could live with you Carl. It would be much too dangerous."

"There's no danger unless you intend to break the law. I don't break any laws."

"Yes you do. You've just said you work for Morris."

"All I'm supposed to do is to report the movements of Russian soldiers; any build up of forces in my sector or anything which could endanger Western Germany. I sent in a report a month ago. All I said was 'nothing to report'".

"How did you do that?"

"I've got various ways. I could send anything urgent by radio but I never do. I would only use that if the Russians were going to invade. What I do normally is to leave a coded letter in a secret place for someone to collect."

"Who collects it?"

"Blessed if I know. Someone collects and leaves a note when they will be coming again. It's very simple."

"So he has to cross the border then. What happens if he gets caught?"

"I don't know that either. I suppose he will have a cover story. I don't imagine he will cross the wire. There must be other ways, I suppose. He could be anybody, even my friendly post-man. My letter box is not in a compromising place."

"Where is it then?"

"Ah-ha. That's my secret."

"Come on. No secrets from your wife."

"You're not my wife yet."

"As the wife of a spy I should be arrested along with you. I love you Carl but."

"Do you still love Charlie?"

"Charlie's married. Nothing's the same any more."

"But that didn't stop you having his baby, did it?"

"He made me. Susan was away in England. I didn't think we would have a baby did I? I thought I was safe."

"Mein Gott, that was rape."

"Oh dear, I shouldn't have said that. No it wasn't rape. He was drunk. In a moment of madness I accepted him. In his drugged sleep he thought I was Susan."

"Glaubst Du das wirklich?"

"I made him believe it. I was wrong, so wrong." Lucy burst into tears and buried her face in his coat. Carl, totally confused by her outburst, hugged her to himself until her cries subsided. He thought how mistaken he had been about the English and their emotionless attitude to life. They rode back to the Kuhnes apartment in silence because although Lucy could shout in Carl's ear she couldn't hear his reply above the noise of the engine and the wind. On the following day, their holiday together over, Carl took Lucy to the station. The steam locomotive, black and streaked with rust, from the east was removed to be replaced by a new, shining diesel from the west. Lucy boarded and leant from the window to give Carl one last lingering kiss. She was holding a handkerchief to her face as the train drew away towards Hannover. Carl mounted his motor scooter and made for Vacha.

****

"Well, what happened? Tell us all about it. Did he pop the question?"

"Yes, he did, several times."

"And the baby?"

"He doesn't mind about the baby. He says he wants to adopt it."

"Lucy, seriously, are you sure that this is what you want?" asked Susan.

"Haven't I thought about it a thousand times? Charlie's married to you now. He doesn't love me any more. How can he?"

"That's not what he said when I was away is it?"

"Oh Susan. Don't you know your own husband? He's weak. He fell for me that night. I seduced him. I didn't set out to ....honestly. It wasn't deliberate. Anyone could seduce Charlie. He's like that but he loves you. Don't you know that?"

"If I believe that I suppose I can believe anything. So what *are* you going to do?"

"I'm going to live with the one man who I really believe does love me."

"But."

"Yes, behind the Iron Curtain."

"That's crazy. You could be in danger. You won't be welcome. They only allow communists there."

"That's not true. Carl explained it to me. They want people to live there, young people. We'll be welcome and he has a good job."

"It's not what they say here. What about all those refugees who come over. West Germany is being swamped by refugees. Suppose there is another war?"

"If there is, nothing will stop the Red Army. You'll wake up here one morning and see their tanks on the lawn outside."

"So when are you going. Is Carl going to come over here to get you?"

"No. I'm having the baby first and then I'm going to England to see Dad. Don't be cross Susan."

"Why should I be cross?"

"I know you are at heart."

"No, I'm not cross but worried that you are about to take a step you might regret."

"I do love Carl and I know he loves me. If things don't work out then we will come back. It's simple."

"It won't be that simple. You'll just join the rest of the refugees. Charlie says that the border is going to be defended."

"We'll go to Berlin and get the army to fly us out."

"Even that won't be as simple as you pretend. Carl is a cold fish. Cold and calculating. Beware of that man. He's got hidden depths. Be warned. He says he loves you. I wonder what sort of love he is offering?"

"Oh Sue, he's not like that. Believe me. You might think he's cold but I know better. He's kind and considerate. He wants to adopt my baby, whatever it is, boy or girl."

Charlie woke in the night. He could hear Lucy cry. He slid from between the sheets trying not to wake Susan but in vain.

"What's going on Charlie?"

"It's Lucy, quickly."

They found Lucy sitting on the lavatory crying and screaming.

"Lucy's waters have broken darling. I'll get her back to bed. Get a towel and then phone for the ambulance."

In the early hours Lucy gave birth to a girl. She was nearly a month premature and very tiny. From the first moment Lucy named her Charlene.

The headquarters of BAOR was alive with news of the scandal. Charlie was interviewed by the Commander in Chief. The Staff was almost equally divided on the issue. Somehow or other the news reached Hugo and Frank. Someone sent Eliza a copy of the camp newspaper. Charlie was held up to be a latter day Casanova. His fellow officers in the mess treated him to endless ribald jokes and humiliating humour. They called him a cad and a renegade. The only person interested in defending Charlie, not on the grounds of sexual morality but for his courage and efficiency in his work, was Brigadier Jim Morris. The clique surrounding the hierarchy tried to persuade the Commander to demand Charlie's resignation on the grounds of 'misconduct, unbecoming an officer and a gentleman.' It was only Brigadier Morris who prevented this dire step which would have ruined Charlie's career.

The censure which reached Charlie was nothing to that heaped upon the head of Lucy. The officers' wives described her as a hussy, a loose woman and worse. Lucy moped in the apartment, too frightened to face the scorn of her peers. Her milk dried up with anxiety and unhappiness. As expected, her security pass was rescinded. Her work in the Ops. Room came to an end because the American officers on the site could not tolerate two identical women with different security passes. She was offered a post in the Kindergarten which she declined.

She wrote to Carl,

Dearest Carl,

I am so unhappy. Charlene is sweet. She was born a month too soon. She was tiny (four and a half pounds) but putting on weight now quite fast. But everyone has been absolutely beastly. They call me all sorts of horrible names and make my life a misery by talking about me behind my back. Charlie is not much help. He gets a lot of laddish banter which he seems to enjoy. I want you so much. You said you would adopt Charlene. I would love it if you did. I don't want her to grow up knowing she's a bastard. She will get so much teasing and it won't be her fault. I can't stand it here any longer Carl. I know Susan would like to adopt her but I can't bear that. I love her too much.

I long to see you again. If you still want me, I will marry you and come to live in your forest.

Please write. I am so miserable shut up in this flat.

Your loving Lucy.

Lucy received Carl's reply after a month.

Liebchen,

Of course I want you. Have not I told you this many times already? I have been to Berlin to the immigration authorities. I have applied for a permit for you to come over and marry me. I have told them that we shall have lots of children. When you get here you can apply for a DDR passport. I am sure that they will welcome you. As soon as you are able to arrange your journey I will meet you in Berlin. We will marry and then I will formally adopt Charlene. Do you mind if we change her name to Carla? I am sure after your recent experience that you will prefer this.

I can't wait to see you again and hope that you will reply soon. The letters take so long to get through that I think you should book your train at least three weeks ahead.

Alles Gute Liebling. Mit lieben Grussen Deine Lucy
Auf Wiedersehen, Carl

Dearest Carl,

I am overjoyed to get your letter. What a pity they take so long to reach me. I will definitely come to you in the spring. I am going back to England for the winter to see Dad. He is still very ill after his stroke. I might not get another opportunity to see him. It could be now or never. Darling, I long to be with you and I hope you will not think badly of me for being away for so long. I will write every day. I do want Dad to see Carla. I am sure that he will be thrilled.

Let's get married in Berlin when I return. I will love your home in the woods. I can get the train straight through from Hamburg to Friedrichstrasse and then I don't need to come back to this horrible barracks.

Bless you my darling. Your loving Lucy.

When Lucy showed Carl's letter to Charlie and Susan, they were speechless.

"Don't you think it's wonderful? Aren't you going to say anything?"

Charlie said,

"There's nothing we can say Lucy. We've been over it time and again. I shall be upset, Susan will be distraught, your father may die of shock, your whole family will be anxious for you. I don't suppose I shall sleep any more."

"I've got my life to lead, haven't I? You said that. Anyway, I'm going to see Dad soon and then I'm going to get the train to Berlin where we shall be married."

"Don't you want a proper wedding Lucy?"

"It will be a proper wedding. We can't afford the frippery and we don't need to prove our love in that way even if you did."

A few days later Lucy and Charlene, (Susan kept calling her by that name right up to the moment of parting), caught the early morning bus from the camp to the station, just as Susan had all those fateful months before.

****

Lucy's train journey from Helmstedt to Berlin seemed to go on for ever. She sat nursing Charlene. The coaches were clean but old and grossly overheated. There was no way to open a window. Every seat was occupied. Two coaches were reserved for armed service personnel, the remaining four occupied by West Germans visiting relatives or else returning home. As the train, which did not stop at any station between Helmstedt and Berlin, slowed through Brandenburg, Lucy viewed, with mixed feelings of alarm and sympathy, the ruins and decrepit trackside coaches. The scars of war were pitiful with whole families living amongst the wreckage of the city. The beautiful strains of the Brandenburg Concertos sang in her head in stark contrast to the devastation before her.

Her father's last pleading, as they parted on the station in Manchester, still kept repeating in her head as if he was sitting next to her. The winter had been severe and Uncle Frank and she had not been able to take him out of the house for weeks. He was no better in spite of the constant care he received from the full time nursing. She had thought he should be in hospital but Hugo wouldn't even think about it. There were many times when their relationship became very strained but Charlene brought tears to his eyes and softness in his voice. He would nurse the baby, sometimes for hours. She remembered the long conversations they had, mainly about Susan and Charlie. She could tell him very little about Charlie's work.

The strangest part of it all was her father's total acceptance and acquiescence of all that had happened between them.

Charlene's cry woke her from her reverie. Lucy had four vacuum flasks of hot water. Since her milk had dried she had to carry powdered milk in her bag. In a trunk she had packed everything she thought she would need for life in the forest. Carl was at the Friedrichstrasse Station patiently waiting for her train to arrive. There were only two trains every day and he had been to the station to meet each one for the last three days. Like a proud father he stood by the barrier with an empty baby carriage, already provided with blankets and a miniature pillow.

Carrying Charlene, now to be called Carla, and her bag, Lucy looked up and saw him waving from the crowd. She saw a porter and asked him to bring her trunk from the van. Carl gathered up the baby from her arms and laid her gently in the pram. Then they embraced. At the DDR Office in West Berlin they obtained a travel permit for Lucy, valid for two weeks. Carl explained to the official that they were to be married and that he already had a permanent post as the forest ranger in the Thuringerwald. The man smiled and wished them luck. He said that Lucy would have no difficulty obtaining a DDR passport once they were married.

On the way to Eisenach, the following day, Lucy became more and more depressed. The journey proceeded through ruined towns and villages. The impoverished people and dilapidated factories made stark contrast with the new buildings, glitz and bustle of West Berlin. In Eisenach Carl had already made a booking at the Registry of Births, Death and Marriages. There were no witnesses to their union other than the staff who signed their certificate. Once outside after the austere atmosphere of the office, Lucy clung to Carl and burst into tears thinking all the time about the lovely wedding which David Brown had arranged for Susan nearly nine years ago. Carla in her pram slept through it all.

From Eisenach they found a bus to Vacha where Carl had left his motorbike in a garage. With Lucy, Carla and luggage following in an old decrepit taxi he led the way to the house.

Lucy's spirits revived when she saw her new home for the first time. From a short distance the wooden house looked charming, perched on a rocky knoll with extensive views over the forest and the valley. The air was fresh and tingled with the sap of the pines. Inside it was a different story. The rooms reeked of stale food and bedding. The windows ran with condensation. The primitive kitchen with its wood-burning range, which had not been cleaned since it was new, made tears spring to her eyes. It was obvious that Carl was not house-proud.

"How do you like your new home then?"

"It could be made beautiful," said Lucy guardedly.

"Do you like it?"

"I will like it darling. I'm going to work really hard to make it a lovely place for you and Carla."

5 THE PLAN

Charlie took a garrison car to Osnabruck station to collect David and the mysterious JD.

Their train from Hamburg was on time. David Brown descended to the platform carrying two bags closely followed by an older man. Both were wearing dark grey suits and trilby hats. Charlie, looking very spruce in his service dress, stepped forward to greet them.

"Hello David."

"Hello Charlie, meet my boss, ' JD'." Charlie snapped to attention and saluted.

"No need for that," said JD as they shook hands.

"Is there a car?" said David.

"Over here, the Humber."

The three got into the staff car, Charlie on the rear facing seat. They shut the interior window as the WRAC chauffeur pulled away from the curb. It was a quarter hour drive to the HQ.

JD opened the conversation.

"How are things at home?"

"On the home front or at work?" said Charlie

"At home."

"At home, not good, bad in fact."

"What's the problem?"

"After Lucy had my child, a daughter, she went to the East and married Carl."

"Yes, we know. We've been thinking about it. We thought that if you had really wanted to play fast and loose you should have been more discrete. It disturbs a tight ship when we have a rogue officer who creates mayhem. You were very lucky not to be sent home."

"Yes, I'm very sorry. It wasn't intended to work out that way."

"We didn't think you had much idea of the trouble you caused. David and Jim Morris put a spoke in the wheel on your behalf. They pointed out the investment we have in you and your experience. No one's indispensable, however. But for them we would have given you the sack. As it is we just hope to God that it's history now, all a seven day wonder."

"Look," said Charlie. "It was unintentional. I was drunk and asleep. I thought I was with my wife. If I'd known it would create such a fracas she could have gone home to have it. We three have known each other since we were kids."

"That's as maybe but you are kids no longer."

"Anyway Lucy has gone to live with Carl."

"Yes, well, all things considered it could be for the best. We didn't really approve of Carl's long distance courtship. It could have blown his cover. At least we may have reached some point of stability."

"With Lucy away, Susan has been more settled," said Charles.

"Will she get over it?"

"Who knows? I expect so. Can I assume the incident is closed?"

"As far as we are concerned, yes. Now to the more important matter of business."

"OK. What do you want to know?"

"I've read your report. It seems that the doors are closing one by one."

"They are indeed," said Charlie. "But it's quite free and easy in Berlin at the moment. The demarcation lines are open. But it's a different story on the Grenze."

"The what?"

"Grenze, the boundary between the Russian Zone and us. The guards at the checkpoints are very keen."

"How did you get on with that Russian guy, General Balashev?"

"I had a terrible time. He's a most difficult man. He got into East Berlin easily enough, in full uniform in his own staff car. We met, as planned in the foyer of the Hotel Marien and went to the apartment. I had to get him up in the early morning to mingle with the rush hour workers. After an argument, I persuaded him to leave his uniform behind and put on some nondescript clothes I had there. We got the S-Bahn from Alexander Platz to Tiergarten. I took him to the airfield and reported to the duty officer. I had difficulty in explaining who he was, which caused a bit of delay. He wanted another uniform but we got him fixed up with a smart suit. All in all it was a terrific coup. We flew out next day."

"Excellent, well done," said JD. "He's being de-briefed in Woolcroft and then flown to a new life in the USA."

David said,

"One up to us I think and a smack in the eye for their Intelligence. I just hope the Russians don't come looking for him. Be careful Charlie. You'll be a marked man if they find out."

The car stopped by the main entrance to the HQ.

"Let's go up and see the CO, David. Charlie, you carry on and we'll see you at ten tomorrow. We've got another assignment to talk about."

"Yes Sir. Goodbye then for now, until to-morrow. See you David."

"Night Charlie."

****

Five men sat round the table in the commander's office, the CO, JD, Brigadier Jim Morris, David Brown and Charlie.

"I suppose this room has been de-bugged," said JD.

"Everyday Sir. Let's get down to it, shall we?" replied the CO. "Congratulations, Jim, on your promotion. How does it feel?"

"No different but thanks anyway Sir. I just hope that I'm worthy of the responsibility for MISU. We've got some very efficient people here."

David continued the discussion.

"Yes Sir, I'm sure we wish you well in your new post and thank you gentlemen for sitting in on this very important meeting. Now Lieutenant Forbes, Charlie, listen very carefully to what we have to say. We are co-operating with the Americans in this project and there are very few agents left who qualify."

"What do you mean qualify?" Charlie asked.

"We think you qualify. You're almost fluent in German, a doctor, proved yourself to be resourceful etc etc."

"Come on David. Cut the flattery."

"The high command is very impressed with your track record. You are the most experienced courier we have."

"Is that what you call me, a courier? I set out to be a doctor."

"We haven't forgotten but this is likely to be the biggest job you have tackled so far - or ever will tackle. The Brigadier will explain the details. If you get this job under your belt you'll be stood down and sent back to England for some long leave."

"Let's have some coffee," interrupted JD. There was a delay whilst this was served and the room once more isolated.

"I think we should stress, for Charlie's benefit, that this operation is to be classified as entirely at his discretion. There is to be no compulsion. If Charlie is not comfortable with the plan then we shall abandon it and leave it up to the Americans to carry on if they feel so disposed," said David.

"Thank you Brown. The chap we want, let's call him Herr X, or just X," opened Brigadier Morris.

"That's a bit corny isn't it?" said Charlie.

"If you sign up to this job Lieutenant Forbes, you'll be subject to military discipline," said the Brigadier somewhat testily. "King's Regulations and all that, we may think of a name later. His real name is top secret. He works for the Russians although the work goes on in the Harz Mountains."

"I've heard about that."

"Oh really. It's supposed to be classified," interrupted David.

"That's a joke. Everybody knows what goes."

"Everybody?"

"Well most of the military at any rate. This base leaks like a colander," said Charlie.

Brigadier Morris continued,

"Be that as it may, X has said he wants to come over to the west and we need him."

"Do we indeed? Are we so behind then?"

"No it's not like that. We need to know where we stand. The whole effort of our intelligence is directed towards monitoring the disposition of the enemy forces, or I should say, potential enemy. The Harz installation was one of Hitler's rocket factories and X was brought up as one of the engineers from early days of the science, going back before the war. What he doesn't know about rocketry probably isn't worth knowing."

"If it's common knowledge that we know what goes in the Harz, then the Ruskies will be making darn sure that we don't get anywhere near the place," said Charlie. "Anyway how are we so sure of our facts?"

"We've an agent over there, working on the inside," replied Brigadier Morris.

"Wow, that sounds dangerous. How reliable is he?"

"Actually, he is a 'she'. We are not too sure of her duties, probably secretarial. Her code name is Rita. She's about thirty one years old. We know she's very reliable. The intelligence we have had from her has been first class over several years. Our side is developing rockets too but we may have to build one that will be capable of intercepting one of their's, a tall order to say the least."

"So where do I come in.?"

"If you agree to join the project I'll give you transport and a driver and in two weeks I shall want a report on the steps the DDR are taking to stop east-west traffic, likely weak places, all that sort of stuff."

"But the DDR isn't a state," said Charlie. "It's a zone. Without the Ruskies it will collapse. Surely, the sooner the Ruskies go away the better. All we have to do is wait."

"That's not as we see it and we have to live with the reality. The Russians will never go away. Their empire stretches from us, NATO/BAOR, to the Pacific and, but for us and the Americans, there is nothing to stop the Red Army marching to the Atlantic. They still could," continued Brigadier Morris.

"But for the Atom Bomb," interjected the CO.

"That's the only thing that will keep them guessing. The thought of an atomic war in central Europe is, well, I won't elaborate. Coming back to this mission. Are you in or not?"

"I've got to know more Sir. Is this only to be a recce?"

"Yes, a fact-finding tour only at this stage. But we must act fast. Patrols are covering the border strip, which has been ploughed and wired and mines laid. We expect that progress will be very rapid. Soon the whole frontier will be impenetrable right to the Med," said the Brigadier.

Charlie said,

"They've sealed the border. I know that. It's been sealed very effectively for some months. There may be a few loopholes but not many. Corporal Tom McGinti and I have been doing some surveys up and down the Grenze all year. Several very daring escapes are recorded in my reports."

"Yes, we've read them."

"But why rely on me? The best ones get into the newspapers. There was that balloon that......."

"Yes, yes, this is not helping our present problem. I'm not talking about a daring escape."

"All right then. I'll do what you ask. Just tell me when you want to fill in the details."

"To-morrow. My office at 0800."

"Wow, that urgent?"

"That urgent."

The following morning Charlie found himself interviewed once more but this time only Brigadier Morris and David were present.

"Well what do you think?" opened David.

"Why me? There must be many others better qualified."

"Not many, a few, but you have one unique advantage."

"Have I indeed, what's that?"

"You know Carl and when we told him about our little expedition he asked about you. He says you two are great friends."

"He's no friend of mine."

"He spoke highly of you though."

"Come on David. You know what happened in the war."

"Yes but he gives you the credit for helping him find his feet after the war and everything that has followed."

"He stole Lucy from us."

"Lucy had nowhere to run and you know it. Anyway according to Susan, Lucy loves him."

"We haven't heard from Lucy for weeks. We've no idea how she's getting on. Why not use Carl? He's on the spot, knows the forest. He's your man."

"No he isn't. We can't use him for this, not after all the resource we've put into getting him established. Carl is back-up to be used only in emergency."

"Oh, I see. He's too valuable so what value do you put on me then?"

"That's not fair Charlie. You have different skills, altogether different and you know it. Besides that, his wooden leg prevents him from overland hikes. At least this time you'll both be on the same side. So what is your decision?"

"I'll think about it. But first tell me more."

"We'll not tell you much more until you sign up."

"So, you'll be asking me to break through the Iron Curtain. Trek to the Harz. Make contact with X. Get him back to the fence and through it. What then?"

"We'll be there to meet you, along with the MC."

"Master of Ceremonies?"

"Military Cross."

"Brilliant, and if I fail?"

"You won't. I knew you would agree."

"I haven't yet."

"Well, you only have forty eight hours to make up your mind and sign on. Sleep on it."

"I will." Charlie said,

"Charlie, this is your work. When I signed you on, I understood that this is what you wanted to do."

"You told me yesterday that this op. is to be at my discretion."

"True, but your continued employment here depends on your performance."

"Do I get to see Carl?"

"That's a difficult one. Lieutenant," said Brigadier Morris. "You'll have to take a lot on trust. Getting Lucy to Berlin was beautifully arranged and we had the perfect excuse. We can't do it again. Not for a long time. Meanwhile we'll just have to rely on his drops. We get them every week. So far everything is going well. Your task is to find ways of getting across."

"So that's what the recce is all about."

"Precisely. We want to press the button about a month from now. The Americans are doing the recce in their zone. You will have from the Baltic to Witzenhausen."

"Is that all?"

"We think it's enough."

"But Vacha is well south of that."

"I'm aware of that. I'm hoping the American recce will cover that area thoroughly."

"So I don't get to see Carl or Lucy?"

"Charlie, this is not a holiday. If you want to see Lucy it will have to be another time.

You'll have a radio. We shall be monitoring you every step of the way. You'll have the latest electronic mine detector. We've come a long way since 1942."

"I think you've talked me into it. I'll check it out with Susan to-morrow."

6 The Zantens

Charlie sat in the Jeep with Tom, the driver. It was raining. The Jeep was facing the wire. The country road was blocked by lumps of concrete. Beyond, in the mist, they could dimly see the watchtower over the top of the high fence. Inside that, they knew the police would be watching them through binoculars.

"Hell. What do you make of it Tom."

"I reckon they've sewn up this area good and tight. If this is a fair sample of the Grenze, it's impregnable to all but the most determined young people. I wonder if we could walk round the end of the wire at Lubeck?"

"Not a chance. We'll go and have a look if you're not convinced. One or two bold fellows have joined the West by swimming round it but it's very chancy. They have to rely on being picked up by one of our patrol boats. The East has more boats than we have."

"So where do we start?"

"I think a barge is the answer."

"How so?"

"There's a lot of traffic on the Elbe, which forms the border from Lauenburg to Schnackenburg, that's the last checkpoint before the barges enter the eastern zone. Here have a look at the map. We'll recce our bank and then pay a visit there to see how thorough they are."

"Takes you back to your trip on the Rhine, I expect."

"Well at least I've had experience and I know where to get help. It's no use asking any of the river skippers here. They could be very uncertain which side they're on."

"Beyond Witzenhausen we're in the American Zone."

"OK then. We'll start from here and work our way south. We've got to the end of the week. Our main target is the Harz."

"Why is that?"

"The Ruskies have an underground weapons factory there. We've got an informer on the inside. The ex-Nazi scientists working there are virtual prisoners. My boss thinks we can get one to come over."

"How the hell are they going to fix that?"

"It's partly up to us. Let's get going."

They drove south towards the Harz. As they approached the hills it became impossible for the jeep to reach the Border in many places. Most of the reconnaissance was done on foot but they could see little of the Grenze. They found the marker posts but nothing beyond, apart from steep rocky hills and thick forests of pine. Once over the line of the frontier they knew that they could meet an armed patrol anywhere. Even if they managed to reach the wire undetected, they would be observed and photographed, even shot.

"This is no place for us," said Charlie. "These Ruskies certainly know how to keep us guessing. We haven't a hope of getting our man through here. If I do manage to find him, getting him to the crossing point will need transport."

"What now Sir?"

"Let's get back to the Jeep. We'll find a bed with our chaps in Bad Lauterberg. It's a lovely spot."

Ten days later Charlie was making his report to Jim Morris.

"In view of X's age, Sir, we've got to find an easy route. We don't want a situation where he is in danger from mines or bullets. I don't suppose he can run very far either. We can't help the danger of discovery, only minimise it."

"Wouldn't it be better if you made out a written report?"

"Very good, Sir, I will but for now I have to say that the best way out will be on a barge. Forget about the wire. There are ways through the wire but only for brave young men."

"How do you propose we organise a barge?"

"Time will no longer be a problem will it? We'll have to get co-operation from a repair yard in Hamburg and money. We'll have to think very hard about getting X on board but if we succeed then the rest should be straight forward. I've had experience"

"How much money?"

"Hard to say. At least ten thousand pounds but don't quibble about that. If you want him out then MISU will just have to pay the price."

"All right then, let me have your report a.s.a.p. like tomorrow but you're wrong about the time factor, Charlie. We are in a hurry. Rita says the Russians are closing down the Harz operation and moving it to the Urals. X and his wife……"

"I don't know anything about a wife, Sir."

"He won't move without us arranging for his wife to join him too and his family."

"That's going to make a whole heap of difference and it will alter the timetable too."

"Well that's how it is. We didn't know about this before yesterday. Just carry on and report back."

"There's just one more thing, Sir."

"Oh, and what's that?"

"We may need a bolt hole. Not now necessarily, but in an emergency. I think I've the ideal place at Vacha."

"OK, put that in your report as well. Don't go into detail now."

"Vacha is opposite the American Zone. I'll explain it in my report. Whatever we do it's going to cost."

"Charlie, I don't think we're price sensitive. MISU just want results."

"Yes Sir."

A week later Charlie attended a meeting in London with David and 'JD'.

"And Susan?"

"She came over with me. She's gone to see her Dad."

"I see. Are things better between you all?"

"Not really. Hugo thinks I'm a turd and that's all there is to it, and she's still mad. Blames me for Lucy going east. She had another bleeding heart letter."

"OK. Can we get down to business?" JD interrupted. "You want us to modify a barge so we can transport our precious cargo. Is that it?"

"I've seen it done. I was on a Rhine barge in 1940. We carried an elderly couple and three teenage girls from Antwerpen to Basle, right under the noses of the river patrols."

"And it worked?"

"Except for one incident."

"What was that?"

"One girl was killed by an inspection party but it was just carelessness. It should never have happened. The hideaway was sound. The bargemaster had a very narrow compartment constructed in steel at the after-end of the main hold. Access was behind a generator in the engine room. Without detailed measurements of the hull it was impossible to detect."

"Have you thought about the bargemaster?"

"I have indeed. Hans Zanten will be the ideal person. We did the Rhine together back in 1940. He is experienced and speaks fluent German and is one hundred per cent reliable. He was the skipper on my trip. I was just a deckhand."

"Don't sell yourself short Charlie. You were all but the mate, especially after Hans was wounded." said David.

"Ok." said JD. "It's go. We'll do it, just as you say."

"I've been to have a look," said Charlie. "There's a damaged barge lying in the docks in Hamburg. The place is a mess. It resounds with scrap merchants and the repair yards are working flat out. We'll never get the work done unless......"

"Oh, we'll get it done all right. We just want you and this Hans Zanten to get over there and set the ball rolling. Check the barge and make sure it's suitable et cetera."

"Who do I contact?"

"I'll make a contact. You just get to see Zanten and we'll all meet in Hamburg in a week. And keep in touch Charlie. We've got to move fast. You're the man on the ground. David will do the admin. OK?"

"What shall I offer Hans?" queried Charlie.

"If you want to go over a thousand pounds, phone David first. OK?"

"Very good Sir."

"This meeting is ended. Phone me from Bern when you land."

****

Hans Zanten was at the airport to meet him. Charlie had fixed the rendez-vous three days previously. He had made it sound like a social call.

"Hello, hello, my old friend." Hans shouted across the concourse. He enclosed Charlie in a bear-like hug almost squeezing the breath from his body. His rugged face was creased from ear to ear.

"It's great to see you again Hans. How's your arm and how are Heidi and the boys?"

"They're fine. The boys are both working now. Working the barges down to Strasbourg."

"They must be skippers now."

"Peter will take his final exam in a month. Jo in two more years."

"And Heidi?"

"She's OK. Older and wiser like the rest of us. She doesn't travel on the barges any more and neither do I unless I'm needed."

"What of La Tulipe?"

"We sold her. I got a good price but it was a wrench. Sometimes I wish I hadn't but she needed a lot of money spending on her. The big boys are moving in on the Rhine trade these days. Family barges are on the way out."

"Let's have dinner somewhere and then we can talk. How long will it take you to get home?"

"Only two hours. Where are you staying?"

"Here, at the airport. We can eat right here. Is that all right?"

Charlie checked in and they relaxed over a drink in the bar.

"Hans, this is not just a social call. I'm on a mission."

"And what might that be my friend?"

"Well, cast your mind back to 1940. Do you still hear from Luc?"

"Of course. He is one of my oldest friends."

"Do you remember how he persuaded you to take a precious contraband cargo?"

"How can I possibly forget? That's how I met you."

"Take a deep breath Hans…… I'm on a similar mission."

"Oh no! Really? And you think an old man will be interested in contraband cargo?"

"You might be and, if not you, Peter and Johannes might be."

"There must be a thousand shady masters who would be but not me. I'm sorry Charlie."

"Listen Hans. This is the tricky bit. It's very secret. I'm a doctor with B.A.O.R. HQ in Osnabruck but that's not all I do. I also work for a special unit getting VIP's out of the east. It's important work. Now we have a VIP in our sights who wants to come to the West. I've told my boss that the best way, if not the only way, is to use an Elbe Barge. Mr X, Herr X, is elderly and we need him. He has a family too and that makes it doubly tricky."

"Well I'll mention it to the boys when I see them. They're down river at the moment."

"I need help now. It's not like 1940 Hans. We're not at war. The journey is from Hamburg to Berlin and back. Lots of barges do it every week."

"Why not ask them then?"

"Come on Hans. You know very well why I can't ask them. Many of them are Communists but we don't know which ones."

"It was different in 1940. I was a younger man and we were saving lives."

"And you were being paid a lot of money."

"Not all of us."

"Not all, but you were."

"I nearly lost my arm. If you hadn't gone off in the dinghy when you did, the bullet might have missed us."

"If, if, if. Let's not talk about the past."

"Well you brought it up Charlie."

"OK, touché. Now, I need help. We, the service, need help and we'll pay. And it will save lives in the long run, - lots of lives." Charlie paused. Hans sat back twiddling his glass. A minute passed before he replied.

"All right then. Tell me what you want."

"There's a barge in the Vulcan Yard in Hamburg, which we are buying, but she's in need of repair and she needs a secret room built in, like we had on La Tulipe. We want an engineer to shack-up on the docks and organise everything, engine overhaul, hull repairs, the lot."

"Well if that's all, I can do it. It will be a welcome change from tending the garden and going for walks with Heidi and the dogs."

"Well it's not absolutely all. We want you to take the boat to Berlin, picking up me and my passenger on the way back."

"I can't do it on my own. I don't know the Elbe and what about locks?"

"No, but you could if Peter and Johannes were with you and I would join you near Havelberg with any luck."

"Luck won't have to come into it on a journey like this. Anyway where's Havelberg?"

"It's where the Berlin Kanal joins the Elbe. There are lock gates there. I've still to do a recce but I've been told the canal runs through forest, a 'Naturpark', so getting to you should not be a problem. I just hope my customers won't mind a bit of a walk."

"Give me a day to think about it. I shall have to make some plans too you know."

"Yes, I can see that."

"If I come to Hamburg I can get the job under way and then, if the boys join in, maybe they can do the voyage. If they don't want to do it then you'll have to find another skipper."

"OK. That sounds a fair proposition to me. We are offering a thousand pounds plus all your expenses."

"OK, a thousand just for getting you afloat, just that and we'll talk about the voyage later?"

"Since it's you Hans, I agree. Let's shake on it."

Charlie met David at Hamburg Airport a few days later.

"It's all fixed David. The Zantens will be here next week. He's accepted a thousand plus expenses for the overhaul. You'll have to cough up more for the trip."

"Was that necessary?"

"David, you got him cheap. He's doing it as a favour to me personally. In 1940 he got over a million Guilders."

"We were at war then. Things are different now."

"This is the Cold War, remember. If he backs out now we'll be in the soup time-wise."

"I agree but next time, consult me first."

"I will but it won't make any difference. His boys will probably do the trip."

"His boys?"

"Peter and Johannes. Peter has his ticket and Jo is experienced. They were brought up on La Tulipe in the war."

"I was hoping that you could persuade Hans to skipper."

"It'll cost."

"How much?"

"Get real David. Only a fraction of what you've spent so far. Morris said money wasn't important."   With that David caught the next BEA flight to Northolt.

Two weeks later Hans and Heidi were living in a small hotel close to the docks in Hamburg.

Work had already begun on the barge, called 'Freiheit', in the Vulcan yard. Hans had decided to construct 'The Black Hole' (the name they gave to the secret room in memory of La Tulipe). He put it about that the new owners were short of money and had hired him to do the welding as well as supervising the overhaul and painting. In fact the fewer people who knew about the work the better.

Toward the end of January a cold snap brought most of the work to a standstill. Freiheit was nearly ready. Peter, now thirty one, joined the barge and was appointed skipper. Hans and he had agreed to do the trip if Johannes would join them.

"I'm going to ask for a thousand pounds each," Charlie told Hans. "And you can cut me in for ten percent."

"You old rogue. I suspected you wanted some of the action. Make it two thousand each and you can have a tenth."

"Shake on it. We officers are always under-paid. You know that Hans."

Charlie visited the yard occasionally, usually after dark, and always dressed in mufti. David was getting anxious about progress. Charlie reported to Brigadier Morris every week and in the meantime went back to his duties in the hospital. The cold snap got worse. The river and the docks were locked in ice and diesel fuel in the freighters turned to jelly. The whole fleet was immobilised and in Berlin the coal shortage caused people to shiver at best and at worst to die of hypothermia.

****

Brigadier Morris received another letter from Rita. When de-coded it read:-

"X is going to visit his family in Leipzig. He has three weeks leave and so have I, since I have to go with him. The snow will delay his return. Frau X, wants to go shopping in Berlin. I've got the company car to take her. You can look after X and his bodyguard at the hotel. X is desperate to get out before the big move. What about his family? Have you thought about that?"

Morris realised that timing was the essence of this operation. If he acted too soon then Freiheit would not have reached Berlin. Too late and the authorities would wonder why the return of an empty barge was delayed, increasing berth costs and holding up other traffic. He discussed the dilemma with Charlie who said,

"I'll join the next road-convoy to Berlin and wait at the apartment and watch to see if X arrives at the Alexander"

"He will have escorts. You may have to get rid of them," said the Brigadier.

"If I do the balloon will go up and they'll be looking everywhere."

"At the moment I can't see a way round that."

"We could spike their drinks."

"That's not practical and anyway it won't ease the situation except to salve your conscience. The balloon, as you put it, will still go up."

"I want to meet this Herr X. and I want a profile on Rita."

"Our Rita, why on earth?"

"I think I may have met her before. Can you check it out with David and see if I'm right?"

"Well, perhaps you have…. And then perhaps not."

She might have been with us on the Rhine in 1940 and she might have been one of the girls boarded at the Refuge in 1941."

" I'm not able to give you anything, sorry."

"In any case, what's the panic? If I can get to Rita or X, I can tell them about Freiheit. I'm not happy about a snatch in Berlin. It could be suicide and not just for me. The Stasi operate on both sides of the line you know."

"What do you propose?"

"I'll think of something in due course," said Charlie with a confidence he didn't feel.

A few days later Charlie hitched a lift in the daily convoy along the Autobahn to West Berlin. It was a perilous journey. Most of the road had been cleared of snow but, in places, it was drifting up to a meter deep. The convoy halted while the bulldozer was unloaded and the snow pushed to one side. On the approach to the West Berlin barrier the convoy halted again while all personnel had their passes scrutinised. Charlie felt sorry for the East German Border Police. It was half an hour past mid-night. He found a room for the rest of the night in the army barracks and slept fitfully. At six he rose and joined the commuters walking into the eastern zone. There were few of them compared to those travelling west. He went to the MISU apartment and changed from his non-descript garb into something a little more acceptable to the reception at the Hotel Alexander.

7 Berlin

"Rita! My God, it is you."

"Too damn right it is. Didn't you know?"

"You don't sound surprised to see me."

"I'm not. I've known for over a month."

"Who told you?"

"Jim, who else?"

"Brigadier Jim Morris, the bastard. He flatly refused to give me anything on you."

"Good for him."

"He knew we would meet, so why didn't he?"

"Jim knows all about you or he thinks he does. He didn't want to rock your little nest. You know how Lucy and Susan feel about me."

"Susan is my wife now and Lucy's gone east, married to Carl."

"Charlie, you don't need to tell me."

"I'm supposed to be sending X's escorts to the cleaners. I don't relish dispatching you.

Don't worry about me. I can hit a moving duck at a hundred feet with my iron. In any case I'm not an escort. Actually I'm coming with you."

"What, and blow your cover?"

"X has three weeks leave and so have I. All we have to do is get rid of the minders. I'm not going to the Urals, even if that's what Jim thinks. My cover should hold."

Rita Smidt and Charlie sat side by side in the hotel reception talking in undertones in the almost deserted lounge.

"Where are they now?" asked Charlie.

"In the first floor suite, room 101. Are you booked in?"

"No, I've got an apartment just off Rosen Strasse. Have you a room here?"

"Of course. Want to come up?"

"Is that wise? Your room might be bugged."

"Do you really think so?"

"Well it's a possibility. I think we'll be safer talking down here. They can't bug the whole hotel. I want to know more about X and his family."

"Well Karen, his wife is with him now and they have a son, aged about thirty five, unmarried but I believe he has a lady friend. Marriage is a probability."

"Why does X want to defect? He seems to be well dug in, a good job and plenty of privileges. Wouldn't it put his wife and son in danger if he came over?"

"Karen will have to come over too. That's a condition. He doesn't seem too worried about the son who has a steady job driving buses in Magdeburg. He's fed up with the system. Dealing in top secret design and technology means he's practically a prisoner. Even when he goes home he has two security men with him. They never get any privacy and no chance to have holidays unaccompanied. By all accounts the son is a good communist."

"Did you think that I'm here to get them out by air?" asked Charlie.

"Yes, I did."

"I don't see how that's possible without a shoot out. The West might have got him on a plane during the 1948 blockade but not now. Things are too tight. We have a plan to get him on to an Elbe barge but it's got to seem like a defection, not a kidnap."

"Let's go upstairs, Charlie. I'm off duty until to-morrow."

"All right then but later. I'm starving."

"Let's snatch something down here."

Over their dinner Charlie and Rita talked about their escape from Belgium in 1940 with her sister and Abe on board La Tulipe. Rita's eyes filled with tears as they remembered how Gretchen had been shot by a German Rhine patrol. For fear of discovery they couldn't give her a proper burial. Abe had made up a short service of prayers as they had consigned her body to the Rhine waters, sewn up in a canvas bag weighted with a small anchor.

They washed down their meal with the best Johannisberg which had been hidden away in the cellars of the Hotel Alexander. Charlie noticed Rita secretly topping up his glass between courses but since he had the same idea he let it go unremarked.

At five in the morning Charlie left the hotel to walk to his apartment. He failed to notice the dark figure which followed him all the way. It was afternoon when he woke from a deep sleep.

Looking out of his window, he noticed a man standing in a doorway opposite. Thinking little of it he washed and prepared to go out. He had arranged to meet Rita and Karen in the ruined church-museum, the Kaiser Wilhelm Kirche, at the end of the Kurfurstendamm. The man was still standing in the doorway. He had been there for at least half an hour. As he watched another figure approached. The first man moved away and the newcomer stood in his place.

"Damn, damn, bloody hell and damn." Charlie thought to himself. "They know me, the flat and probably Rita as well."

He went into the bathroom. Above his head was the trap door. He lowered the ladder and climbed into the radio room.

One short message to Osnabruck would suffice. It was already encoded for just this eventuality.

"All aborted, close down, homing, out."

He stripped out the wiring, placed the transmitter in the bag and descended three floors into the basement boiler room. Opening the fire door he threw the equipment and his code book into the furnace. Ascending once more to his room he wrote a note to Rita. It said,

"The op's blown. You may be in danger. I'm going home. I advise you to be on the next convoy."

Then he packed leaving a salacious paperback in German for the titillation of the Volkspolizei on the table. He carefully wiped all the surfaces and then poured a generous tot of schnapps into a glass, shouldered his bag and descended once more into the street.

With a disarming smile he approached his shadow still standing patiently at his station. The man looked up, saw Charlie holding out the tempting drink but moved away without acknowledgement. Charlie placed the drink on the pavement and walked in the opposite direction. He didn't look back.

Half an hour later he was being interviewed by an American duty officer at the east-west checkpoint. After the American had phoned Osnabruck he said to Charlie,

"And what do you want us to do?"

"Just get rid of my tail for me, that's all."

"You guys are a real pain. You just walk in here and expect us to do your job."

"Listen Yank, I'm meeting Karen X in an hour."

"Karen who?"

"Just check it out with your HQ. OK?"

"If you say so but we can't stop those spooks. They've every right to walk in here."

"Hold them up. Ten minutes is all I need. I'm going home on the first convoy tomorrow so I won't be in your way. I'm blown."

Charlie walked across the city. He saw them before they spotted him. They were climbing out of the U-Bahn station, two ladies out on a shopping spree. He was early. The meeting time was still a quarter of an hour away. The church was a magnet for tourists, all anxious to see the memorials to the bombing. Near the door was a small iron cross made of nails from the old Coventry cathedral in England. He stood near it reading the blurb, all about the Coventry blitz illustrated with photographs. Rita and Karen entered. He held the door open for them and passed his note to Rita as he left.

8 Magdeburg

The thaw had come at last. Charlie and Susan kissed and hugged, glad to see each other after the tension of the past two weeks. The MISU car had collected him from the crossing at Helmstedt and returned him to the HQ. The following morning he went to see Brigadier Morris.

"And where's Rita now?" he said.

"She didn't show. I suppose she stuck with Karen. I hope to God she's OK. She's taking a terrible risk."

"You're a menace and a fool Charlie. My best operator possibly blown and all because of you."

"It was a plan doomed from the start, Sir, if you don't mind my saying so. I only went to Berlin to get information. With two minders for Himself and Rita for Karen how was it supposed to succeed? Freiheit ice-locked in Hamburg. I couldn't have kept X and Karen under cover for two weeks."

"So what's the fall back?"

"I don't see a fall back at this stage, Sir."

"There's got to be a way. Got to be."

"What do the Americans say?"

"They've washed their hands of it. Too many cooks. It's up to us. Do you mean to tell me that the Freiheit Op has been a total waste of time and money?"

"No Sir. Certainly not. I want to get him out without sparking off another row. An overt snatch in Berlin or anywhere else is going to cause a rumpus. We have to get him on board. After that it will be plain sailing, to coin a phrase. I hope I can use Rita or at least the information she carries. X is not under arrest, just surveillance. He goes home nearly every weekend. All we have to do is to persuade him and Karen to rendez vous with me."

"How will you do that without the minders being aware?"

"I don't think I can without a lot of back up. We'll have to see if Rita has spotted a chink in their armour."

"Well don't take too long over it. The Harz installation is to be shut down."

"I'm well aware of that Sir. Will you arrange a planning session and we could do with David here as well I think?"

"Good. I'll be in touch. Probably the day after tomorrow."

His interview over, Charlie walked back to the flat, collecting Charles from his nursery on the way.

"Well, how did it go then?" queried Susan.

"Difficult. He accused me of compromising Rita. Rita Smidt."

"Rita, who's Rita Smidt? Not Rita from Antwerpen?"

"The same. I've known her since 1940. You remember."

"I remember all right. You had her in the cellar at The Refuge."

"Actually she had me but some things are best forgotten, OK."

"Charlie, seriously. Many wives would have divorced you."

"Rita! You and I weren't even married."

"I'm talking about Lucy."

"She seduced me. I thought it was you. She got me at a very vulnerable moment."

"So you say."

"Anyway, Rita Smidt is Brigadier Morris's spy in the Harz."

"A master at changing the subject, aren't you?"

"She should have got out. I was rumbled. Maybe she was too. I don't know."

"So what's going to happen now?"

"There's to be a meeting the day after tomorrow to discuss alternatives"

"Will it involve you going back?"

"Yes, almost certainly."

"Here, read this. It's from Lucy."

Charlie read Lucy's unhappy letter.

10th March '53

Darling Susan,

I'm so miserable and homesick. My new home is beautiful. It is a log cabin, on the edge of the forest, but it is so hard to keep clean and nice. Carl is not at all house-proud himself but he expects me to keep everything perfect. He's not the man you will remember. Sometimes he's like a stranger and at other times he's kind and loving. I've still got my problem but I can't tell Carl about it. Could you possibly come over on a weekend visit? You could get a train from Berlin to Eisenach and we could meet for a meal and a chat. If I have another winter here I think I shall go mad. It's so isolated and Carl doesn't like me going into the village by myself.

Please write. Your loving Lucy.

"That's awful. How long have you had this?"

"It came the day you left. What are we to do? If you go back perhaps you could go to see her."

"It's a thought. I'll have to mention it to Jim."

"He'll never allow it, not after what's happened. I'm sure he'll think it would be too dangerous. Why can't we go and see her? Just get passes and go. There's nothing wrong in that."

"OK. Let's think about that. Perhaps we could get someone to look after Charles and then get some local leave. I'm due for it anyway. We could just go couldn't we? No need to tell anyone where to."

****

The meeting with the Brigadier continued with David present.

"As I see it," said Charlie, "We've got to get the minders out of the way. If we do it by force then the whole operation will become an overt snatch. They'll take one of our's and bargain for X's return. Ideally, X should just defect but they watch him too closely for that."

"So what are we left with?" said David.

Charlie said,

"One – he has to defect with Karen, that's essential. Two – he can't do it unaided. That's where we come in. Three – our involvement must be secret. There must be no hint that we have been responsible."

"All right then," said Jim Morris. "That leaves us with the problem of arranging his defection so that it coincides with Freiheit. It shouldn't be impossible. What do you think, Charlie?"

"Bribery."

"Eh, what's that?"

"He means," said David, "that's where I come in, money, real money."

"I think I should make contact with their son. We might be able to bribe him into setting up a family celebration of some sort. Anything to get X out from under to noses of the Vopos and the minders."

"Sounds a bit far fetched to me," said David.

"It's worth a try. How much do you think X is worth to us?"

"Millions," said Brigadier Morris.

"Well then. Doesn't that put things into perspective? If you don't trust me, David, then you'd better come over too."

"If the son…. What's his name by the way?"

"Friedrich. We call him Freddy."

"If Friedrich is a good communist, telling him the plan will blow it up. You'll never get away with it."

"Listen, Sir," said Charlie. "Everyone has a price. It shouldn't take much to persuade a bus driver to drive on the other side for a spell. If David writes me a blank cheque, I'll do it. It may take time but I'll do it. Getting Freiheit into place will be more difficult, believe me. I can't do it alone. I'll need help from here."

"You'll get all the help you ask for, Lieutenant, from me personally."

"I'll need a car with a marine radio, some cash and a shooter."

"The car will have to come out of the pool in Berlin. When will you want it?"

"I'll have to let Berlin know about that at the time. I shall need Rita to meet me. Dare I suggest the airport. Rita will have to make the contact with Freddy."

"Is that all?""

"All for now. I've got Freiheit and the Zantens. We can't fail."

****

"Well?" said Susan.

"Very well, thank God. Jim started off by being very offensive but I talked him round."

"You could talk anybody round. You could sell ice in the Arctic."

"Ha. Where did you hear that one? Anyway it's up to me to get them out. I've got a half baked plan which involves going over again. I'll make contact with Rita and X's son and bribe him into helping me.

"You seem very confident."

"Well there's no use being diffident about it. It's got to succeed if we want X out without any fuss."

"Do you know his name yet?"

"No, but I'll find out on this trip. I've got so used to calling him X that I don't really care any more what he's called."

"Now what about Lucy? I suppose with all the excitement making secret plans with your buddies you've forgotten all about my sister."

"Far from it, but she's safe where she is and just as soon as this op. is over, we'll go. We'll bring her back here if you like."

"Well I'm not so sure about that but I am anxious about her and Carla. When are you going?"

"Very soon. X's leave runs out in a week but we've got two days to relax. We could have a family outing. Requisition a car and do shopping in Hannover and take Charles to the fair."

****

The Dakota circled Templehof before descending through cloud and making a bumpy landing. Charlie climbed down the steps and made his way to reception. He was in his Medical officer's uniform. Rita, dressed in nurses' uniform, wearing clear spectacles and bleached hair, was there to meet him. They stayed that night in the BAOR hostel. Eyes, watching from the perimeter fence, saw nothing unusual in the passenger complement of service personnel

The following morning Charlie, wearing mufti, took a taxi to the DDR Passport Office and asked to see the Commandant. He showed them a recent copy of the East German newspaper, Die Zeitung, and his British Passport. He said he intended to apply for the advertised vacancy at the Magdeburg General Hospital. He explained that he had been black listed in Britain due to the evil influence of his father-in-law and that there were plenty of opportunities in the DDR due to wholesale defections of the medical profession. He said he was AWOL from the RAMC. He asked for a temporary work permit.

Meanwhile Rita, early the following morning wearing dowdy working clothes, mingled with the crowd crossing into the eastern zone of the city. She boarded the ladies-only coach of a train travelling to Magdeburg. She carried a new but battered identity card and work permit which Charlie had brought with him from Brigadier Morris. On arrival she went to a small hostel near the station and booked a double room for three nights. Charlie caught up with Rita the following day. They met in the station café at twelve noon.

"How did it go Charlie?"

"Smooth, no probs."

"The immigration officer seemed delighted to meet me. I must be an odd ball, travelling in the opposite direction to the general flow. He will report back I'm sure. It's anybody's guess how far they'll go. Brigadier Morris will act his part I know but it could be a bit awkward if they go right back to Hugo. They won't. At least I hope not. In any case we should be out of here before they can."

"Well, do you want to ask me anything?"

"Of course I do. Tell me all."

"Well, I rang Freddy. He wants to see me. We've not seen each other for about a year. I told him I had something special to tell him about his Dad. I told him that the installation is to be moved over the Urals. He wasn't pleased about that, I can tell you."

"Anything else?"

"Yes. Some not so good news. He's broken up with his long-time girl. We've got to see him to-morrow when he comes off duty. He's on shifts and finishes at one."

"That could be a bit difficult. I'm due at the hospital at two, to-morrow."

"Freddy can borrow a car. He'll pick us up. I told him about you."

"Oh, you did. What did you say then?"

"I told him you are AWOL but applying for a position at the hospital. He seemed very interested in that."

"Shall we go for a walk around the town? I've one or two things we need to plan."

"There's a park down the road. We could go there. We can't be overheard."

"OK."

****

Freddy picked them up from the rail station after he came off shift. They went back to his home. Friedrich Schultz lived in an apartment on the edge of the city. As Charlie read the name below the bell button on his front door he realised that, at last, the secret of X's identity was out. Freddy's rooms were immaculate and furnished in a modern style. He was very pleased to see Rita but a little more cautious in shaking hands with Charlie.

Rita and Charlie had decided that the best way to tackle Freddy would be to tell him the whole story, in Jim Morris's words, 'to lay the whole pack on the table'.

"We've come with some good news and some bad, Freddy," Rita opened. "It's to do with your father. He's getting on in years and not as robust as he used to be. It's been a privilege for me to work as his secretary for so long and your mother and I are good friends. We go shopping together whenever we can. He told me recently that when he retires he wants to reside in the USA and Karen and I feel that way too. Unfortunately he has now been told that he will have to move with the rocket lab. to a new location east of the Urals and that his contract has been extended for another five years. He has no choice in the matter. If he refuses to go he will be accused of being a western sympathiser. He could even be imprisoned."

"How does this concern me?" asked Freddy.

"Charlie here has been sent by the British Foreign Office. His job is to persuade you to help your father. He wants to defect to the West before the Harz operation shuts down."

"I don't see that I can be of any help whatsoever. In fact it could put me in danger. What my father does is entirely up to him. If the authorities here find out that he accepted help from the British to defect that could start a war."

"No chance of that, Freddy, but it would start an international slanging match and maybe your chaps could snatch one or two of our people in order to do a swap. That's the usual procedure we want to avoid," said Charlie.

"So where do you go from here? I could go straight to the authorities now and have you both locked up."

"That's true Freddy, but it's in your interest to hear me out. When I've finished if you still want to go to the authorities then do but I would advise against it. You could be dragged into a nasty enquiry as well."

"Are you threatening me?"

"No, not at all, but…. Tell me, do you enjoy being a bus driver?"

"My job pays well enough. I'm not particularly ambitious. I'll get married one day and have kids. There are plenty of other jobs much worse than the one I've got. You said you have good news, yes."

"We want you to throw a party to celebrate something really good, say for about a hundred guests. We want you to invite your Dad but without bringing his bodyguards. I want you to lend him and Karen your car so that he can drive to meet me at a place where I will get him over the border. It's what he wants."

"So he can sell his knowledge to the Yanks."

"So he can retire and live a life of freedom in the West without being in a virtual prison. I don't think he can tell the Yanks anything about rocketry that they don't know already. Your scientist Werner von Braun has seen to that."

"This party, it's going to seem very odd isn't it at the very moment when he disappears. I'm going to be in it up to my neck. Anyway, I've no reason to throw a party and in any case I can't afford it."

"We can afford it. Rita and I have permission to reward you well. In fact we could help you into the west too you know."

"I could go to the west any time I like without your help. I could drive a bus in the west just as well as here. I could go to Berlin. What's the party for anyway?"

"We've got to get your Mother and Father away from their bodyguards without them raising an alarm until it's too late. Can you think of a better way?"

"Suppose not. I don't want to be involved."

"You will be involved anyway Freddy if they use you to get your father back."

"Scheisse!!"

"We were sorry to hear that you've broken up with your girl. I was hoping you'd get married. That would be a cause for a celebration."

"No chance of that. She's marrying another fellow. Good riddance."

"I'm sorry," said Charlie.

"Don't be. I could marry Rita though, that's if she's not already married to you."

"That's a thought…. No, Rita and I are not married".

"Charlie," exclaimed Rita. "I'm still here…. Listening…. I'm not a piece of baggage."

"Well you could."

"No, I could not. Freddy and I are not lovers or even in love."

"Think of the Empire. Think of the Allied cause."

"Fuck the Allies. I'm not marrying Freddy for a cause."

"Would you Freddy?" said Charlie, who had been watching his reaction to this exchange.

"Like a shot. I've been in love with Rita since the day we first met but I'm not so much in love with her blond wig."

"It's not a wig."

"Well dye then. I'll overlook the dye. Rita was one reason why Greta and I broke up. She found a letter I'd written Rita."

"It's not dye. It's bleach actually. I never got a letter."

"No, it's here, still, in this drawer. Do you want to read it?"

"No thanks."

"I think I'll have to go now." said Charlie. "I've got an appointment at the hospital but, before I go, I have to say that we can make you a very rich man. Think about it"

"Charlie don't go now," said Rita.

"I must. See you back at the Hotel Bahnhof, say about four. Bye."

****

Charlie left the hospital after his interview. He had found the buildings unimpressive but had only words of praise for the hard work and devotion of the nurses and doctors. Taking a tour of the wards and theatres with the Direktor was like taking a step back in time. Herr Direktor said he was very pleased to meet him and would follow up the details of Charlie's experience. He had said,

"We shall meet again next week, shall we? In the meantime if you have nothing better to do perhaps you would like to spend some time in our Casualty Ward, on an unpaid basis of course."

"I shall have to look around the town for some accommodation."

"No need for that. You can stay here at the hospital for the foreseeable future if we are able to offer you a post. I shall know by next Thursday. Meanwhile I must consult my colleagues in the hospital and the city authority."

Charlie returned to the hotel to wait for Rita. When they met later, she asked how his interview had gone.

"Very well I think. They certainly have need of more qualified staff. Herr Direktor said he would be checking up on my qualifications. I don't know how he's going to do that but he sounded very confident. How about you?"

"Freddy and I are engaged to be married next month."

"You've got to be joking."

"No I'm not. He popped the question after you left. Down on one knee and all that. He's very quaint."

"What's the catch?"

"No catch. I've just got my eye on half of the million Brigadier Morris is going to pay us. In any case I want to sacrifice myself for the Empire."

"Now I know you're joking."

"The plot is:-   One, Freddy and I will announce our engagement tomorrow and put it in the local rag. Two, he will issue invitations to his colleagues at work and book a reception room in the Rathaus. Three, we will have a jamboree of a party to which his parents will be invited. If the minders turn up we'll get them drunk or spike their drinks. Four, Freddy and I will go on our honeymoon taking his parents with us. We'll go to the West, preferably to the USA. Freddy and I will get divorced and split the million D-Marks between us, fifty-fifty. Perfect don't you think?"

"Brigadier Morris said half a million," said Charlie.

"He'll budge. If he doesn't then the deal is off. It's off anyway if we fail."

"You've got a nerve I must say."

"One has to have nerve in my business. How do you think Gretchen and I got out of Antwerpen?"

"That's a long time ago. How did you get to be Schultz's secretary?"

"That's another story. I'll tell it when I write my memoirs."

"Knowing you Rita, I can guess. Are we sharing a room at the hotel? I'd better move out."

"Why?"

"Now you're engaged."

"Don't you want us to have a good time together?"

"You're incorrigible. Yes. Of course I do. Suppose Freddy finds out?"

"I shall merely tell him I am honouring a prior commitment. Come on let's go back to the hotel."

"Your plan won't work. You think MISU are going to cough up a million D-Marks just to get Schultz out? How do you know they'll pay up?"

"I'll tell him I want the money up front."

"One of us will have to go to Berlin. We need cash and I need the car that I've asked for and a gun. If you think you stand a chance of getting your money out of Jim then you'd better go. In any case I've obligations at the hospital."

"I'll tell Jim it's the only way. It will work. I tell you. It will work. Have confidence."

"Rita, I have complete confidence in you. So long as you fix me up with the car. I'll do my bit once you deliver the goods."

"Why the mystery? What's so difficult? We could just fly them all out from Berlin."

"No way. The Stasi will cover every door once they know X is missing. They'll shoot him sooner than watch him defect. I've arranged an exit plan. All you have to do is to get him to me."

"And I'm not supposed to know how this miracle will be."

"No point."

"OK then. So your confidence is not quite complete. Oh, by the way, see if you can get a supply of Rohypnol from the hospital."

"Shouldn't be difficult. They seem to be pretty lax. Oh, and while you're away, if the hospital doesn't need me for a couple of days, I'll take a trip down to Vacha. I worry about Lucy. It must be a rugged life and she's not used to that sort of thing."

"What sort of thing?"

"Well, you know, life in the raw. She's the product of posh schools."

"Uh, you've got a funny idea of posh schools. She'll cope."

"I hope you're right. I'll ask Herr Direktor to give me a travel permit on compassionate grounds."

"And if he doesn't."

"Then I won't go. It's as simple as that but I would like to see the bridge."

"What's so special about the bridge?"

"I'll tell you later."

"Secretive bastard."   After dinner they went upstairs to bed.

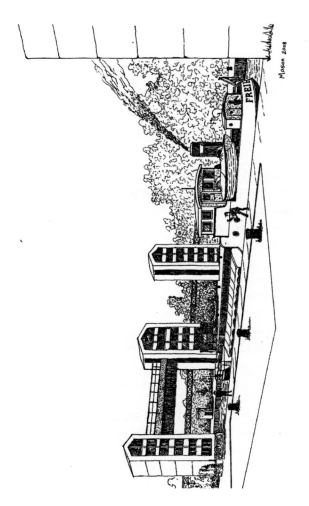

"Freiheit" leaving the lock at Geesthacht, River Elbe

Mason 2008

9 The Elbe

"Let go for'ard, let go aft." Peter spoke into the barge's telephones. The longshoremen unhooked the cables and let them fall into the river as the barge sheered away from the quay with a half load of house coal. Hans and Charlie had decided that there was no point in taking a full load.

"We're not going into the coal business," remarked Charlie. "Just get there and back safely. That's all." Johannes on the foredeck and Hans aft coiled the warps and stowed them neatly. Back in the wheelhouse, Hans said,

"Coffee anyone?"

"You don't need to ask, Dad," answered Peter.

"And me, two sugars, black," said Johannes.

"You'll rot your guts Jo," retorted Hans.

"I like to live dangerously."

"You'll be sorry you said that. There'll be no shortage on this trip. Believe me. This is not the Rhine."

"OK Dad. I got the message."

"There's a checkpoint at Lauenburg and after that we've got the Commies on the north bank to Schnackenburg and after that on both banks all the way to Berlin because the Elbe is the border from Lauen to Schnacken." Just then Peter turned Freiheit sharply to starboard as she left the coaling dock at Altenwerder and entered the Suderelbe.

"Ten kilos and then we join the main river. Leave the red buoys to port," said Hans.

"Aye aye. Just relax Dad. I am qualified, remember? Where's that coffee?"

As soon as she entered the current of the main river Peter opened up the throttle. The engine roared and Freiheit surged ahead. Hans went below.

"Have a look at the pilot-book please Jo. What time do you think we'll reach the lock at Geesthacht?"

"It's thirty-two K's. At this speed over the ground we should make it by five."

"We'll get through it this evening and then moor up. Make an early start to-morrow."

"Aye aye."

Freiheit made good progress against the Elbe current and at five o'clock, almost to the minute she entered the Schleusenkanal, the channel which bypassed the weir at Rönne. Peter throttled back out of the current and scanned the lock-gates ahead for the signal lights. The barge glided in between the formidable walls and under the first gate, which was lowered slowly behind her. Peter manoeuvred alongside the wall on the port side. Johannes and Hans threw warps into the waiting hands on the edge of the lock. The inrush boiled and foamed as the sluice was opened to admit the water from upstream. Slowly Freiheit rose to the level of the upper river. The top gate was raised and twenty minutes later the voyage resumed.

"That's the only lock until we join the Havel at Havelberg," remarked Peter, "but the next stop will be at Lauenburg in the morning. That's where we shall be inspected. We'll moor up here and have a good meal cooked by Dad. Is that all right by you Dad?"

"Doesn't seem as if I have much choice. How about that steak pudding Mum made before we left Hamburg?"

"Wonderful," said Peter and Johannes together.

As Freiheit approached Lauenberg in the early morning twilight the deckhouse was picked out in the glare of a large red stop-signal mounted on a pillar almost in mid-channel. At the checkpoint Peter stopped the barge alongside a wooden quay. Die Ostdeutsche Wasser Polizei came aboard. There were five of them. Peter cast his mind back to the inspections they had suffered on the Rhine all those years ago.

"Nothing much has changed has it Dad? I thought peace had broken out."

"They may not shoot but in their eyes we are the enemy now," cautioned Hans.

The officer in charge asked for the ship's papers and the passports of the crew whilst the other policemen asked for the tarpaulins to be rolled back. Every inch of the accommodation was inspected in detail. Satisfied at last Freiheit got under way again but this time with a police launch as an escort.

"How long will they follow us? All the way to Berlin?" queried Johannes. "Surely we're still in the British Zone. The Grenze is on their bank."

"Who owns what is in dispute," replied Hans. "The DDR claim the border lies in the middle of the river."

"That seems fair enough. Surely we can keep to our bank," remarked Jo.

"The problem is that the deep channel crosses from side to side of the river. On a starboard bend we almost touch their bank but the treaty says we have a right to navigate all the way to Berlin. We'll just have to get used to surveillance. On the way back we've got to pick up Charlie and Herr X. If we have an escort all the way that's going to be tricky to say the least."

Soon after passing Boizenburg the river did indeed enter a long right hand bend and the deep channel took Freiheit to the north bank. The patrol boat roared up alongside and the officer gesticulated for the barge to move to the centre line of the river. Hans moved to the side deck and waved, smiled and then shrugged but soon they reached Radegast where the dredged channel, marked by beacons, crossed to the south bank. Soon after that the launch turned away. Peter handed over the helm to Johannes whilst Hans prepared another meal. They continued the voyage to Schnackenburg which they reached in the late evening.

"Moor on the British frontier post," said Hans. "They'll give us clearance in the morning and then we'll cross the river to get clearance from the DDR. After that we shall be totally inside East Germany."

"Where do you think we'll be this time to-morrow?" asked Johannes.

"It's another 53 kilometers to Havelberg. I don't suppose we'll get much beyond there. It's where we leave the Elbe and join the Havel. There's a lock there which could hold us up for quite a while if there's a lot of traffic. It's not a double lock and it can only take one barge at a time so we'll be in a queue. We'll try to get through tonight and moor on the waiting quay just upstream."

The following morning the voyage was resumed. The German river patrol came aboard.

After examining the ships papers and their passports, the officer said,

"Warum so leicht?" Hans intercepted the question.

"We are not sure about the draft in the lakes, officer. We decided to play it safe. Besides which, we only had a sale for 500 tonnes. Our finances would not permit us to buy coal as a speculation. Perhaps on our next trip we will carry a full load."

"So Sie gehen nach Berlin, You could always deliver halb in the DDR, at Brandenburg or Potsdam. Wer ist Ihr Kunde (Customer)?"

"The British and American Forces."

"Sie Können weiter gehen."

Johannes cast off the warps as the officer stepped back on to the DDR patrol boat.

Peter opened the throttle and the engines responded once more with a throaty roar.

"There are seven locks between here and the Westhaven, not counting this one. After we leave the Elbe we shall be ditch crawling," said Hans.

"What do you mean Dad?" asked Johannes.

"He means the river will be narrow and when we get to the lakes it gets shallow as well, but with this light load we'll manage OK in the shallow places," said Peter.

Hans continued,

"We should be there to-morrow evening if all goes well or, failing that, early the day after. The distance is 160 kilos but I've allowed an hour at each lock. We should average about eight knots between them. We get into a chain of lakes after Brandenburg but so long as we stick closely to the buoyed channel we should be all right. They used to land Sunderland flying boats on them during the blockade. Halfway up the Jungfernsee we shall meet the checkpoint into West Berlin at the narrows between Riesterhorn and Quapphorn. There may be a chain across the fairway. At the very least there will be patrol boats. We'll have to slow down so they can board us. Then after Spandau we join the Berlin Ship canal which takes us to the west dock to unload."

"How long will that take?" asked Peter.

"Allow two days. Then we have to wait the signal to start back."

"Where shall we meet Charlie and the mysterious Herr X, Dad?"

"Somewhere near Havel. Actually I don't know the exact place yet. The most important thing is to keep a strict 24 hour watch on the radio. When Charlie comes on he will expect an immediate response. He could be in danger. If we let him down it could cost him his life. We are, quite literally, his life-line. If you feel sleepy on watch then come and wake me straight away. I can manage easily on four or five hours a night."

To the surprise of Freiheit's crew, there was little fuss on entering West Berlin. An officer of the Border police examined their papers, stamped their passports and wished them 'Bon Voyage'. It was to be a different story on the return journey.

10 Eisenach

Charlie got off the bus five kilometres from Vacha. The bus driver said he was unable to take any passengers to the centre unless they had a special pass.

"The new regulations are only a week old," he said. "This is your terminus now unless you live in the zone. Folk living near the border need a special stamp on their Identity Card. If you haven't got one then you must report to the guard post here."

Charlie digested this new obstacle with dismay. He decided that he had no other course but to tackle the authority head on.

"I wish to see my sister-in-law, Lucy Wogart. She lives near Vacha. Her husband is a forester," he said to the border policeman. "I have a position at the hospital in Magdeburg and I have only received permission to travel for two days."

"We have no authority to issue a permit here. You should have obtained a pass in Eisenach but that would take about a week assuming your application is genuine."

"Oh, it is," Charlie replied. "No mention of this was made when I applied for my travel permit."

"The regulations are quite new. The people in Magdeburg may not be fully informed."

"What do I do now then?"

"I'm sorry. There is nothing more I can do. You should return to Magdeburg. Write to your sister and arrange to meet. She could travel to Eisenach without difficulty. She must have clearance to be living in the protective zone."

Sadly, feeling defeated, Charlie turned away. The bus on which he had arrived returned an hour later and took him back to Eisenach, twenty kilometres away. During the journey he struck up a conversation with a passenger, a man obviously in his late sixties or early seventies.

"I came here to see my sister," Charlie said. "She lives in the forest with her husband, Carl Wogart but I have no pass."

"We all need special permission to live in our own homes and our relatives can no longer come to see us." the man replied. "It's very irksome. I'm going to get a few things for my shop."

"Do you know Carl?" asked Charlie hopefully.

"Oh yes. We know him all right and Lucy and little Carla. They're quite famous. Carla goes to the clinic and the nursery next to my shop. We're 'neighbours.'"

"If I stay overnight in Eisenach could you get a message to them to meet me tomorrow. I'll pay you for your trouble."

"No need for that. Yes, I'll be home this evening. I'll see to it that they are informed. If I get back in time I may see Lucy before she goes home. If not I'll cycle up."

"That's very generous. I would like to reimburse you. I really would."

"Not at all. It's a pleasure to be of service to her."

The following day Charlie waited anxiously at Eisenach for the bus from Vacha to arrive. At last his vigil was rewarded.

"Charlie, Charlie." Lucy's unmistakable voice echoed across the bus station.

He turned and saw them, Carl carrying Carla on his arm and Lucy carrying a bag. He ran.

"Dearest." Stuck for words and with a large lump in his throat he swung Lucy off her feet. Carl stood watching this display of affection with reserve. Placing Carla down, he stepped forward and shook Charlie firmly by the hand.

"Are you well?"

"Yes thanks Carl. Are you all well?"

"We are, as well as can be expected."

"That doesn't sound too good."

"We're not leading an easy life, you know."

"Oh Carl, let's not spoil the day. Charlie, I can't believe it. I couldn't believe it last night when Herr Gruber came to our home with the message."

"I didn't know about the zone. I don't have a pass. It was lucky I met a neighbour of your's on the bus."

"Charlie, how do you come to be here? It's incredible. I thought I would never see any of you again. We've so much to talk about."

"It's a long story, and classified too. I can't go into details. Let's have some lunch. There's a café over there."

Later as they sat over their meal, Charlie said,

"Susan might get a visa to come over and see you both. She could probably get clearance at Helmstedt, if not then Berlin. What do you think about that?"

"I would love it," said Lucy enthusiastically.

Carl interrupted,

"We're very content with things as they are. It is a hard life but not an impossible one. The thing which troubles me the most is the possibility of being resettled."

"What do you mean, resettled?"

"People living close to the Grenze need special passes. If you can't get one or have it withdrawn then the authorities will direct you to live elsewhere. They will provide accommodation but maybe not in a nice area."

"That's terrible. You mean to say that one can no longer choose where to live?"

"If I found work in a place, I could go and live there, - no problem -, but not in a protected area and that includes the area close to the border."

"Five kilometres, the bus driver said."

"Look at it from their point of view Charlie. Russia was devastated in the war. They need protection. We are having a difficult time now but in future years the new system will prove its worth. You'll see. But we are hampered all the time by the West. The West Germans, supported by the Allies, America etc, are tempting all our best people away. Some towns and villages are left short of skills, some completely without. Doctors, nurses, teachers, scientists and engineers have been flocking to the west. It's got to stop and the only way to do it is to block the border."

"You speak like a Communist, Carl," retorted Charlie.

"I'm not a communist but I do see things in a different light from this side of the border. The people I meet in Vacha are good people. They need our help. Lucy is helping in the village Kindergarten and when Carla grows up we'll see she gets a good education and learns the true history of socialism, all for one and one for all, equality, fair shares, an end to poverty, the good life."

"Bla, bla. I came to see Lucy not to hear a political speech. And if the good folk don't want your brand of equality then it's the bullet."

"It's not my brand. It's the system."

"So where does that leave you and Lucy?"

"In spite of our difficulties I like it here. Lucy has made our home beautiful and today we're buying a car, here in Eisenach. You see we can save up and buy nice things. I've been promised a little truck, a Trabant, brand new. It will be so useful and we will be able to get about more. It means that when Carla goes to school I'll be able to run her there every day."

"You've been very quiet Lucy. What have you to say to all this."

"We're expecting a baby." Charlie sat in silence while this bombshell landed.

"So, you've kept the best news till now. Congratulations to you both," said Charlie, with a show of joy he did not feel.

"Carl only knew last night. I went to see the doctor. He comes to Vacha once a week. We're thrilled."

Later that day Charlie caught a train back to Magdeburg after tearful good-byes were exchanged. He had seen the Trabant, with the proud owner, Carl, at the wheel, disappearing through the streets of Eisenach.

11 Ivan Rostovski

The outstanding memory of childhood retained in the brain of Ivan Rostovski was his first experience of school. He was a puny boy for his age with a slight stutter. It got worse when he was angry or frightened. At the age of eight he was a month late joining his class since his parents had only recently moved to Moscow to find work. His father had been offered a job at the gigantic coal-fired power station on the outskirts of the city near the river. Their apartment was in a large precinct block, newly completed after the recent civil war.

It had been a bleak day, bleak in weather and bleak in achievement when he was set upon by a group from school. Crossing a barren corner of the park, they chased him into a lavatory block, stole his new bag with his books and pushed his face under the icy water with which they had filled the hand basin. They left him unconscious on the cold concrete floor.

Very late for supper, he stumbled into the apartment that his parents called home.

"Where have you been? Just look at the state of you," his mother challenged, "and where's your bag? I suppose you left it at school."

Ivan ran to his mother, burying his face in her voluminous skirt.

Mrs Rostovski sat in the family armchair and put her arms around Ivan as he crouched, foetal-like, on her lap. She rocked him to and fro until his sobs subsided. Gently she coaxed his story of the day's events from him, from the moment he arrived at the school until he returned home. She was in the process of consoling him when his father came in from work.

Rostovski was an intolerant man. A giant at six-feet-four, he exuded strength and dependability from every pore. That day he had shifted ten tons of coal from the stock yard to the furnaces and it showed.

"What's going on here? Sorry I'm late. Is my bath ready? I had to work extra because we were short handed to-day. What's the matter with Ivan?"

"The boys at school have stolen his bag. They nearly drowned him. Left him for dead," his wife replied. The father looked down at his snivelling son and was ashamed. He wondered how he had brought such a runt into the world. Without a word in reply he stripped naked, dropped his coal-stained garments on the floor and stumped off in a temper to the bath.

"Go out to play," his mother advised.

Ivan suffered another hellish day at school. When he returned home there was a stranger in the kitchen. His father was there also.

"Ivan, this is Yuri. He's a fighter….a professional. He's going to teach you to fend for yourself."

For the next eight years Yuri taught Ivan all he knew, the exercises and runs he needed to do every day to build his strength, and the high protein foods to support this regime. At first Ivan hated Yuri. Every week he would visit the apartment. He would wrestle, throw, box and knock the boy about until he was covered in bruises and crying, pleading for Yuri to stop. Nevertheless he gradually mastered self defence, the holds and throws needed to paralyse and inflict maximum pain on his attacker. By the time he was sixteen he was able to hold his own with Yuri and anyone else who crossed his path. His stutter had long since gone away and the bullying had ceased. He had hated his father for bringing Yuri into his life and his mother for doing nothing to protect him any more. She too was afraid. With strength came self confidence. Yuri had successfully turned Ivan into a ruthless fighting machine, who knew his own capabilities and how to use them without mercy to his victim. When he was eighteen Ivan joined the Red Army. When he was forty-five Colonel Ivan Rostovski was the chief security officer at the Harz Missile Factory.

12 The Wedding

Rita watched as the train slowed to a halt. After a minute Charlie alighted and walked to her. They kissed.

"Well, how did it go?"

"I'm worried about those two."

"What's the matter?"

"They're not getting on. There's too much tension. Lucy was glad to see me but I could tell that Carl wasn't. He's a worried man although he pretends otherwise."

"What was their house like?"

"I never got to the house. There's a five kilo zone by the Grenze. Only those with a pass can live there. Even relatives can't visit their kith and kin. I got a message to them and they came to see me in Eisenach."

"So you never got to see your precious bridge."

"No. Pity about that but I'll get some photos later from the other side. Now then, tell me, how's it going with you?"

"Freddy and I are going to get a bus to see Karen in Leipzig, probably tomorrow. We've got to see how the land lies. If Karen has cold feet then the deal's off and I'll lose half a million."

"Hold on a minute Rita. It's not your's to lose. Anyway, tell me what happened in Berlin?"

"Easy, like I said it would be. Jim was a walk over."

"You managed to convince him that your plan is going to work?"

"You convinced him the last time you two had a meeting. We just talked details….and the price. He was taken aback at first until I reminded him of his own comment to you."

"Oh, and what was that?"

"He said that X would be worth millions didn't he? That says it all doesn't it? We are the ones taking all the risks."

"True. Report back soonest."

"OK I will."

"By the way, I'm going to move into the hospital when there's a room. They've given me temporary employment in the casualty ward for six months."

"That's a shame, just as I was getting used to your smelly socks. I need some cash."

"I can give you a grand to be going on with. How soon before Jim comes through?"

"He's opened a bank account in the name of Frau und Herr Friedrich Schultz with the Deutscher Bank in Hannover. He's agreed to put in five hundred grand, half a million. A courier will be coming here from Berlin in two days time. I have to meet him at the station. He's going to bring about twelve grand in Marks, that's Ostmarks, about a thousand pounds, for expenses and a car for you, Magdeburg registered."

"Sounds OK to me," said Charlie. "Let's drop in and sort out a few more details with Freddy."

"No, I don't think we should. The less you have to do with Freddy from now on the better. As far as the watchers are concerned, I'm his fiancée, Doctor Schultz's secretary, ex-secretary."

"So how far have you got?"

"Well for a start he's cock-a-hoop about me. Admits he's had a crush on me since we met two years ago. We'll leave the wedding reception to go on our honeymoon the only difference being that Karen and Eric will be coming with us."

"Are you in love with Freddy?"

"Now you've got to be joking. I'm doing this for the Empire, remember?"

"At a price."

"Joke if you must. We'll dump his parents at a Gasthaus I know near Stendal. After that it's up to you. Meanwhile we'll drive without stopping to East Berlin, park the car and mingle with the rush into the west in the morning. I've fixed it with Berlin. The Brits will be expecting us and will fly us out the same day, first stop Northolt. Poor Freddy. He wonders what's hit him. I hope he has no regrets. I've promised him a year of non-stop sex when we get to America."

"Do you think Jim Morris will really come through?"

"He'd better otherwise I'll sell it all to the New York Times."

"Rita, I have to take off my hat to you. Better get your hair bleached again love. It's beginning to show. If the minders recognise you we'll all be done. Pad yourself out a bit too. Make it look as though you're six months."

"OK, OK, Charlie. Even you won't know me."

Frenetic activity took over the lives of Rita and Freddy. The civil union was scheduled for noon on the first Saturday in April, 1950. There were only a few weeks in which to make all the arrangements and to send out over a hundred invitations. Freddy was worried that he hadn't got a hundred friends but then relatives he hardly knew started to ring up and write, inviting themselves. Soon the numbers had reached the desired figure including many of the bus drivers of the city. He was worried that the city authority would prevent many attending since it would cripple the service for most of the following day. Rita's wedding gown caused some difficulty since she couldn't admit to the gown shop that she intended to stuff a small cushion down the front. She had to make the necessary modification herself.

The receptionist at the Station Hotel stopped Charlie as he returned one afternoon from the hospital.

"Herr Forbes, here is a packet for you." Charlie collected his room key and the packet. In the room he opened it to find a car-key and a note which gave a time and the name of a street near the station. The car had been delivered. Later he found a service revolver in the glove pocket and a silencer which attached to the muzzle. There was a separate pack containing twenty-four rounds of ammunition.

"They were using these in the Boer War," Charlie said to himself. "Never mind it's better than nothing I suppose." In the boot was the marine radio. He tuned in to 2182 kcls and listened to a bit of radio traffic just to make sure it was working but he didn't try to transmit.

Charlie kept the Daimler in the car park at the hospital. He was concerned that with such a machine at his disposal questions would be raised about his story in the minds of medical colleagues. On the other hand any car parked in the car-free streets of Magdeburg received curious stares from passers bye. He wished that the car pool in Berlin had not been so generous. True, this was a battered pre-war model with more than two-hundred-thousand kilos on the clock. There were some other staff cars too, so he thought that the Daimler would attract least comment if he parked amongst them.

Rita and Freddy's wedding day dawned fine and bright. Charlie was still on duty at the hospital and had no intention of being at the ceremony. At the end of his shift he said a mental goodbye to the hospital and in the twilight took the road north to Stendal. He had no difficulty finding the Gasthaus Holzern. He drove past and eventually came to a narrow track about a mile further on. He reversed into it and parked where the car would be concealed from the road. Walking back to the rendezvous he stationed himself in some foliage overlooking the forecourt and waited.

****

Amid great excitement, in mid-morning on the wedding day, Eric and Karen Schultz arrived at Rita's hotel in a large Mercedes driven by Eric's most trusted bodyguard Hermann Klein-Schinkler. Eric and Hermann went back a long way, to 1938 in fact, when Doctor Schultz was head of the Faculty of Physics at the University of Leipzig and Hermann his chief demonstrator and assistant.

Hermann, unlike his name, was a large man, tall and well built. For such a heavy man he was light on his feet and spent half an hour each day in physical exercise. He was quite capable of carrying the diminutive frame of Eric as he would a child. When Eric was ordered to join the experimental staff at The Harz in 1940, Hermann, still unmarried, went also. At the end of the war the underground rocket factory fell into Russian hands. Captain Hermann Klein Schinkler found himself enrolled into the Security System under a Colonel of the KGB, Rostovski, but secretly his first loyalty was to his friend and master, Eric Schultz.

For the first time Rita explained the details of the plan to Eric.

"We shall leave the reception at about five," she said. "You should slip away about half past four. There will be a taxi waiting to take you to Freddy's flat where we shall have left some clothes suitable for the journey, good stout walking shoes included. We'll call at the flat, change and then take Freddy's car. We'll drop you at the Gasthaus Holzern five kilos north of Stendal. We have booked a room for you in your own names because they'll ask to see your identity cards. We'll just have to risk that you're not well known in the area. After dropping you, we'll drive on to East Berlin through the night. Early on Sunday morning we'll mingle with workers walking to West Berlin.

My friend Charlie will pick you up from the gasthaus. You'll be in safe hands, I promise. He's planning to fly you to England. Freddy and I will be waiting for you there."

"What about Hermann?" said Eric

"Oh yes. I forgot to explain about him. By three o'clock he'll be unconscious. We'll make him drunk and failing that we'll drug him," said Rita.

"That won't work. He never drinks on duty."

"What, not even to toast the bride?"

"Knowing him he'll want a soft drink for that,"

"We'll work something out - make sure he's in no fit condition to follow you."

Two hours later the Registrar solemnly intoned,

"Im Namen der Deutsche Demokratischen Republik erkläre ich Sie Friedrich Schultz und Sie Rita Smidt Mann und Weib."

At half past four the party was still going well, the food consumed, speeches made and toasts enjoyed. Eric went to the toilet. Before he returned Karen went also. They took the taxi, which was waiting outside, to Freddy's flat. One of the well meaning guests woke Hermann, who had fallen asleep in an easy chair, to offer him some more food. He looked around the room. Some of the guests were chatting in small groups. Many of them were dancing to a string quartet. In a separate room children were playing games. Hermann struggled to his feet, somewhat alarmed and very dazed. He strolled about looking for his charges. He was told that Freddy and his bride had left the reception five minutes ago but that the groom's parents had left some half hour previously. He came to the conclusion that someone must have drugged him, either in his food or in his orange juice. This thought added to his anxiety. He went to the men's room and was promptly sick. As fast as he was able he left the Rathaus and climbed into the Mercedes. Attempting to think coherently, he decided that the only possibility worth following was a search of the area where he guessed Freddy would have his home. Freddy would know what had happened to Eric. Some months ago, at Karen's request, he had posted a letter to their son. He struggled to recall the address. However he knew Freddy had bought or hired the Volkswagen that had been parked outside the Rathaus for the honeymoon. He headed for the north of the city and stopped to ask in a shop if someone could direct him. The people, in the shop, seemed to know the area where Freddie lived. It was not hard to find the car. It was in a quiet residential street of apartment blocks. It was the only one. Unable to memorise the number plate he fumbled in his pocket for a pencil and wrote it on his shirt cuff. Then he parked the Mercedes in the next street and walked back to where he could watch the apartment block near the car.

His head throbbed with the effects of the drug and his legs ached abominably. He wondered how long he could last as the evening shades began to lengthen. He had almost made up his mind to walk up to the apartments and ring the bell, any bell, when, to his relief and satisfaction the four of them emerged carrying their bags. He returned as quickly as his aching legs would allow back to his own car. He was just in time to see Freddy's car move off. On reaching a main road he turned to the north, away from the city. He had no certain means of knowing that he was heading in the right direction but his hunch proved to be correct when he spotted some tail lights ahead. He drew closer to verify that it was the same car and then dropped back to a safe distance. Freddy was not driving fast. Two hours later they passed through Stendal and headed out towards Wittenberge. After another two kilometres he pulled off the road in front of the Holzern. A single lamp over the front door illuminated the forecourt.

Hermann saw Eric and Karen go into the gasthaus after Freddy drove away. He decided not to confront them. He had made up his mind that they would be staying the night and he could meet them in the morning. It was plain that they were not returning directly to their home in Leipzig. He let his car roll quietly on to the edge of the forecourt and sat agonising over his next move. He knew that his first duty would be to report these developments to the Head of Security. On the other hand his first loyalty was to his friends. He guessed that there was nothing sinister in their behaviour but, to play safe, it would be better to liaise with 'Ivan the Terrible' in order to keep his 'nose clean'.

At last he entered the Gasthause. He showed the sleepy janitor his Security I.D. and verified that Eric and Karen were indeed asleep in their room. Then he asked to use the phone. He dialled the night staff at the Harz. It started to rain as Hermann returned to his car and the long vigil. He suddenly felt very weary. He drank most of the bottle of Vodka he kept on the glove shelf and fell into a deep sleep.

Charlie came out of his hiding place and approached the Mercedes with great caution. He had witnessed Rita and Freddy leave Eric and Karen. Now he was watching the second car parked in the shadows. He could see the driver had slumped forward over the steering wheel. Stealthily he walked up and opened the driver's door. He thrust the silenced revolver to the man's temple.

****

Heino, a senior staff member was driving Ivan. Behind was another car with four more security soldiers. They were armed with light machine pistols. Ivan said,

"It's one-hundred and eighty kilometres. We'll be there by three o'clock. We will arrest Schultz and his wife at breakfast or before if they try to leave. Meanwhile I want the place surrounded. I will interview any night staff ."

The cars approached to within a hundred meters of their target, doused the lights and then approached on foot. Ivan saw Hermann's car parked under some trees nearby. Signalling his men to disperse around the building he approached the

121

car and shone his torch into the interior. He was shocked. The body lay across the front seats, a dark patch on his left temple. Who could have done this terrible thing? He opened the door and reached for his wrist. Relief flooded into his body. Hermann had a strong pulse. Ivan shouted for help. Two of his men came running. Between them they pulled the unconscious security officer from his car.

"Get water." Minutes later Hermann began to stir. They shouldered him towards the open doorway and sat him on a sofa in the foyer. There was no one on duty at this time so Ivan examined the register. He was intrigued to see there were few guests. Herr Schultz and his wife were booked into room five. All the guests had signed in except one, Herr Hessler.

Ivan placed his thumb firmly on the alarm button which was placed on the Janitor's desk. After a minute the man appeared from a back room rubbing the sleep out of his eyes.

"Was in allerWelt (What is going on). Wer sind Sie?" he asked roughly.

Ivan didn't reply but merely held up his warrant card for the janitor's inspection.

"Verzeihung,. What can I do for you?"

"Tell me," said Ivan. "Wer ist Hessler? Has he cancelled his reservation?"

"No Sir, ich weiss nicht."

"Then when did he make a booking?"

The janitor opened a drawer and pulled out a book. He said,

"All the reservations are listed here. See for yourself. The girl does it. That's her handwriting."

"Where is she?"

"She lives in the village, ten minutes cycle ride away. I am her father."

"Ring her up. I want to speak to her."

"We don't have a phone at home Sir."

"Then go and get her. This could be urgent. I'll get my man, Heino, to drive you."

Ivan turned to Hermann who was lying on the sofa.

"Hermann," he said. "Wake up, wake up."

He shook him roughly. Hermann sat up slowly and yawned.

"What happened to the young Herr Schultz and the girl?"

"They drove off."

"Time?"

"Must have been about midnight."

"I've got to find them. I need them for questioning. Who is the girl?"

"Rita. Rita Smidt. The Doctor's secretary."

"Indeed."

"They told me they were having a honeymoon."

"Did they say where?"

"Berlin."

Twenty minutes later Ivan was questioning the hotel's receptionist.

"Who was it made the booking?"

"A woman Sir. She didn't give her name, a reservation for Hessler. She didn't know his name at first. I could hear them talking."

"Is that all?"

"Yes Sir, but."

"But what?"

"She wasn't German; I don't think."

"What then?"

"I don't know Sir."

"Polish, French, British?"

"No Sir. Not any of those, not American, definitely not. Could have been Dutch. She said he might be late getting here, about nine; I think."

"Dutch you say. Hermann, isn't Rita Smidt Dutch?"

"Yes Colonel, she is," he replied.

"Making a booking here for Herr Hessler? Smidt, I wonder. All right then. You may go. I'm sorry to have disturbed you. Heino, please will you run the lady home. Hermann, I want cover on every gateway into Berlin. Give the Statsi a description. You have the number of the car. They may ditch it of course and take a train, so I want the main stations in Berlin covered too. See to it."

"Yes Colonel."

"Oh, and whilst you're at it, put two men on every train from Brandenburg. It's just a hunch but if I were them I would take a train into the city. I'm going for some rest."   To the janitor, Ivan said,

"Have you an empty room?"

"Ja Sir, plenty. Take your pick."

"Thanks, I'll have room four if it's available."

The janitor took the key off a hook and handed it to Ivan.

"Wake me at seven Heino and make sure that the occupants of room five don't leave."

13 Rendez Vous

Charlie witnessed some of these events from his hiding place. The enormity of what he had been about to do hit him like a wave. He broke out into a cold sweat in spite of the rain.

"I must be losing my wits," he thought. It had been a close run thing. His finger had taken up the tension in the trigger before the reality of what he was about to do came over him.

"I was about to commit murder," he whispered out loud.

The soldiers had surrounded the Holzern. He saw the car driven by Heino go and return a little later. He could only guess at the events in the gasthaus but he came to the conclusion that there was nothing more for him. His plan had obviously been blown. He made his way carefully round the soldiers standing in the rain and then almost ran back to his car. The track was now a small stream of running water, down the slope away from the road. He started up and slowly engaged the clutch in first gear. The rear wheels started to spin and moved sideways off the track. He felt the back of the car sink into a rut. Pushing the heavy car would be impossible. He decided to wait until daylight, four hours away. If necessary he would have to search a nearby farm for help. He switched on the radio, put on the earphones and listened to the river traffic for a few minutes. Then he switched to the working frequency, pressed the button on the transmitter and spoke,

"Hello Freiheit, hello Freiheit, this is Diamond? Over. After a few seconds the deep guttural voice of Hans Zanten filled his head with sound.

"This is Freiheit receiving you strength three. Over."

"Goods unobtainable. Order cancelled. Meet on the north bank opposite Wahrenberg at twenty hundred, two zero zero zero, today. Over"

"Wilco. Out."

"That's my babies," Charlie thought. "Completely reliable."

Resigned to the fact that he could do nothing until daylight, he closed his eyes and went to sleep.

At the same moment that he was woken out of deep slumber by the dawn chorus of birds in the wood, Ivan was brought back to consciousness by his orderly, Heino, suitably armed with a cup of black coffee. Charlie set off across the fields towards a nearby farm while Ivan set off toward the breakfast room and an encounter with the Schultzs.

Charlie explained his predicament.

"I had a puncture," he lied to the farmer, "and then it got too late so I slept in the car. This morning it got stuck in the mud. Please can you help me? I'm late already. I'll make it worth your while. Will five hundred marks be all right?"

The farmer didn't need any further persuasion. Half an hour later Charlie was back in business.

"Another two hours and I'll be in Wittenberge", he thought. "What then?"

He pulled into the side of the road and studied the local map. There was only one bridge over the Elbe to reach the town. To the west the next bridge was in the British Zone, out of reach due to the Grenze. The next bridge to the south-east was at Tangermunde, too far. He had no alternative.

About a kilometre short of the bridge Charlie came to a gentle left hand curve in the road. He slowed down and saw ahead that there was a police car on the bridge-head and a barrier. He stopped and reversed. Once out of sight of the bridge he turned and drove back. Two more kilometres and he saw the bye-road to Seehausen. He parked by the church and walked to the square where there was a café. He went in and ordered some breakfast. After three coffees he decided to leave. He went to the church. It was open so he sat in a pew away from the door planning the remainder of his day. He left before the Sunday service began. First he must radio Freiheit again and fix another meeting.

He returned to the Daimler. There was no one about in the quiet Sunday afternoon in Seehausen so he switched on the radio and picked up the microphone.

"Hello Freiheit". Do you receive me. Over?"

"Loud and clear Diamond. Over"

"Meeting now at Wahrenberg, at the church, same time, south bank. Repeat south bank. Over"

"Understood south bank, wilco. Out."

****

"Good morning Doctor." Ivan greeted Eric, striding across the room with hand outstretched and a broad smile on his face. Karen looked up and went deathly pale.

"May I join you?"

"Please," rejoined Eric, trying hard to smile also but making a poor job of it.

"You have to serve yourself if you want breakfast," Karen said.

"Only coffee. That will do me. Now Doctor, why have you come so far out of your way home?"

"That's easily explained," Eric replied. "I came because my son dropped us here. He's on his honeymoon, touring the countryside, and we wanted a good chat. A private chat you see. I knew we could get a good night's rest here."

"How did you intend to proceed this morning without a car?"

"I expect Hermann to be here or failing him a taxi to Magdeburg station."

"Why did you proceed without Hermann?"

"He was drunk, flat out, in no condition to drive anywhere. I left him a note to tell him where we are."

"I see you have thought of everything Doctor. Well I have to tell you that you are needed at the Harz. Finish your breakfast, no hurry. I have some unfinished business here. It may take me most of the day. Hermann will take Frau Schultz to Leipzig and I will be pleased to give you a lift later. It's easier by car. Meanwhile please wait here for me."

With that Ivan left them and mustered his men on the forecourt.

He said to them,

"Someone was here to collect the Schultzs. I'm sure of it. Hermann has a bruise on his face. It must have been given to him while he was sleeping. I want you to spread out and search everywhere. Heino, they were heading north. We'll get help from the police in Wittenberge. I've already put a block on the bridge. Every car will be stopped and searched. The rest of you search around here for some evidence of a spy."

Two kilometers north they found mud on the road. The rain was washing it away but it was obvious that a car had been pulled out of the wood by a tractor. Ivan and Heino followed the track-marks back to the nearest farm. Ivan found the tractor, its wheels caked in mud standing in the farm-yard. Its engine was still warm. He met the farmer just coming out of his house.

"You were helping a stranded motorist I believe?"

"Yes, that's right," said the farmer guardedly. "Who wants to know?"

"What time would that be?"

"Oh, I don't know, About two hours ago."

"And the make of the car?"

"That's difficult. It was black, definitely black and I think it must have been a Daimler. Big it was, big and rather old looking. Yes, I'm almost certain it was a Daimler. Do you mind telling me who you are?"

"Police," replied Ivan. "The car was stolen. Did you get a good look at the driver?"

"Yes I did. Young man, spoke with an English accent, mid-twenties, light brown hair, thick set."

"Is that all? What was he wearing?"

"Grey denim, I think. Like an overall but smart."

"Thanks for your help. Wiedersehn."

Ivan and Heino continued on the road to the bridge.

"Very good," said Ivan. "Well done so far. We need co-operation from the local police. Two cars are not enough. We must scour the area. Ask for a report of any black cars, almost certainly a Daimler."

Ivan made his temporary base at the Wittenberge Police Station. About two o'clock he got a call.

"Jenisch here Sir, Seehausen. There was a Daimler here. The owner went into the church and was there for about an hour. Nobody saw him drive away."

"Very good Jenisch. Put a car on the main road at the Seehausen turn-off and wait. If they see a Daimler I want the driver arrested."

****

Eric and Karen felt badly let down. Rita had assured them that they would be met by a courier from England instead of which the head of security from The Harz had turned up at the Gasthaus. They knew Ivan as a very efficient officer but Eric allowed himself to be lulled into a false impression that all was well by Ivan's apparent acceptance of his account the day before. He knew that once back at the Harz factory his future would be tantamount to internment. He thought quickly. "Karen's with me. Friedrich should be safely over the border. I've no reason and certainly no wish to work for the Russians, whom I hate. Ivan's away for a bit looking for the 'Englander'. This is my last chance to make a break." But how was he to do it?

Karen walked out onto the forecourt. She tapped the window of the car, where Hermann had slept the last hours of the night. He woke almost immediately and blinked in the daylight. Karen stepped back as Hermann opened the door and swung his legs to the ground.

"I am to leave with you, Hermann, and you are to take me back home, to Leipzig. Have you had any breakfast? I can see you haven't. There is some laid out for you. Please go in and have it because I want to leave as soon as possible." Grumbling about his bad headache Hermann staggered to his feet and started to fumble with the keys.

"Leave the car. I'll do it when I have my bag." He handed her the keys and went slowly towards the main entrance. Karen watched him as he entered the dining room. Then she went for her bag and for Eric.

"How will I get out and what about air?" he asked.

"Peel off the rubber seal. I'll get a pillow for your head." Eric said,

"I can open it from inside when you unload. Get Hermann to carry the bags upstairs when we get there."

Two minutes later Eric, covered in a blanket with their bags, was shut in the boot of the car. Hermann, carrying his small case, came out of the gasthaus wiping his mouth on a paper napkin. Karen handed him the keys. She said,

"All set now?"

"There is a change of plan. I have just taken a call direct from the Harz. Where is Eric? I need to explain the details to him." Karen looked embarrassed by this turn of events. Hermann had the keys. Putting on a brave face she said,

"I've just shut him in there. I wanted to take him with us."

"I see. Quite a dangerous thing to do Frau Schultz. Let's get him out."

"I'm sorry Hermann. I didn't intend to compromise you."

"As it happens you haven't. Things will work out I'm sure. My superiors have given us instructions not to interfere with your travel arrangements. Orders have been relayed from Berlin. Your son has been detained and ordered to meet us in Brandenburg. I will drive you there."

"But Colonel Rostovski told my husband that he would return with him to The Harz. I am to go home to Leipzig."

"At the moment the Colonel will be unaware of these revised orders. He has gone to Wittenberge and won't be back for some time. Apparently the KGB wishes to exploit the situation. I have no further details except to say that they think that your husband will be of more use to them in the west. His work in the field of rocket design is at an end anyway. That's all I can tell you. As soon as possible I will get a message to the Colonel. He will meet you in Brandenburg for sure. It's going to be all right. Trust me."

****

Two Polizei were standing at the crossroads when Charlie approached. It was now dark and raining again. They had been standing there for three hours. They saw the lights of a car, stood in the road and held up their hands in a futile gesture. Charlie spun the wheel, mounted the grass verge and continued over the crossing towards Wahrenberg, ten kilometers away. Shaking themselves into action after their long vigil, the Polizei ran to their car and gave chase. After two kilometres they came across the Daimler parked near some trees well into the left side of the road   Charlie was in the passenger seat, the window lowered and his right arm holding his revolver over the side of the door. They slowed down and drew abreast. Charlie smiled at the Polizist sitting beside the driver and then at close range he shot their tyres. By the time they had recovered their surprise the Daimler was fifty meters down the road. Charlie had dowsed his lights relying on his memory to stay on the black-top. They let loose a volley of shots with their machine pistols. One bullet penetrated the fuel tank and the rear and front wind-shields were shattered. Charlie felt the shock of the bullets as he crouched below the steering wheel but he wasn't hit. When he was about two hundred meters further he switched the lights on again, sat up in the driver's seat and trod on the accelerator.

At Wahrenberg he parked the Daimler near the church. He opened the bonnet and took off the car battery. Already there was a pool of petrol on the road and a thin stream making its way into a ditch. He wrenched a piece of wire off the radio leads, placed the battery in the petrol stream in the ditch and created a bright spark by short circuiting the terminals. There was a flash and in seconds the car was an inferno. He ran to the river bank. The blazing car illuminated his way. Peter was waiting there with the Freiheit's rubber dinghy.   Charlie jumped down the bank as Peter opened up the outboard. They saw the headlights of an approaching car and heard the siren.

"They must have had back up Peter," Charlie shouted above the noise of the engine as they motored into the black night.

Minutes later the dinghy caught up with Freiheit, showing no lights. They clambered aboard as Hans opened up the diesels. The image of wild bursts of automatic fire from two silhouettes, with the blazing car as their background, burnt into Charlie's retina. It was a scene he would always remember.

Ten kilometres to go to reach the border at Schnackenburg. Meanwhile the outwitted Polizei returned to their station in

Seehausen and telephoned Ivan confessing failure. Ivan alerted the river patrol at the border check point.

For the next ninety-six kilometres after the check point Hans knew that the Elbe was the border between East and West. Fast launches, both British and East German, patrolled this stretch of the river. With the current the barge could do about ten knots making the time to Lauenburg five hours twenty minutes. After that both banks would be in the British Zone. The throttles wide open Freiheit surged forward, black exhaust smoke pouring out from her stubby funnel.

"Nearly there," muttered Hans. "Just round the next bend. I wonder what sort of reception we'll get at the check point."

"They'll shoot at us for sure. Anything to stop us and arrest me," replied Charlie.

"They don't even need to stop us. Their launches can do twenty five knots. You lads get below."

"What and not see the fun, Dad," replied Peter.

"If Charlie and I get hit you'll have to take her. Now do as I say, please."

Suddenly the two hundred tons of barge hit the chain at full speed. There was a tearing and grinding of tortured metal as the shock of the impact shook the vessel. The anchorages were torn out of the riverbanks but the heavy chain was embedded in the stem. Like a bit in the mouth of a horse, the drag of the chain slowed them down to two knots as they pulled the concrete blocks along the river bed.

Meanwhile Hans steered close to the south bank which was now in the British Zone but he knew that would not make much difference to the Vopos. Freiheit was illuminated by a powerful searchlight on their starboard side as a German launch easily caught up with them. With the roar of their diesels drowning out all but shouted instructions, they heard a loud megaphone,

"Anhalten, zum Stehen kommen. Sofort. Sofort." After a further minute the Germans opened fire. They shot at the steel side of the vessel as a warning. Then they broadcast the warning again, this time in English.

"Halt or we open fire."

Charlie and Hans threw themselves on the cabin sole as bullets shattered the bridge deck windows. The patrol boat came alongside and two men armed with machine pistols jumped on the side deck. A third man followed holding a rope which he used to tether the two vessels together. Hans, Peter, Johannes and Charlie stood in the wheelhouse. A German entered and pushed them aside. He shut down the engines.

"Guten Abend." An officer was speaking. "Wo ist der Kapitan?"

"I am." Peter and Hans answered simultaneously.

"Well who?" the German asked impatiently. Hans spoke,

"My son, Peter, is the Captain but he was following my instructions."

"You have damaged our control point and infringed navigation rules. You will board our vessel please and hand over your vessel to us. Please board our boat immediately."

"Can we take our personal belongings?" asked Peter.

"You have two minutes," the officer replied.

Suddenly, out of the darkness another patrol boat came alongside on the port beam. A very British voice spoke through a loud hailer.

"I say, what's going on here?" Charlie pushed his way out of the crowded cabin and vaulted over the rail of the barge on to the deck of the British boat.

"The Germans are trying to arrest my crew. Quick do something." he shouted.

"Leave this to me." A naval officer climbed on to the barge.

"This ship sails under the West German flag. I demand that you and your men leave immediately. You are now in the waters of the British Zone."

Hans spoke.

"We hit the chain. It's illegal to restrict navigation on the Elbe. We are making water and down by the head. We must restart the engines and pump the bilges now."

The German officer said,

"My superiors will hear about this incident." He then ordered his compatriots back into their launch and they motored away into the night.

"Put the engines full astern Peter, we must shake off the chain."

"Aye, aye." Hans, Johannes and Charlie went up to the bows to survey the damage. The slack chain dropped away and Freiheit was free to go ahead.

"Slowly, slow ahead Peter. The bow is holed near the waterline. Take it easy and keep the pumps going."

"Aye, aye," Peter replied.

"Well, Hans, Peter, Johannes, this is goodbye," said Charlie. I hope you have a safe voyage back home."

"She's a good ship, this one," remarked Peter. "If you've no further need maybe we could buy her."

"No doubt I can fix that. Leave it to me. What are your plans?"

"Well…. not on the Elbe, that's for sure, but there's plenty of business to be had elsewhere. The damage is easily put right."

"I'll be in touch. She belongs to the British Government at the moment. Goodbye for the present," said Charlie as he stepped aboard the British patrol boat.

The last he saw of his Dutch friends, they had anchored Freiheit near the British zone bank. He guessed that by the evening of the following day they would reach Hamburg and the yard. He would make a point of asking Jim Morris to expedite repairs.

****

Colonel Ivan Rostovski's car drew up at the East German Border post in the early hours. Having spent the night in a futile attempt to arrest the man responsible for Hermann's bruise he was not in the best of tempers. The River Police explained,

"We only had half an hour's notice."

"Surely that should have been time enough," exploded Ivan.

"Our boat was down river. We got it back in time but the British patrol interfered with our arrest since the barge had passed the border control. They were under British jurisdiction by then."

"That shouldn't make any difference on a matter as important as this. I believe we nearly got our hands on a spy who was arranging for one of my scientists to defect to the west. Such an eventuality must be prevented at all costs, all costs. Do I make myself understood?"

"Yes Sir, Colonel."

"Such incompetence will not go unremarked. Your superiors will hear of this."

Ivan stormed out of the control building and Heino drove him back to the Gasthaus. He arrived late for breakfast. His temper was not improved having forgotten to ask the river patrol for Charlie's description.

On his arrival in the dining room he discovered from the waitress that Eric and Karen had not had breakfast. With mounting anxiety he questioned the receptionist who rang their room. There was no answer. They had paid their bill and vanished. Furthermore Hermann and his Mercedes were also missing.

Ivan was a worried man. It seemed that Hermann was already obeying his order to return Karen to the Schultz residence in Leipzig but in that case why had she not had her breakfast and where was Eric? He phoned the Leipzig police. He asked them to keep watch on Schule Strasse 334 and to arrest the owners should they arrive.

14 Brandenburg

"Darling, we don't need the car in Berlin. It'll be safer to catch a train in Brandenburg and get off at the Ostbahnhof. From there it's only a short walk to the bridge on the Oberbaum Strasse. There's a crossing point over the Spree. We can stop in a café I know until the morning rush. We'll get through all right. No problem."

"I know that bridge," Freddy said.

"They do checks but on a random basis. It seems as though the Border Police decide for themselves who to stop and search. If it's a cold wet morning you are more likely to get through without question."

Freddy drove through the night to Brandenburg. They left the hired car in a side-street near the station. Rita said,

"We'll get the first train. There's one in about half an hour." They huddled together in the cold waiting room waiting for the first signs of a new day.

Presently a man entered the waiting room. He took out a newspaper and started to read. After about ten minutes he put it aside and with a snort of impatience stood up.

"Do you know the time of the next train?" he said. Rita was asleep, resting her head on Freddy's shoulder. He put his finger to his lips as if to tell the stranger to speak softly and shook his head.

"How does it happen that you wait here so long?" the man said.

Freddy sensed danger as Rita stirred and sat up.

"We were misinformed about our connection." Freddy lied. "We live in Magdeburg and hoped to get the last train to Berlin. We were married yesterday and this is our honeymoon."

"My job is security," the man continued. "I hope you have a happy time in Berlin. I expect you will want to walk the Unter den Linden like most loving couples. Please will you tell me your names."

"I'm Friedrich Schultz and this is my wife Rita."

"Thank you. Now I must go. Safe journey. There is a stopper quite soon now which will take you to the Ostbahnhof." With that the man left.

At last the train drew into the platform, the locomotive issuing jets of steam and making metallic noises signifying that it was in need of a major overhaul. Two hours later they were sipping hot chocolate in the café near the Oberbaum Bridge.

About ten minutes after sitting down, a man, who had been at a nearby table, got up and approached them. He was wearing the standard grey raincoat of the Stasi.

"Herr Schultz? It is Herr Schultz isn't it? Do you mind if I join you?"

"Please sit down." Freddy's legs turned to jelly. He wanted to get up and run but he knew that would be futile.

"Just a moment, who are you?" Rita said.

"I have been sent with a message to help you. My name is Luger."

"Oh, and what might that be, Herr Luger?"

"My colleagues have been concerned about you. They have asked me to inform you that your mother and father have been detained in Brandenburg. They are in the care of Colonel Rostovski at the Hotel Astoria. He has asked that you return to Brandenburg. Don't be alarmed, he has good news for the four of you but you should go straight away. I have a car here. It will be much quicker than the train."

"Have we a choice?" said Freddy. "Can we believe this?"

"We must believe it Freddy. It's your Mum and Dad we are talking about. Let's go. We are ready Herr Luger."

An hour later Herr Luger stopped the car in front of the hotel in the main street of Brandenburg. The old building bore the pock marks of bullets in its stucco. He opened the rear doors.

"Please," he said. "Colonel Rostovski will meet you inside."

As they ascended the short flight of steps the Colonel came out and held out his hand in greeting.

"Welcome to Brandenburg, Herr Schultz. Welcome to all four of you. I mean that most sincerely," said Colonel Rostovski, smiling from ear to ear. They entered a private lounge where Eric and Karen were already seated.

"Mama and Papa," exclaimed Rita as she ran towards them. "Are you all right?" They kissed.

"Please sit down and make yourselves comfortable. I will order coffee," said Ivan.

"What do you want with us Colonel?" said Eric guardedly.

"I want your help Eric. You don't mind me calling you Eric?"

"I've no objection Colonel. You know our names; my wife is Karen, my son Friedrich. Rita you know but you may not know that Rita and my son were married yesterday."

"Thank you Eric and please call me Ivan. Married eh, well I suppose congratulations are in order. Now, this is a friendly meeting you understand. The circumstances may be a little strange but we are both men of the world, are we not?"

"Why, yes, I suppose so."

"Colonel Rostovski, let's be frank with each other. Please stop playing cat and mouse with us," interrupted Karen.

During this exchange Freddy and Rita sat together on the couch holding hands. Rita was very frightened.

"I assure you Frau Karen that it is not me. It is you who are playing the cat with the mouse. I was unaware that my orders had been countermanded. Why did you not inform me that you were leaving the Gasthause? I have lost a night's sleep in a futile search for a spy and then I returned to the Holzern only to discover that you were in Brandenburg." Ivan said,

"We are truly sorry for the trouble Ivan but we didn't know until you arrived here of any change. What is this leading up to?"

"Hermann tells me that you have had clearance to enter West Germany. He thinks that you may have been in touch with the British Secret Police and that they have sent a spy to help you cross the zone boundary. Is this so?"

"It is true that I wish to reside in the west, with my family of course. I intended to obtain the necessary papers tomorrow in Berlin. It is also true that the British immigration authorities said they would send a courier to help with the formalities. I understood that when my contract expired, which it did at the end of last month, that I would be free to leave."

"No one leaves the employment of the Russian Space Agency without clearance from me personally. You do know that Eric."

Karen interposed,

"I think I am to blame for the whole fracas. You were to send me back to Leipzig while my husband was to be taken by you to the Harz. He told me, that once there, he would be a virtual prisoner. How was I supposed to react? I reacted like any wife would in similar circumstances. I took what steps I could to remain with my husband. In Berlin we would have made contact with the DDR minister responsible for internal affairs. My husband has not broken any laws. We have had no contact with a British courier."

"Your husband is in possession of secret information vital to the USSR and the DDR. It is essential that he should be prevented from selling or disclosing any of it to enemy forces."

"Enemy? What is this talk of enemy?"

"NATO forces are the enemy. There is an alliance between the USA and certain European nations to destroy our way of life."

"Nonsense. That's utter nonsense."

"The Americans have the atom bomb. They can destroy us at any time they choose."

"What good would that do them? As regards my speciality, the Americans have their own rockets, more advanced than ours. I could teach them nothing."

"Stop it," screamed Karen. "Stop these semantics. They are leading us nowhere. It just so happens that Hermann had prior information. Your bosses, Ivan, gave instructions that Eric should be allowed to travel to the west, to the USA to be precise. I had hoped that we would reach West Berlin to obtain travel documents to Britain."

"Well then, as I said at the beginning, this is to be a friendly discussion. It also happens that I have been asked to smooth away the normal obstacles to your departure in exchange for certain guarantees."

"Does that include my wife and me," asked Freddy.

"I'm not going anywhere without my son," interjected Karen.

"We shall discuss your son's position and that of Miss Smidt presently."

"It seems as though we may have an impasse Ivan," said Eric. Can we get back to what you want from me?"

"Quite simply, we want your friendship and co-operation. We think that you will be of much more use to us in the West than here. All your pioneering work has been overtaken by others. There is nothing left for you to do in the Harz. In any event we are moving the entire installation to the Urals. I doubt if you would want to be there."

"That's correct."

"Well then, we want you to be our contact inside the American Space Effort, NASA. Furthermore we want details of proposed American rocket locations. We have information that they may have plans to surround the USSR with long-distance rockets capable of delivering atom bombs. If this is so we need to know about them. We also need information on nuclear weapon design. The USA is developing Doomsday weapons of extreme power. If true, the Soviet Union and the countries we protect could be in terrible danger. We think that, with your knowledge, you will be able to gain access. Need I go on?"

"Very good then. I have the picture. First let me say that we have no enmity towards the Soviets or my fellow countrymen in the eastern zone. Neither do we bear ill-will towards the British or the Americans. My desire is to live at peace with everyone in quiet retirement. I have chosen to live in the West because it will be more fun for me and my family, my future family. That's all."

"That's not all Eric, as a man of your intelligence, having held the privileged position as one of our top scientists, should know. How will you live? You will lose all pension rights here."

"I shall find work.... Teaching probably and Karen too. Besides that I have a brother who lives in Philadelphia. That's where we would like to settle."

"Have you indeed. I didn't know that."

"He went to the USA in thirty-six."

"Listen both of you. Try to be sensible about this. You have a clear choice."

"Oh and what is that?"

"Isn't it obvious? You can live in disgrace here, with no pension or you may help us by sending reports from time to time about British and American rocket science after you have moved to the west. In return we will continue to pay your salary into a Swiss Bank of your choice."

"All right then, put like that Ivan, it seems we have no choice. We agree. I'm sure I can speak for all of us. Of course I can't guarantee results. I have firm promises from the British but nothing yet from the Americans. One other thing. My son and his wife must accompany us."

"That will not be possible. It is only fair to warn you that, should you not keep our pact, the long arm of the KGB reaches around the world. I need reassurance that you will continue to work for the good of the Soviet Union. Your son and his wife should return to Magdeburg. He can continue bus driving and I will see to it that Rita is given a job."

At this announcement Rita burst into tears and buried her face in Freddy's lap. Freddy turned as pale as a ghost. Karen stood up in anger.

"No, no, no. That's tearing my family apart. Is there no way…. no alternative?" she shouted.

"For the present that's the best deal I'm empowered to offer you. You should be pleased with the outcome of this discussion. Friedrich and Rita will be working in the DDR as they have been for some time. Your husband will be doing a vital job for us and receiving a good salary also. He will probably get payments from the Americans too. You should be pleased."

"Pleased? How can we be pleased?"

"You will be able to visit your son here, Karen, whenever you wish. This is the best possible contract I can offer. No Karen, there is no alternative."

"Sit down dear," said Eric in a calm voice. "Let us talk sensibly to Ivan. I don't think we have an alternative either."

"I'm glad you're beginning to see things my way," said Ivan

"It will take time for us to settle in. Please don't expect anything useful until I become part of their establishment. Let's just say I'm on probation for the next twelve months. I've already been given a temporary post at the English Electric Company's missile base in Luton, Hertfordshire. Their guided weapons are still in a very experimental stage."

"One last thing," said Ivan. "I need to know who is the British agent?"

"He's not a spy, just a courier," said Rita.

"Do you know this man?"

"Not personally. I contacted British Immigration in Berlin and they said they would send a courier to meet us and smooth our path through West Berlin," said Rita, beginning to sweat under this cross questioning. She worried that one lie could lead to others.

"Was he planning to entice Doctor Schultz into the west?"

Eric interrupted,

"Not at all. I had made up my mind to travel to the West as soon as my contract expired. I can assure you that the KGB has nothing to fear from this man."

"Do you know him then Eric?"

"Certainly not. We've never met. We were due to meet at the Holzern but I imagine it was your men that frightened him away."

"We think that he left a burnt out Daimler car in a street in Wahrenberg. The same car was being used by a medical doctor at the hospital in Magdeburg. We know the registration number. This same man obtained leave from the Direktor to go to Vacha. As you know Vacha is in the border area. I am making enquiries to find out what he intended to do in Vacha. If you can help in any way then please tell me now. Rita?"

"I know nothing about Vacha, Colonel. If anything should turn up I'll pass it on."

"Very well then. It will be necessary for me to question the inhabitants of Vacha. A big task but not impossible. In the meantime enjoy your new life in the west, Doctor Schultz. Let us drink a toast to our future collaboration." Freddy jumped up at this and said,

"I'll order wine." He left the room closely followed by Rita.

"What's going on Rita?"

"Your Dad's just agreed to spy for the Russians in exchange for our freedom. Sounds like a fair swap to me."

"Sounds terribly dangerous to me. If he's found out, he will be executed."

"Don't be silly. The British don't do that sort of thing. Klaus Fuchs has only got 14 Years after disclosing all the British atom secrets to the Russians. At the worst he could be swapped for one of their's and sent back here."

"What about our deal with Brigadier Morris?"

"For heavens sake Freddy. Shut up. We may be overheard in a place like this. Ivan knows about Jim for sure. If our plan gets out we'll be linked straight back to Charlie. Just get the wine ordered. We haven't time for recriminations. My thoughts about what could happen are making me sick."

After a meal at the hotel Ivan announced,

"We shall stay here for the night and in the morning we shall disperse. Friedrich and Rita shall return to Magdeburg in order to make a new start. Eric and Karen, you may wish to go back to your home in Leipzig to collect some belongings. Hermann will accompany you and deliver you to Berlin. I am sure the English will find a way to fly you to London. It is important that you are believed to have defected without our help. We have managed to recover your car Herr Friedrich. I think we may be asking Rita for some help in catching the British spy but I shall be making enquiries in Vacha and hope to pick up his trail there."

15 Vacha

Colonel Ivan Rostovski sat behind his office desk. His elbows were planted firmly on the leather surface supporting his head on cupped hands. Eyes tight shut, he was deep in thought when the expected telephone call jangled the instrument.

"Rostovski."

"Colonel, is this line secure?"

"Yes Comrade General. I am assured it is completely protected. You may speak freely."

"What was the outcome of your meeting with Doctor Schultz?"

"As you instructed, comrade, nothing was done to obstruct his flight to England. He is staying overnight at a hotel in London, The Cumberland. We expect that the English ministry will provide accommodation for him and Frau Schultz at Woolcroft Manor in Berkshire for de-briefing. The outcome of this by MI6 is uncertain. As soon as I have some information from our agent about his movements you will be informed. Meanwhile I can report that his son, Friedrich, and daughter-in-law have taken up residence in Magdeburg at Friedrich's apartment. The manager of the bus service has re-engaged him and also Rita Schultz, who has been promised a clerical position. The manager has been made aware of our arrangement and that he must contact me immediately should anything change."

"Very good Colonel. I support your actions so far but I wish to make it clear that I hold you responsible for your failure to apprehend the English spy. It is apparent that MI6 has infiltrated your organisation. We need to deal with this situation as a matter of extreme urgency."

"I have a man in the town of Vacha making enquiries about a possible link with the Englishman. We know that an English officer, a Lieutenant in the British Army Medical Corps, took up a temporary post at the Magdeburg hospital. He obtained a permit to visit Vacha. He told the Direktor of the hospital that he wished to visit a relative. That is all I know for the moment. He would have been unable to visit Vacha, which is in the restricted zone, but, so far, I have not found out what he did do. Another link is his car. He had a Daimler first registered in Magdeburg in 1937. This car, or one very like it, with the same illegal licence plates was found burnt out in the village of Wahrenberg after the local police failed to apprehend it. We believe that the English spy was using it and that he ultimately escaped on a barge."

"Do you suppose that the medical officer and the spy are one and the same?"

"Yes. It is almost certain. Rita Schultz claims he was a courier sent by the British Immigration Service."

"Do you believe that?"

"No I don't."

"Then why didn't you arrest her?"

"I can at any time I choose. She's going nowhere. She used to be employed at the Harz as secretary to the Doctor. I think she may be of more use to us as a co-operative source of information if she's not in prison."

"Do you think she has been passing information to the British?"

"Possibly, but we have no proof of that. Even if she was to be convicted and sentenced to a long prison term we would be no nearer finding more enemy agents in the Harz or anywhere else. The enemy agent has escaped back to the British Zone. Of that I am sure."

"How sure?"

"Because of the barge incident. He was probably picked up at Wahrenberg after setting the car on fire and taken down river to Schnackenburg. I have two descriptions of the man, from the Direktor at the hospital and from the farmer who pulled the Daimler out of a ditch. Our border guards have been informed."

"Very good Colonel. Please keep me informed of progress. If we get this man we can use him to uncover all the enemy spies in the DDR and maybe beyond."

When Ivan put down the receiver he found himself sweating. He mopped his face and pressed a bell on his desk. Presently Heino entered.

"We're driving over to Vacha, Heino. Ist der Wagen fertig?"

"Ja, my colonel. Fünfzehn Minuten."

"We can stay the night in Eisenach and be in Vacha first thing to-morrow. I want another man with us, armed."

"Yes Comrade Colonel."

The town of Vacha has nothing to recommend it to the casual tourist. It stands on the banks of the Werra river by the side of the Grenze. On the other bank in the middle distance is the neighbouring town of Phillipsthal, in the western zone. The main road, from there, comes to an abrupt end by the red sandstone multi-arched bridge over the Werra which is about a hundred meters wide at this place. Local historians will tell you that Napoleon led his army over this bridge before the famous battle of Austerlitz. The Grenze crossed the bridge in the shape of a high wire mesh firmly bolted to the western parapet. Nearby a high concrete watch tower, in which there were always at least two armed guards, kept the crossing under constant surveillance. The Werra is heavily polluted and devoid of all life due to the effluent from the nearby potash mines. The fast flowing river is inky black.

The Colonel and his bodyguards took up residence in the only hotel, Die Rhön. On the second day Ivan interviewed Herr Gruber.

"My man has been making enquiries here for nearly a week now. Surely, Herr Gruber, you were aware of this? I now discover that you know of an English woman who is married to the local forester, Herr Wogart."

"I must protest Colonel. I only heard about your presence in the town yesterday. That is why I have come forward. Yes, it is true that there was an English lady living with Herr Wogart. She may still be there but it is about a month ago that she stopped coming to the Creche and the Clinic with her baby. I have not seen her since then."

"Very good Gruber. I want you to go with my driver and bring her to me for questioning."

The Mercedes wound its way up the tortuous track through the pine woods. The surface was eroded and pocked with deep holes. Eventually, in the centre of a clearing, Heino stopped the car by the front of the cabin. All was quiet, the house apparently deserted. They got out of the car and stood listening to the gentle breeze stirring the tops of the trees. Herr Gruber climbed the short flight of steps on to the wooden veranda and put his face to the glass. He could dimly see Lucy asleep on a couch. By her side was a sleeping baby. He tapped on the glass. She woke and sat up in alarm.

"Frau Wogart, it's Gruber here. I have a message for you. Lucy came to the door. She stood in the opening looking pale and unsteady.

"I'm not well Herr Gruber."

"I'm so sorry to disturb you. I hope you are not in a serious condition. You are needed in Vacha. It is urgent." Heino swung his legs out of the car and stood up. Lucy faced him in fear of his uniform.

"You must come with us into Vacha. You are to be interviewed by my boss, Colonel Rostovski. He wants to know all about you," said Heino.

"I've done nothing wrong, I promise," said Lucy in a voice filled with alarm. "If my husband comes home he will be very angry with me for leaving here."

"I shall see that he knows you had no choice, Frau Wogart. I will ask Herr Gruber to remain here to explain. I see you have a truck so your husband can bring him back to the village. Where is your husband?"

"He works in the forest. Contractors have been called in to cut many of the trees along the border. My husband is supervising the work. What about my baby?"

"Bring the baby."

"I need a coat."

"Yes, get a coat. I shall be waiting."   Lucy came out carrying Carla in a wrap. Heino supported her as they walked to the car.

Lucy started to cry. Her only comfort was that she knew Gruber as the man who kept a shop next to the clinic in Vacha. As the car proceeded down the steep track Lucy's questions and sobs filled the silence.

"What is the trouble? Is something wrong? Why not speak to my husband, Carl? He will tell you anything you need to know."   Heino remained impassive.

Ivan heard the car arrive and greeted Lucy at the door of the hotel with a jovial smile.

"I am Colonel Rostovski; I work for the Security Service of the Russian Army in this area. I am so sorry to bother you like this Frau Wogart but there are several questions which are causing me difficulty and I have to report back to my superiors; you understand?"

"I've done nothing wrong, I swear," said Lucy in a shaky voice. "My husband will be very angry with me for leaving our home without his permission." She sat in a high backed chair trembling.

"Is that why you are so upset? You have nothing to fear from me. I assure you. Does your husband beat you?

"He has done when we quarrel, sometimes, a smack," she said in a whisper.

"Please Frau Wogart. Compose yourself. Dry your eyes. Now…do you wish to leave your husband?"

"No, not really. What would become of me if I did?"

"I could probably arrange for you to go into a hostel."

"With baby Carla?"

"I'm sure we can arrange something."

"No please. I would like you to explain to Carl, my husband, that I had no choice but to come here."

"Of course. Now can we come to the reason why I need to ask you a few questions?"

"Yes, please."

"It has come to my notice that an English doctor, working in the hospital at Magdeburg, made a visit here about six weeks ago. Since you are also English, I believe, I am asking if you know about this visit."

"Yes, my brother-in-law Charles Forbes, Charlie, came to see me but not here. We met in Eisenach for about an hour. It was over six months since we last met. I was overjoyed to see him again."

"I can understand that Frau Wogart. Excuse me but what is your first name?"

"Lucy Sir."

"You should address me as comrade."

"Yes, comrade."

"Lucy. Ah-ha, 'light', well perhaps you will shed some light on my problem.

"Sir, er, comrade?"

"Your brother-in-law, Charles is a doctor, yes?"

"Yes comrade."

"Does he also work for the British Secret Service?"

"No Sir, comrade, I'm sure he wouldn't. He just came to see me and Carl, to say 'hello'. That was all. He couldn't come to our home so we met in Eisenach. It was the same day that Carl bought the truck."

"I ask you now; if ever he decides to visit again that you contact your local police. We need to talk to him. Do you know where he is at this moment?"

"Unless he's in Magdeburg I expect he has gone back to his unit. He's married to my sister Susan and they live in Osnabruck."

"Why do you suppose he came here to the DDR?"

"He said he knew there was a vacancy in Magdeburg. He said that he is getting very little experience in Osnabruck."

"You are not happy to be here, are you?"

"I was very happy at first comrade but now I am expecting another baby in about six months. I know it will not be easy. I would like some help. Maybe if we lived in a town I would be able to make some friends."

Outside they heard the noisy Trabant truck arriving. The door was slammed shut and Carl's wooden foot echoed down the passage. He burst into the room.

"What's going on here? Herr Gruber told me I would find you here, Lucy."

"This is Colonel Rostovski, Carl. He brought me here to answer some questions."

"What sort of questions?" Carl's loud voice woke up Carla who began to cry.

"I think I have all I need for the moment Herr Wogart. Your wife has been very helpful. She will tell you what has transpired. I suggest that you both go home now. It will soon be dark. Once again Lucy, thank you for your help and co-operation. I'm sorry you were troubled. I bid you both good night."

After Lucy and Carl had departed Ivan turned to Heino.

"We've work to do Heino. I must get back to the Harz. Drive overnight. We'll get this Charlie. It's not a question of 'if' anymore but 'when'. How would you catch a fish Heino?"

"Colonel?"

"With bait, yes. I think I know where we can find some bait."

The following day Ivan held a meeting with his assistants, Hermann and Heino amongst them.

****

It was a beautiful sunny morning a week later. Carla was fast asleep tucked under covers in the pram on the veranda. There was no wind. All was silent as if the whole world was waiting for the baby to awaken. The air was heavy with the scent of the pines. The quiet was broken by the distant growl of an approaching vehicle. Lucy paused in her ironing to listen. Carla stirred in her sleep. Presently a black Mercedes drew up at the Waldstation. Two heavily built women, dressed alike in grey habits, alighted. The chauffeur waited until they had shut their door and then turned the car ready for departure. One nun went over to look at the baby and the other rang a brass bell which she found hanging beside the front door of the dwelling.

Lucy came to the door.

"Guten Morgen Frau Wogart."

"Morgen," replied Lucy squinting in the sunshine as she pushed back an auburn lock.

"Colonel Rostovski asked us to call. We are from the Convent in Bad Salzungen. May we enter?"

The other woman, without being asked, wheeled the pram to the door and followed inside. Carla woke and looked up, wide eyed. This was a new experience for her. Lucy bent over the pram and whispered in the baby's ear,

"It's alright Carla," she said. "These ladies are friends."
Then turning she said,

"Come in and sit down, welcome."

When they were seated,

"Would you like coffee?"

"No thank you," they said. "Where do you get coffee? It is very expensive."

"My husband does a lot of the shopping. I imagine he gets it in Vacha. Now, I suppose you are here to see Carla."

"That is correct. First we shall introduce ourselves. My colleague is Sister Kratze and I am Sister Martfeld. Our work is at the Convent where we care for baby orphans and we are also house visitors."

"Well, as you can see baby Carla is well cared for and happy. I am sure you will give me a good report. Is this visit routine?"

"Partly routine. Yes. But we have been asked by Colonel Rostovski to call. We have been told that he interviewed you and among other matters you informed him that your husband can be violent. Is that correct?"

"No, that's not right really. He does get cross with me sometimes, when I do wrong that is. I don't always understand his German. He likes to speak in German all the time. He says it's good for me and I am quite fluent."

"The Colonel is worried for you and for baby Carla."

"Oh. Please assure the Colonel that Carl would never lay a finger on his daughter in anger. He is so good with her."

"I see. I am sure Sister Kratze will agree with me, you should be very careful. Always be present when your husband has charge of her."

"I assure you everything will be all right."

"Nevertheless the Colonel has asked us to look after Carla for a short time."

"Very good. You may visit here when ever you like. I am nearly always here, except Wednesdays when we go into Vacha for supplies."

"You don't understand Frau Wogart. We cannot come here. We shall make room for her with the other babies in our care at the Convent. You may visit us of course. We are only twenty kilometers away. Just let us know by letter when you would like to come."

"But ......"

"No buts Frau Wogart. We have to do what we are instructed. It will be for the best. Maybe until you and your husband separate or until we have re-assurance that he is unlikely to attack you or the child."

"This is unbearable," cried Lucy bursting into tears. "Wait until my husband returns," she said through her sobs. Carla started to cry at the sound of the raised voices.

"You see what we mean Frau Wogart. Quarrels are not good for the correct development of the baby."

"Sister Kratze. Please take Carla to the car. I wish to speak to Frau Wogart alone."

"No you shan't." Lucy moved forward but Sister Martfeld was too quick for her. She wrapped her strong arms around Lucy's slender figure while the other lifted Carla from the pram. Lucy screamed and struggled to no avail and watched Kratze run across the clearing and get in the car.

"Calm yourself, Frau Wogart," said Sister Martfeld but, when she released her, Lucy ran across the room, outside, across the clearing to the car but the door was locked. She picked up a stone to break the window.

"Stop her," shouted the Sister. The chauffeur was ready. He blocked Lucy's path, took her arm and led her firmly away.

"If you damage the car that will be a felony," he said as he gently prised her fingers off the stone. He tossed it away. Sister Martfeld got into the car. The chauffeur started the engine as Lucy sank to the carpet of pine needles and put her head on the ground. Two hours later she was there when Carl found her. He ran.

"What is it?" He crouched. He shook her shoulder.

"You should have been here. They've taken her. Taken my ....our baby."

"What is this? Who's taken our baby? What's happened?"

"The Sisters from the Convent. They came here soon after you left. They could have been watching us to make sure you were out of the way."

Carl lifted her up. Lucy leant on him in her distress and together they walked to the house. She went to the bedroom and flung herself across it burying her face in the pillow. Carl, unable to consol her, went for a tot of brandy. He lit a fire in the stove and made a meal. Presently Lucy came to the door of the living room. She made her way unsteadily to a chair. Slowly and quietly she related the events of the morning.

"But why, why, why?" Carl remonstrated angrily. "There must be a reason. Is it something you have done? Did they find fault with us? What reason did they give?"

Still sobbing Lucy could only think slowly.

"It was on Rostovski's orders. He wants information about Charlie. I told him that we know nothing about Charlie, but he knew that Charlie has been to see us. I told him we met in Eisenach but he wanted to know more. I told him we didn't know any more. He thinks Charlie is working for the British Secret Service. I denied it of course but he doesn't believe us."

"Foolish girl. I told you ages ago never to mention Charlie to anyone. You have brought this on us. May God give me strength."

"I'm sorry Carl. Really sorry but Rostovski knew. He knew already."

"And you, silly girl, confirmed it. Now they'll be watching us. I thought there was more activity. They've got a lot more Vopos in the forest, patrolling this area."

"Don't please Carl. Don't make me more miserable than I am already. Please, please don't."

"We'll have to think this out very carefully. It's obvious to me what going to happen next."

"What's that Carl?"

"It will be Charlie or Carla. It's easy to work out. If we can give them Charlie, then we can have Carla."

"That's unthinkable Carl. They'll kill him. At least they won't kill Carla, a little baby."

"They could threaten us. If they do, what do we do then? We can't call their bluff. It wouldn't be bluff." Carl stood and started to raise his arm.

"I couldn't help it. Please don't."

"Go to the bedroom."

The following morning, with Carl out of the way, Lucy sat down to write a letter. When she had finished it she hid it in the lining of her overcoat intending to place it under her secret stone later.

16 DISMISSED

"Lieutenant Forbes on the line now Sir."

"Charlie, where are you?" asked the Brigadier.

"In the officers' mess Sir."

"I've David with me. Get your arse over to my office and be quick about it."

"Sir, I'm on my way." Charlie slammed down the receiver and started to sweat as he ran across the BAOR HQ Campus. He saluted as he entered.

"So you're back. I need a full report. I believe you had problems."

"Yes Sir, big problems."

"They've made us look foolish. Our girl…."

"You mean Rita Smidt."

"I do indeed. Did she mislead us intentionally? She's gone over hasn't she? Married a bloody commie?"

"I don't think Freddy is really a commie. He wanted to come over to the west."

"Well, I don't think I need to congratulate you on your role in this affair."

"No Sir. I did have a narrow escape though Sir."

"Tell me about it."

"Gladly. Everything went smoothly up to the point where Rita got Eric and his wife Karen…"

"Eric. You mean X."

"Yes Sir, the same. I was to pick them up at the Holzern Gasthaus but the bodyguard, Hermann, who was supposed to be drugged out of his mind, turned up. He followed the four of them there. Freddy and Rita drove off for West Berlin but Hermann got the security chief to come from the Harz. I knew the game was up and made an unplanned exit on Freiheit. God, wasn't I glad to see them."

"You bungled the whole plan by supplying Rita with the wrong knock out pill."

"How did you find that out, Sir?"

"Never you mind."

"I think Rita is sound, Sir. She married Freddy out of duty not love. Now she's stuck with him. She blew her cover in Berlin. At least I think she did, so she could be in peril right now. As it is she's caught in Ivan's trap in Magdeburg."

"How did she blow it in Berlin then?"

"My cover went when they discovered the MISU flat in the east the day after I spent the night in Rita's room at the Alex."

"Damn fool! We had a big investment in her and in the flat."

"We did a deal with those two, didn't we? Rita told me you would pay them a million D.marks to get Eric out."

"They didn't get Eric out. Eric got himself out. He and Karen turned up at Tempelhof. There's no way I'm parting with more government money over this affair. Thanks to you we've paid for a barge and a crew, both redundant. Also we've lost the base in East Berlin, a valuable radio set and the Daimler….a total waste of money, public money. I'm not parting with any more. You're too expensive Forbes."

"The crew want to buy the barge, Sir. That way you'll get a lot of it back. It needs a repair though, in the bows and it has a few bullet holes in the hull."

"Well, we'll see about that then."

"Sir, may I make a suggestion?"

"Yes, go on then," the Brigadier said somewhat testily.

"Has it occurred to you to wonder how Eric got out so easily? There is very tight security at the Harz."

"Yes, as a matter of fact it has. Do you take me for a fool? David, your chaps are debriefing them now. Is that right?" David, having taken no part in this exchange so far, sat up straight.

"Yes Jim. We have no plans to let him into the Luton site. In fact we intend to offer him to the Yanks. It'll be a relief to pass the buck to someone over the pond."

"Good. Let me know what happens. Meantime Lieutenant Forbes, you are to consider yourself 'stood down'. You should report back to the hospital and resume your training. We may send you back home."

"Sir, is there any reason why Susan, my wife, and I should not visit Susan's sister in the Thuringerwald? Lucy is very unhappy at the moment and would welcome a visit."

"Yes Forbes, there is every bloody reason not to go over. I forbid it. If the Stasi got wind of it you would be shot or imprisoned. I don't know which would be worse. You said yourself some time ago that this HQ leaks like a sieve. You could be forced to give away my whole operation. See what I mean?"

"Yes Sir."

"I'm surprised you asked. Now this meeting is at an end. I want a full report in writing this week."

"Yes Sir." He snapped his heels together as he saluted, turned and left.

****

As Charlie walked back to his quarters he choked on his own bile. He couldn't go back in this state. He would have to tell Susan everything. He sat on a swing in the playground gathering his thoughts and angry at his humiliation in front of

David. Once more in control of his bitter feelings he strolled back thinking about their future. He found Susan slumped over the kitchen table in tears. In her hand was a crumpled letter.

"Darling, whatever is the matter?" said Charlie as he crouched and hugged her to him. It was several minutes before she had calmed sufficiently.

"Read this," she said as she smoothed the letter on the table. "It's from Lucy."

"I guessed it would be …. Bad news."

"It could hardly be worse. Read it." He read the letter.

Darling,   *30ᵗʰ May*

I've lost my two babies.

I'm at my wits end because Carla has been taken to a convent at Bad Salzungen. Carl is furious with me for letting them take her. I couldn't stop them. My little one, due to be born in August, was stillborn. It was a boy. It began because I was taken into Vacha for questioning. Carl forbids me to go anywhere unless he comes too.

What's Charlie been doing? There's a Russian Officer, Colonel Rostovski looking for him. He thinks Charlie is a spy. He's not is he?

When Carl found me in the village being questioned by this Colonel he took me home. We quarrelled. I tried to reason with him. He became violent. I ran away and fell down the veranda steps. My waters broke and he had to take me into Eisenach Hospital. They discharged me after two days. The nurse saw my bruises but nothing was done about it. To give Carl his due, he is absolutely devastated by it all and asked me to forgive him, which I did of course.

Unless you rescue me I could be sent to Siberia. I'm sure of it. Yesterday Carl told me that we are to be moved. Rostovski sent the local police to tell us. I've no idea where we shall finish up. I hope it isn't Siberia. I've been told it's a death sentence. I will write every week. If my letters stop coming then fear the worst.

I'm sure the sisters in the Convent will look after Carla well. I suppose they meant it for the best but I don't know when I'll see my daughter again. They have taken her away since the authorities think I may be in danger from Carl. I had told the Colonel that Carl would hit me if I left the house on my own. I shouldn't have done that.

Luckily I have made a friend of the postman who comes here, otherwise I wouldn't be able to reach you. I don't expect to get all your letters Susan. I think Carl must intercept them at the post office. Sometimes the postman will leave my letters under a stone near our chalet. It is our secret.

Darling Susan, I don't expect you to understand this, but I'm not a good wife for Carl. I don't get the fun that he does from love-making. I know I'm an emotional mess but it's just the way I'm made. I used to dream about being married and all that. I envy you but now I am married it doesn't seem to be enjoyable any more.

Love Lucy.

"God Susan. Our poor Lucy. How were we to know it would come to this? The man's a menace. Why didn't we spot it sooner? Anyway Carl has killed his own baby, if that's any consolation. I can't believe we're talking about to same man we met during the war."

"The war must have left very deep scars. It's turned him into a barbarian. I wonder if, in some way, we are to blame?"

"How can that possibly be?"

"Oh, I don't know. I expect this is nonsense but our cabarets at the mansion did appeal to a man's worst side. Aroused something deep down even they did not recognise."

"Forget all that. It's Lucy we need to do something about now. There's no point in going over all that old stuff. At that time you and Lucy were doing something honourable to protect the other girls. Just remember that, OK?"

"I suppose you're right." Susan said with resignation.

"We'll get her out. Have you had any other letters like this?"

"No, of course not. Not as bad. There have been others, about three, all saying how homesick she is."

"Why didn't I see them?"

"I didn't want to upset you. You …. We knew she would be homesick and we thought she would get over it. The life that Carl offered sounded idyllic."

"Did you know he was violent?"

"No, not really. She did mention that they had a quarrel but I put that down to getting used to each other. There has to be give and take in every marriage. You should know."

"All right, point taken. So this is the first really bad one, is it?"

"It certainly is, and I agree we must get her out as soon as we can."

"If it's true, what she says, that he never lets her out without him going too, then it's going to be almost impossible. How could she apply for an exit visa without him knowing about it and she can't get out without one?"

"We'll have to get her out somehow. Think of something Charlie. We've got to do something. If you don't I will. Now you've been 'stood down' you should be able to get leave. You haven't had any leave since we got here and that's over eighteen months ago."

"I agree. We must and will do something, but what? The Brigadier has forbidden me to go over. He says I'm too hot."

"Since when did you ever take notice of orders when they conflict with your own ideas? We've got to get her out," said Susan raising her voice.

"Easier said than done. This is not."

"You're losing your nerve."

"Joke if you must. This is a serious project."

"If you go I'm coming with you."

"What can we do even if we do go? I suppose we could get DDR permits for a limited stay but apart from meeting your sister we can't really do anything."

"We've got to get her away from Carl. She's obviously not in love with him any more, even if she really was in the first place. Don't you think that marrying Carl was a desperate act?"

"I don't know what to think. Anyway even if we did do as you say, what's to become of Charles and what would become of him if we never came back. No, the whole thing's much too risky."

"Risky, of course it's risky. Just about everything you do is risky. What's changed?

"Well I won't have MISU behind us for a start. In fact if Jim gets to find out he may even obstruct us."

"Let's go back home for a few days. We ought to be able to get entry permits in London. I've heard of other people doing it."

"Have you? Who?"

"Well… people. They have to let some people in on business for instance. The problems start with people coming out not going in. You even got the offer of a job on your last trip."

"Yes I did. A nice man, Herr Direktor. I feel quite guilty letting him down."

"I've got an idea."

"Oh?"

"We'll go over and let Lucy use my passport to get out."

"What good will that do? What about Carla? How will you get out?"

"You and Lucy travel together and then you return with the passport to get me."

"That won't work. They always cancel the permit as you leave the DDR."

"You'll have to get two more permits."

"Impossible without you being there."

"Lucy could be me. You could get them in Bonn."

"Carla?"

"We'll add Carla to my passport. You could get that done at the passport office in London too."

"They'll never allow it. We can't produce a birth certificate for her."

"That's where you come in. Get David to pull a few strings. He owes you a favour, a hundred favours after all you've done for him.

"Well I must say you make it all sound delightfully simple. There must be a snag somewhere. Let's sleep on it."

****

A week later Charlie got his leave. Susan, Charles and he left for England the following day. Susan rang Uncle Frank from London.

"How's Dad, uncle?"

"Sinking fast Susan. I think you've got home just in time. I was going to ring you tonight. He had another attack yesterday. He may recognise you but he may not. It's hard to say. Can we get Lucy over?"

"Oh dear. I'm so so sorry uncle. Charlie and I are staying overnight in London. We'll catch an early train to-morrow. I'll send you a telegram. As for Lucy, we can't reach her by phone. We will write but she'll have to apply for an exit visa. It could take weeks."

"That will be too late Susan. Let me know which train you're catching. I'll be waiting."

17 Cleethorpes

Two weeks later Susan, Charles and Charlie were on the stopping train from Leeds as it drew into Cleethorpes Station. Eliza, Bert and Peggy were on the platform to meet them. Hugs and kissed were lavished on each of the travellers amid shrieks of joy at their safe return. Eliza said,

"I'm so sorry to hear about Sir Hugo, Susan. What a shame that Lucy couldn't get over for the funeral."

"It had to happen, Mum. He had no life. He hated being in a wheel chair. After the first stroke he seemed to rally and we thought he might recover but the last two years have seen a slow decline. I know he was a difficult man. Lucy and I used to hate him, the way he treated us, I mean, but he thought that what he was doing was for our good in the long run. I feel sorry he didn't live long enough to see Charles grow up."

A lump came into Susan's throat when she saw and remembered the old house on the promenade and her escapade with Lucy when they were girls. She wondered whether she would see Lucy again. Nothing seemed to have changed at Number Two except that Bert admitted to giving the whole place a sparkling coat of paint. Even the flowers in the front garden looked the same. Charlie said,

"It's like old times Bert. Let's go for a stroll like we used to and let the ladies natter. Susan will want to tell them what's it's like to be an army wife, and Mum and Aunt will want to make a fuss of Charles."

Soot, the terrier, chased the gulls along the beach albeit with less enthusiasm than Charlie remembered. The two men strode along, side by side. Bert was obviously still a very fit man.

" Tell me all about your adventures. You seem to have been away a lifetime."

"It's about eighteen months Bert, and a lot of water has gone under, as they say. I don't know where to start really. Most of what I do is secret of course. I've been acting as a courier, getting people out of Eastern Germany, the DDR, Deutsche Demokratische Republik, so called.   It's anything but democratic."

"Sounds dangerous work."

"Not at first but it's getting dangerous. The Ruskies and the German Commies are working like mad to stop people crossing the Grenze."

"The what?"

"Grenze, the border between what used to be the Allied Zone and the Russian Zone. Now the border is being strengthened, the two halves of Germany have become two countries. You remember Carl?"

"Vaguely but we've never met."

"Well he and Lucy got married in the east and they live in the Thuringerwald. They have my child, Carla. Carl adopted her as his. Lucy was about to have another."

"Was?"

"She lost it."

"I am sorry," said Bert. "What happened?"

"Judging from her letters, the man's a swine. He beat her up. That's what happened. She's desperate to get back here but she won't leave without Carla, that's for sure. I've got a letter to show you. You could be a real help to us."

"Oh, really? What can an old man like me do then?"

168

"Well I've got to get help from somewhere and it won't be from my boss. He's forbidden me to have anything to do with the problem."

They reached the pub at last. Soot knew his place and sat patiently by the door as they went in. Three pints each later the bell rang and a voice shouted time. Feeling decidedly unsteady in the cold night air they set out for home.

The following day was Sunday. Peggy had done her customary roast. She said,

"Some things are still rationed you know, meat for one. We'll have to get you temporary books if you're staying."

Charlie said,

"I've only got two weeks and then it's back to Osnabruck. We've got to make some plans to get Lucy out. Carl will do his best to prevent us, to say nothing of the authorities over there. Bert, what do you say?"

"Goodness….me, at my time of life?"

"Well if you both came back with us, Mum could look after Charles and you could be our back-up in case things go a bit awry."

"Sounds like a tall order to me Charlie. What would be involved? I don't mind a bit of skulduggery but I got my fill of that in the first scrap. I'm nearly sixty now."

"Don't worry Bert. Don't worry about that. For a start you can help with the planning and then you can set us on the road to buying the kit we might need. Lastly, we shall need a sort of quartermaster.

"Well, put like that Charlie, I'm your man but what's the great plan?"

"Susan and I have already talked about it, of course. The first job is for us to get visas from the East German Embassy in London. We'll have to go there in person to get our passports stamped. We can get Lucy out by swapping passports but she won't leave without Carla. I think we can get Carla added to Susan's passport. Susan and I will get Carla away from the convent. We'll get Lucy and Carla through the Helmstedt crossing. Then Susan and I will get out by swimming under the bridge at Vacha. The old medieval bridge over the River Werra there carries the Grenze. It is a high steel fence bolted to the parapet on the western side. There are steel bars blocking the arches but they are badly corroded. It's the one weak point in the whole of the Grenze. The river banks will be mined, I'm sure, but I know how to deal with them."

"How do you know all this?"

"Well I got a good look at the barrier from our side on a recce I did some time ago. We shall have to buy a car, actually two cars, one for you. You can get the rest of our gear, a gas cylinder, small one, and breathing masks. Also a couple of ex-US-Army Walkie Talkies. They have a range of about two miles. And some tools like a hacksaw, bolt-croppers etc. Let's have some ideas from you."

"Sounds as though this could be a major operation."

"It could be."

"Why not get back-up from your colleagues, kit as well?"

"My boss at HQ has grounded me. Forbidden me to cross over. He says I'm hot, too well known. This has got to be a private op."

"What about Lucy? Does she know any of this?"

"No she blooming-well doesn't, nor will she until I roll up at her house. I don't know how I'll get her away. Carl keeps her under guard or behind a locked door. I'll cross that bridge when we come to it."

"I can't say I like it, Charlie. Too many unknowns, too many holes. Do you mind if I ask a question?"

"No of course not," replied Charlie.

"Why does Susan have to go with you? Why don't you just go and get Lucy, either legally or illegally. Susan doesn't even need to be involved, in danger."

"You don't know Lucy, Bert. It's not that she isn't brave but she couldn't do it. She's not the type. If I shot a German soldier she'd go to his aid rather than scarper with me. She's like that. She would rather go to prison than cause anybody any trouble."

"I see. She sounds a bit like my old Mum used to be. Always sticking up for the under-dog however unworthy. All the same I think you'll be awfully lucky to pull it off."

"OK Bert. You just go over what I've said and make a note of the dangers and we'll cover for them if we can."

"We're taking Charles for a stroll on the beach," called Eliza. "Coming you two?"

"Just a moment everybody," said Peggy.

"What's the matter, Peg," said Eliza.

"Here, on the Obits page of the Tele. Mary Brown (nee Gray) beloved wife of David Brown, and their son, Richard, aged four. Both killed in a car crash. Is that the David Brown that you know Charlie?"

"My God, let me see that. Gosh, what a terrible thing. David will be …… Well I don't know what he will be, do I, silly of me. I'll write. I don't know his home and it isn't mentioned here. It says Box 200, Esher. It's got to be him. What will the poor man do now? Get some leave and then just carry on I suppose."

"Come on everybody. Let's go for a breath of fresh. Time to think about that later Charlie."

****

Bert and Charlie were scouting for their equipment.

"Are you really sure you can't get exit visas?"

"We can in London but it would take too long to get two more. We'll have to use them to get in and Lucy will use Susan's to get out and then it would have to be renewed. I would have to go with her to get Susan's passport back. The whole thing would be much too complicated. We would be spotted making two crossings within a day or so. It will be too suspicious. We can get the permits in London and maybe repeats in Bonn but they must pass information to and fro on a daily basis. It would be crazy of them not to pick that up. As it is I'm going to ask David to wangle Carla's name on Susan's passport. I hope he can manage it. If we can't get Carla out then Lucy won't come out either."

"Would that be so bad? She could probably get an exit visa in due course…. Maybe next year."

"And what would she be suffering in the meantime? No Bert, that's no good at all. If you want to know the score then read this. I kept it, sorry it's so crumpled. By the way, my leave will soon be up. I've asked for an extension on compassionate grounds…. another week. After that I must get back. Here." Charlie passed a crumpled envelope. Bert read.

"Blimey. That's dynamite. I see what you and Susan are on about. Surely there is a legal way to get her out. If the man's violent and liable to commit murder then the authorities should know about it."

"These things take time Bert and time is what we haven't got. In any case they could protect Lucy just like they've taken steps to protect Carla but that doesn't mean to say they'll give her a visa."

Charlie and Bert took the ferry to Hull. In a back street near the docks they found one of Bert's many friends, a ships' chandler, who had a whole range of second hand and discarded marine stores.

"This is John, Charlie. He says he can help us. This sort of gear is not easy to come by but it was used by a firm called in to clear the docks of war debris."

"Pleased to meet you Charlie," said John shaking Charlie's hand vigorously. "Do you know how to use this stuff? I've filled this small bottle. It will only last about half an hour down to depths of about five metres. With two people it will only last a quarter of an hour of course. What's your idea?"

"I've got to get out of East Germany the hard way, John. It involves swimming under the wire."

"Blimey, that sounds dangerous. Funnily enough I was only demobbed last year. I spent some time in Dortmund. I was in the sappers. We had to do some work in the Rhine so I learnt a bit about diving. How about if I take you down to the baths? The manager is a friend of mine. I'm sure he'll let us have a go down there."

"That's a fantastic offer John. I'll take you up on that. Tomorrow OK?"

Bert said,

"As always Charlie, my boy, you've landed on your feet."

"I have, for sure, and I'll bring Susan too."

"Susan?"

"She's my wife, John. She's going to be my buddy. We'll both have to manage with the one bottle. It'll be good to get practice before the event."

"It's not as easy as you might think, Charlie. I can let you have extra tube but you'll have to try swimming arm in arm. What about fins?"

"Fins?"

"Those things that go on your feet."

"Oh, you mean flippers."

"Fins, Charlie. We call them fins in the trade."

"Sorry John. No. We'll manage without them. The less we have to carry the better. Getting to the river bank will be difficult enough. It will be mined. That's why we only want one bottle between us. Once we're in the water we'll just drift with the current."

"Take one pair at least. You can't make much progress without them. Here, feel these. If they're too big you can always take a little slice off them."

"All right, I'm persuaded."

"How far are you trekking before you get to the river?"

"Hard to say. It could be ten kilometers."

"You'll never do it and how long will you be in the water?"

"Say an hour."

"The best thing for you will be a Siebe-Gorman Rebreather. It's called a Tadpole. It's not available on the market but I've got a set, second hand of course. The idea is to use pure oxygen and to re-circulate it. It's very technical but taken as a whole the kit is much lighter. You'd have to be a superman to carry an air bottle for two hours plus everything else. How important is this trip?"

"It's not important; it's vital."

"It'll cost"

"How much is this little lot going to set me back then John?"

"Well since it's you and it's in a good cause, how about two hundred smackers?"

"Two hundred quid, phew. I didn't expect that."

"It's in the valves. You don't want any problems in your game. These valves have only been used once. I can guarantee them. There's a big demand for this stuff. I can't sell them for less."

"OK. Perhaps I can sell the kit back to you once the job is over."

"That's understood. I don't mind buying it back if it's in good nick."

"See you tomorrow at the baths then. What time?"

"OK. It'll be after hours, say ten in the evening. Are you coming too Bert?"

"No count me out. I've got plenty to do. This fellow needs other gear besides diving kit."

"I should be able to teach you all I know in about an hour, Charlie. After that it's up to you to get in some practice"

The following week Susan received another letter forwarded from Osnabruck. She opened it the day before they left Cleethorpes.

"Charlie, have you read this?"
"Let's see, phew."

Darling,   *10th June*
We are not to be moved after all. This is just a short note to say that. Rostovski has changed his mind about moving us but we don't know why. I do hope you can get permission to see me.
Love Lucy
PS The sooner the better. Since I lost the baby Carl has been a model of self control. Actually he has been acting a bit strange. I think he may have found another woman.

"Now Bert, we've got to think about two cars. I suggest two Volkswagons, ex-army. I'll get them lined up ready for you and Eliza coming over. It's got to seem like a holiday for you two. If Brigadier Morris gets wind of what I'm up to I'll be cashiered and probably given time in the cooler as well. So, we'll have to keep all the gear out of sight. I'll carry the bottle in my kit-bag and the other stuff, if you can bring the croppers, life vests, etc."

"That's fine."

At tea time that evening Eliza said she had an idea.

"What's the big idea then Mum?"

"There's no need to mock Charlie. Mums do have ideas from time to time. I'm not coming to Osnabruck. Bert can go on his own."

"What about Charles?"

"Charles can stay here with Peggy and me. We'll have a wonderful time, won't we Charles?"

"No mummy then?" said Charles.

"It will only be for a little while dear. Mummy will come to see you as soon as she can," said Eliza.

Mummy's going to send us telegrams almost every day. Won't you Susan?"

"Whenever I can and you must send telegrams to me too."

"What's a tell-gram?"

"I'll tell you all about it at bedtime instead of a story if you like and tomorrow we'll go to the post office and practise sending one," said Eliza.

"I've ordered the taxi for six o'clock. Susan's all packed up, said Charlie. There's a main line train which stops at Doncaster. We should be able to get the ferry tomorrow evening and have a sleep on board. We'll send you a 'gram from the base and hope that Bert can make it early next week"

The following morning Eliza, Peggy and Bert lined the pavement as the taxi drew up at Number Two. Eliza and Peggy wore anxious faces.

"I hope you know what you're doing dear," said Peggy. "I shall be worried stiff until I hear it's all over."

"Where's Charles?" said Charlie.

"Still asleep. It's better this way. Would be a shame to wake him."

"Don't worry aunt. Bert will keep you in touch. There's a post office on the camp. We can send you telegrams, suitably worded of course. We'll have Lucy safe at home next week, if not sooner."

"Bye my darling, do take care," said Eliza as she hugged him tightly. "We'll see you in a few days, won't we? I'll be in agony until I hear you're back."

"And you take good care of Charles for us, OK. Come on Sue. The taxi's waiting."

18 The Trap

The Camp Bus stopped beside their apartment block at BAOR HQ.

"How much does that lot weigh?" Susan said as they humped the bags up the steps.

"About fifty pounds I guess," replied Charlie.

"We'll never get it to the river bank."

"If we don't then we'll just have to swim without it. That doesn't bear thinking about. I'll manage. Don't you worry. I'm off down to the Transport Depot, the MT. Mike, the sergeant, down there is a good friend of mine. He's in the RASC. We were at school together. I'll tell you all about it when I get back. Let's go down to the Mess for a meal later, shall we?"

"I'll unpack and hide the kit," said Susan.

When Charlie returned he had some good news.

"The plot is, firstly, they've got an old Beetle down there which is for sale. It was pranged and written off a month ago but the chaps have put it together again so it's road worthy, just, but in no fit state for the Regiment. I've bought it for us. Mike's going to put the badges back on.

"Why badges and why are they called Beetles?"

"'Cos they look like them. BAOR use hundreds of them and we'll need badges if I'm to join the morning convoy to Berlin."

"What's second?"

"Mike says we can borrow a jeep for Bert."

"How's that then?"

"Well it's off the record but they lend them to officers going to the sailing club on the Möhne See and to the Golf Club at the weekends. I can sign the requisition before we leave. He says there won't be a problem."

"Sounds a bit hairy."

"Darling, don't worry about that. Mike is very sympathetic. I told him what's happening to Lucy. He is horrified and wants to help. What's more, he can get a forty-eight and join us. That's a good offer."

"OK. When do we leave?

"As soon as we can after Bert gets here. Hopefully in two days. Mike's doing a mod. on the car. He's putting the oxygen bottle in the petrol tank along with all the diving kit. It means we can't carry much petrol but I'm going to put two jerry cans under the front-hood. Hopefully we'll get everything through. Our bags can go on the back seat, nothing incriminating there. When Bert gets here we'll have a final briefing, with Mike too. I'll fit out maps for them and a compass. We'll need one too. With luck, we'll get in touch by radio once we get to Vacha. I'm hoping we'll get away on Thursday morning at about three so I can join the convoy at the Helmstedt check point about six."

"Is that necessary? I'll be stranded in Hannover for ages, until the first Berlin train."

"I can't see any alternative. You'll be alright. There's a waiting room for service personnel. You can use that. We'll get the car and load it after the MISU staff have gone home. They only leave the radio geeks on overnight. Jim will be out of the way."

"What about the paperwork?"

"It's all in my pocket - passports, the lot."

"What about registration plates?"

"Mike's taking care of those. Two sets, an army number and a civil number."

"What about Ostmarks?"

"I've plenty left over from my last trip and I've got a train pass for you."

"I'll make a pile of sandwiches. There's a cake, a thermos, fruit and a gallon can of water."

"Sounds great. We should take food for a week, and some nappies for the baby, just in case. Do you think you can trip down to the NAAFI and get two bottles of Schnapps or Vodka. Not for us… bribes, just in case?"

"Is that all?"

"I hope so. I'll be thinking about it. Oh. We need sleeping bags. We can buy those in the NAAFI too."

"Of course."

"We'll have to go through everything very carefully when Bert gets here. He's probably brought stuff we haven't thought about."

After Susan had gone on the errand Charlie sat down to work out the final details.

"It's getting to be more like a military op. every minute," he thought. "I'd better have it all worked out by the time Bert gets here. We should get to the forest by Friday night. That means we'll see Lucy on Saturday, tell her the plan and get some clothes for Susan from her. Then we'll go and get Carla, back to get Lucy and then take them to Helmstedt. Once she's over the border we can plan our exit. With luck we'll get back to Vacha on Sunday night. Speed is the essence. Any delay will make us more likely to be arrested. I hope Susan can stand in for Lucy until I get back."

Soon after making some notes Susan returned with more tinned food, drink and a doll.

"I couldn't carry all the stuff at one go," she said. "In any case Bert might bring the sleeping bags. Let's leave them till he gets here."

"Good thought," replied Charlie. "I've been making a few notes. What's that for?"

"The doll? It's just a hunch. It might come in useful."

"Let me run through it. If all goes well the whole op. should be over by Monday, Tuesday at the latest. It's about three hundred and fifty kilos from Berlin to the forest. We'll meet in Berlin at the Zoo Bahnhof at about five, seventeen hundred that is. For heavens sake don't fall asleep and ride on into the Eastern Zone. I'll make arrangements for us at the barracks. The following morning we'll drive to Thuringerwald, aiming to get there in daylight so we can find a place to hole up for the night. I think we'll have to manage without the car in the restricted zone. Getting overland shouldn't be a problem," he said. "I'll get some large scale operational maps from the map room and if poss. an aerial photo. I've got the locations of the MISU stations. It's what happens when we get to the chalet that's the problem. Lucy will be pretty shocked to see us turn up out of the blue and from what we know already, Carl will be reluctant to see her leave, to put it mildly."

"We can tell Lucy what we plan about getting Carla. We can't get her without Lucy."

"Yes we can. We must. We'll drive down to Bad Salzungen together."

"Will it work?"

"Why not? Of course it will work."

"No, that's too risky. My dress will give me away. We'll have to get some of Lucy's clothes if you want me to do that. I've got some western clothes for Lucy. She can take the bag."

"Look darling. When I get back from work tomorrow we'll have a planning session. Bert should be here on Friday. Come on then, time for some nosh."

"Hang on Charlie. Give me five to put on my face. Why don't you ring Bert and ask him to bring the sleeping bags? The NAAFI ones may not be so good."

"OK, I will but it may take a long while to get a line. It might be better to send a telegram. Let's leave it till later. I'm starving."

****

Two days later they were standing by the stop waiting for the camp bus from the station. It was dead on time. Bert was the first to alight carrying two heavy bags.

"Bert. Wonderful. Did you have a good journey?"

"Not so bad thanks. You won't believe this but I got a bit sick on the ferry. Must've been summat I ate." Susan swung on Bert's neck and planted a big kiss on his cheek. Charlie enclosed him in a bear-like grip. The camp bus drew away leaving the trio standing on the pavement with the baggage. As they carried them up to the apartment Charlie said,

"Gosh Bert, you've got more stuff here than the camp quartermaster. What's in there?"

"Bolt croppers, like you said and a long rope, just in case."

"And here?"

"That's my clothes and the rest of the tools, a spare valve and some more hose. Goggles too, John's were crap. I've got three black boiler suits, better than wet suits under the 'circs', sleeping bags an' all. I can't see you tramping five K's in wet-suits."

"Bert, you're wonderful."

Later.

"We'll check everything through one last time. OK?"

"You're the boss Charlie."

"Anything incriminating goes in the petrol tank so hand it over and you can come with me down to the MT lines. Mike's going to sort it. The tools can go under the hood. I'm not sure about the bolt croppers. We'll have to ask Mike what he can do about those. I'll need a metal rod to search for mines. It'll be like old times. I hope Mike doesn't get a hold-up. We must get away on Thursday. The weather's in our favour and we shall have moonlight."

****

"Susan, wake up. We've got to get going. It's two o'clock."

"God Charlie. I've only just got to sleep."

"You've had five hours. I'll drive. You can sleep in the car. Everything's loaded. We can be away after we've had some breakfast."

"I'm not hungry."

"OK then, take your time but we must be away by three otherwise I may miss the convoy. It's your sister that we're going for so please make an effort."

"My bloody sister, always, always, ever since we were at school together."

"Come on, don't be like that. You love her. I love her. Whatever she's done we've got to help."

"More like a rescue if you ask me."

"Darling, enough of this. I'll bring you a cuppa."

Charlie drove up to the guard house by the main gate of the HQ Campus. The corporal held up his hand. Charlie was wearing his uniform.

"Where be you going Sir at this time in the morning? Is it a call out?"

"No Corporal. My wife and I are on leave and we want to catch the convoy to Berlin."

"OK Sir. Just come in the guard room and sign out if you please."

As they drove away the Corporal saluted and said he hoped they would have a pleasant journey. Just outside the town they came to the Hannover Autobahn, one of several built on Hitler's orders in the 1930's. Charlie's planning went well. He stopped in the centre of the city and helped Susan find the Forces' waiting room in the station.

"See you this evening darling. Give us a kiss and don't forget to get off at the Zoo Bahnhof. You've got your passport and the train pass haven't you?"

"I've been through it all before. Now don't fuss. I shall be all right."

They kissed. Charlie didn't want to drive through the checkpoint on the East German side at Helmstedt without the protection of the convoy and the presence of Susan would only have complicated matters. In this way he felt sure that the Beetle would cause no comment. He was hoping that Brigadier Morris would be ignorant of his early return from England.

The Army convoy passed through the checkpoints at Helmstedt and at the entrance to West Berlin, Griebnitz See, without much delay having travelled along the Autobahn without stopping. Charlie began to wonder if all the trouble that he had taken to conceal the tools and the diving kit had been necessary. That evening he was standing on the platform at the Zoo Bahnhof when the Hannover train arrived.

"We can walk to the army barracks. It's not far."

"Why, where's the car?"

"The local RASC are painting it black and changing the plates. From now on we belong to Frankfurt. We can collect it in the morning."

"How did you work that one?"

"The last time I was here I needed transport in a hurry. They got me on the convoy. Luckily the sergeant remembered me and the work I was doing."

"Gosh I'm hungry."

"Let's have a bite here then."

"What, on the station? Haven't you any romance left in you?"

"OK then. You choose."

"We want a nice cosy restaurant tucked away in a side street off the Kurfurstendamm."

At eight o'clock on the following morning the car, covered with scratches and mud over the new paint, now looked more like a beetle than ever.

"We'll go a bit out of our way and I'll use the gate at Baumschulenweg to check through the Grenze. It's on Sonnen Allee. Have you found it? You read the map and I'll drive for the first two hours."

"OK darling. It means we'll have to go all round the city on the south side. It's miles out of our way. We're wasting time and fuel."

"I know. Never mind that; I got filled up this morning. Just aim for Leipzig. If I was spotted yesterday they may be looking out at the western gates. Just a precaution."

"Do you seriously think that their security service is the slightest bit interested in us?"

"Well, I haven't a clue really, except that they shot quite a few bullets in my direction a month ago. With you here I'm taking every precaution. Lucy told us that Rostovski questioned her at some length. So when we get to the Chalet we may run into trouble."

"I think you're exaggerating. They can't possibly know that we are here and even if they do what possible harm are we?"

"Don't underrate them. Anyway, keep me on the small roads as much as possible and I'll keep my eye on the mirror."

"I'm more wary of Carl than I am of Rostovski."

"Carl's on our side. He works for Jim, the same as I do. I just hope that he'll be glad to see the back of your sister."

"I hope so too but I wouldn't bet on it. The man's a maniac. Reading between the lines he's been a perfect beast to poor Lucy. Let's not talk about it. I'm going to have a doze. Just follow the signs for Leipzig."

At Taucha, on the outskirts of Leipzig they came to a police checkpoint. A Vopo (Volkspolizei) in a dark green uniform held up his hand for the car to stop. As Charlie wound down the window, he said,

"Verzeihung Comrade. But where are you going and what is your business?"

"I'm on holiday with my wife. We are touring your beautiful country and hope to get to the Thuringerwald for some walking days."

"May I see your passports please and your travel permits?"

Charlie reached into the glove pocket and handed over the documents as Susan woke up.

"How long do you intend to stay in the Republic?"

"Oh. Not long. I am on leave for a few more days. I have to be back with my regiment by next Wednesday."

"I shall have to inspect your baggage. Please will you both get out of the car?"

They obeyed.

"Are you carrying arms?"

"No, of course not," Charlie said truthfully.

"Stand still please." Charlie stood while the Vopo ran his hands down his clothing. Charlie was conscious that two other Vopos had joined them. They were carrying light machine pistols which they slung on their backs in order to reach inside the car for the bags. They examined the bags and looked inside the front-hood. They checked that the jerry cans were really being used for petrol.

"Where will you stay the night?"

"We have not booked anywhere," replied Charlie. "I have been told that there is never a problem finding accommodation. I will stop driving at about five o'clock and look for a gasthaus."

"That is good. I hope you have a good holiday and get some good walking. Be careful in the forest because of the wild boar and remember that you must not go within the restricted zone. It is marked with red and white posts and is five kilometers before the Grenze."

"We shall take great care," said Charlie. "We don't intend to go anywhere as near to the border as that. Thank you all the same. Auf Wiedersehen."

Auf Wiedersehen," repeated Susan.

The Vopos stood back as Susan took the wheel and drove off.

"That was pretty thorough. I hope we don't get many more checks like that. I wonder if they have instructions to report any foreign cars to their headquarters?" said Charlie.

"Well it's no use worrying about it. If they do then they do. We can't stop them."

"No we can't. Our best defence is speed. Let's hope we can get back home on Monday"

"Once we get through Leipzig we'll stick to minor roads, like you said. OK?"

"OK. Tomorrow's our first big day."

"I know. I'm dreading it. Suppose the nuns won't let us take Carla away. Have you a plan for that?"

"No. How can we plan for something we know nothing about? You'll just have to use all your charm my dear and pray."

It was nearly five o'clock when they reached the village of Trusetal in the Naturpark. Charlie found a quiet place to park not far from the forest track but well concealed.

"This is it. We are about thirty-five K's from Vacha here. Tomorrow we'll move up to the edge of the restricted zone and then walk the rest. With luck we'll get to the chalet about eight. Let's hope nobody comes to bother us tonight. Serve up the grub my good wife."

"Yes my good leader."

"Then we'll get some rest. It should be getting light at about five so we'll get away from here about half past four."

"Let's have another look at the map."

"Good idea, before it goes dark. The aerial photo doesn't show much because of all the trees. We want to keep away from habitations. We'll have to be very careful because if there are dogs about they'll raise hell and alarm everyone."

After a meal of sandwiches and fruit, they reclined the seats as far as possible, pulled up the sleeping bags and tried to sleep. Charlie hoped they would wake at the appointed time.

****

In the main security office, deep underground in the Harz Factory, Ivan was seated with his assistants at a long table.

"Comrades, we have an urgent problem of security which concerns us all. There is a spy in our midst and he or she is in contact with the British Secret Police. The British have placed a very competent and active agent in our area. I have it on good authority that his name is Forbes, Charlie Forbes. That may not be his real name, of course, but for operational purposes we have to accept that it is. He is an officer, a lieutenant in the British Army stationed at their Head Quarters in Osnabruck. His cover is quite simply that he is a qualified doctor. He recently took up a temporary post at the main hospital in Magdeburg. So much we know.

"We nearly caught up with this man, or so we believe, when Doctor Schultz and his wife defected to the West. He made his escape on an Elbe Barge named Freiheit and we believe that he would have taken the Schultzes with him. As things have turned out we have other plans for the Doctor which may work to our advantage.

"I am convinced that this Forbes may have orders to help other scientists move to the West. Although our border security is good we must do more to prevent the escape of our scientists, those in possession of secret information. The British and the Americans will do all in their power to penetrate our secrets.

"Forbes has a sister-in-law who is married to Carl Wogart, the forester for the Vacha area. They have a baby girl aged about nine months. I have arranged temporary accommodation for her at the convent in Bad Salzungen. Their home is in the forest about four kilometers south of the village. I believe that Forbes may use this house as a refuge from time to time. I know that he arranged a meeting with Lucy Wogart in Eisenach recently. I expect he will do the same again when he has the opportunity.

"Now to my orders. One, every piece of mail posted in Vacha must be inspected. Any letter addressed to the West must be brought to me for scrutiny. Two, Frau Wogart may try to gain access to her child at the Convent in Bad Salzungen. The Mother Superior has instructions not to allow this. I want a twenty four hour watch placed on the Convent and the Wogarts' Home. When this crisis is behind us I shall arrange for their resettlement. For the time being it suits my purpose to leave them where they are.

"Three, the Border Police at Helmstedt must be put on special alert for Forbes trying to enter the DDR. Unfortunately we do not have a photograph, only a description. All entry points must be alerted especially Berlin. Have you any questions gentlemen?" No one had.

A brief report landed on Ivan's desk.

For attention of Colonel Rostovski

Berlin, Griebnitz See -- Kontroll bf1610 hrs – 20th June

Convoy K3 Hannover / Osnabruck to Berlin
25 Vehicles. Twenty Freight   Five Personnel.

Remarks:-   This convoy contained a Volkswagen,   Reg Number   356 OS 742   driven by a Lieutenant of the BAOR Medical Corps. There were no other passengers. This may have been the agent that you are hoping to intercept for questioning.

Signed   Nickolai Berens, Kapitan.

Ivan picked up the phone.

"Heino. I want all the gates on the west side of Berlin to be put on alert. It's possible that our man is there and may be leaving at any time. He is using an army VW with BAOR, Medical Corps insignia.

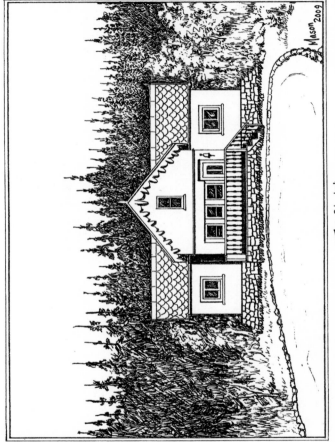

The Chalet

19 The Bait

They woke as the first fingers of early dawn infiltrated the misty pines. Charlie opened the door and put his unshod feet on the ground. He leant forward and tried to rise. He couldn't.

"Susan, wake up. I'm stuck."   Susan stretched full length and slowly flexed her limbs one by one. Presently she was able to get out of the car. She walked round to Charlie and pulled him to his feet.

"Come on old man. What's the matter with you?"

"I'm stiff, that's what. I feel a hundred, as if I've been beaten all over."

"Go for a walk while I organise the car and get the grub, cornflakes, cold meat and cheese."

"OK."

Half an hour later there was enough light to steer the car down to the track. Susan drove while Charlie read the map. They passed a group of woodcutters standing by a logging machine and a huge pile of logs. Charlie smiled at them as they drove slowly passed. Susan waved her hand out of the window and smiled also. Some of the men whistled at them, making suggestive gestures, but no-one tried to get them to stop. Presently the track joined a metalled road. They drove for an hour and then Charlie started looking for a new place to conceal the car. The road they were on was devoid of traffic. Charlie didn't know whether this was because of the early hour or whether it would be a quiet road anyway. Presently he said,

"Turn off at the next track on the left. We'll drive about two 2K's into the forest and hide the car. We mustn't leave anything in it. Any food and kit I'll put in a cache some distance away. I'll take out the rotor from the distributor."

"What's best to wear?"

"Walking shoes, slacks and a waterproof. Hopefully Lucy will lend you some clothes and shoes for the Convent."

Charlie needed all his map-reading skills to find the Chalet in the trackless forest, but the army maps they had brought were excellent. They laughed as they thought that they were probably using prints that Lucy had created in the Ops Room.

"Not far now. I reckon we should see the chalet near the top of this hill."

"Gosh Charlie, I hope so. I'm jiggered and the day has hardly begun. I'd no idea what it would be like. Have you any idea where we are?"

"Shhh. Whisper. Of course I know where we are. These op. maps are good and the photo here shows up the forest tracks. We're well inside the restricted zone now so anyone we see must be illegal like us or on patrol, so we must stop and listen from time to time."

"It's scary."

"It is a bit. We don't want to be taken by surprise. Let's have a rest for about fifteen. Then we shall need a vantage point and hide. We'll keep watch and see if they're awake yet."

Later on Charlie said,

"Come on. Let's do a bit more. We want to be there at least by eight, before if poss."

"I don't think I can manage any more at the moment. I didn't sleep much last night. You were snoring most of the time."

"We must move now darling. Have a choc bar."

Half an hour later they had scaled the hill from the east. The chalet was about five hundred meters away. There was a distant bang. The shutters had been opened and folded back from inside. They could hear a man's voice faintly. The front of the chalet was still in shadow. Charlie reckoned that it would be mid-morning before the sun came around. Meanwhile it was difficult to make out the details.

Charlie kept the field glass trained on the building searching for the first signs of either Lucy or Carl. His head and his arms ached with the strain. Susan lay asleep beside him. At last, movement. The door opened inward. Lucy came out with a bucket and besom. She swept the veranda and washed it. Then Carl came out dressed for work in a leather jerkin. He went round the chalet out of sight. The last Charlie saw of him he was disappearing into the trees carrying a chain saw with a heavy haversack on his back.

"Come on darling. Let's go."

"What's happened," Susan said in a sleepy voice.

"Hurry, wake up. Carl's gone out, maybe for the day or at least the morning. We've best part of half a mile to cover. Let's go."

Charlie picked up the haversack and started off down a steep path winding through the trees until at last they found themselves on the edge of the clearing, the chalet before them. There was no sound, not even bird noise. The stillness of the morning seemed oppressive. They walked slowly forward. Charlie pushed Susan in front of him.

"You go first, but quietly. She'll be frightened out of her life. Just gently ring the bell. Not loudly mind. Just tap it with a stick. Here's one. Then stand back so that she can see you without coming outside," he whispered.

He saw Lucy before she saw him. She was standing at the window. She saw Susan. She put a hand to her mouth and then her heart. She stepped back into shadow. Then came forward once again.

"Susan, is that you?" in a faint voice.

"Yes Lucy it's me. Charlie is here too. Can we come in?"

"I can't let you in. The door's locked. The only windows I can open are too small or too high."

"Charlie," said Susan in an urgent voice. "She's locked in; what can we do?"

"Easy."

Charlie ran up the two steps onto the veranda and aimed a kick at the door lock. There was a splintering of wood. At the second attempt the door gave way under his onslaught. The door crashed open and they were in. Susan ran past Charlie and stooped to pick up her sister who was crouching on the floor. They clung to each other, Lucy in terror, Susan protectively.

Lucy started to cry and tremble, then she started to kiss Susan, saying,

"Take me away from here, take me away, take me away," between her tears and kisses. Charlie, at a loss how to behave, sat quietly on a chair on the veranda waiting for the torrent of emotion and joy to subside. Presently,

"Charlie is here too Lucy, now stop crying and pull yourself together." Lucy slowly released Susan from her grasp but, so as not to loose her entirely, led her sister to a sofa where she sat and pulled Susan down beside her. Susan, in a matter of fact voice, said,

"Now tell me Lucy. Where is Carl and how long have we got before he returns?"

"Susan, and Charlie, I can't believe it's you, both of you. You've come to rescue me haven't you? Say you have. This is not just a visit is it?"

"No, this is not just a visit."

"Oh Susan, I'm so sorry. How you can forgive me for what I did. I'm so grateful and so over-joyed to see you… and you Charlie. I'm going to cry again."

"Now Lucy, please," said Susan.

"You have forgiven me haven't you, otherwise you wouldn't be here," said Lucy as she wiped her eyes yet again.

"Lucy, there'll be all the time in the world to talk about these things when we get home. Please concentrate on the job in hand. Pleeeease. Tell me where to find things, Charlie and I need a cup of coffee or, better still, tea."

"It's all there Sue, on the side, sugar as well and the milk's under the cloche. There's more outside in the back. Hot water in the kettle on the hob."

"How long have we got?" said Charlie in a business-like voice.

"What do you mean Charlie?" said Lucy.

"How long before Carl returns?"

"Most of the day I guess. He'll be back before dark."

"We've got you a passport, Susan's, and we've got to get you over the border at Helmstedt."

"But I can't go without Carla, Charlene, I can't."

"We know that. We've just called here to get some clothes for Susan and then we've got to go to the Convent to get her. We'll come back here for you and then I'll take you to the check point."

"That's no good. They'll never let you have her. They have their orders. I'm not allowed to take her away because she has been taken into care. They know Carl has been violent, not to her but to me, so they won't let her come back here. The only way I can get Charlene back is to leave Carl and go into a hostel."

"Why didn't you do that Lucy?" said Susan.

"I thought about it…. seriously but the postmistress in the village told me how awful the hostels are."

"OK then," said Charlie. What do you propose then Lucy?"

"I've got to come. Let's all three of us go to the convent."

"What difference will that make?" said Susan. "We don't want you to be a drag."

"I know the way and I know a lot about the Convent inside. I can be useful. I won't be a drag, promise. It would be better for me to go in. They know me for a start and maybe I could persuade them to let Carla meet her aunt."

"You know Charlie; I really think Lucy's got the answer. We'll take the big holdall and Lucy can wrap up the doll in Carla's clothes and take her back to the nursery. If we can't take Carla out of the Convent with their consent then maybe we can get her out using the doll."

"So that's what you were up to. You got the doll from the camp crèche didn't you?"

"It was just a hunch, not even an idea. I thought we may be able to do a switch."

"Lucy, we'll pack the holdall with clothes for the nuns. They might be grateful for some things even if they only use them to give away. The holdall's in the car. Come on now. Let's get moving. We don't want Carl on our tail. We've got a long tramp ahead to get back to the car"

"I've got to take some baby food and milk for Carla. I hope it's not gone off. It's a month old. I'll fill a couple of thermos and take some ordinary milk as well. If only I'd known you were coming I could have prepared something."

The trio started on the long trek back to the car. Charlie laid the map on the ground and took a compass bearing.

"Follow me girls. This will be a piece of cake. We'll pick up the landmarks we saw this morning. Give me the bag Lucy. Now hurry. We've a lot to do."

"What will we say to Carl when we get back?" said Lucy.

"We're not going back. Not now. I thought we might have to leave Susan at the chalet overnight but not now. We're all together and we'll see you over the border with Charlene."

"But what about you two?"

"We'll be OK. We're going to swim under the bridge at Vacha."

"You can't possible do that. The river is poison. It's absolutely black, black as ink."

"Who says?"

"Everybody in Vacha knows that. It's because of the salt mines. The factory just outside Vacha produces potash but a lot of it goes into the river. It's caustic. Swallow some and you're dead."

"We don't intend to swallow any but thanks for the warning all the same. If it's that bad maybe there won't be so many mines. What do you say Susan?"

"Shhh. Keep quiet both of you. I heard something."

"Down, both of you." Charlie whispered.

They lay still, conscious of their exposure in the open floor of the forest. Then they heard voices. The voices seemed to be coming nearer. Charlie whispered,

"Here you two. Here's the map and the compass. Susan, we're here and there's the car," Charlie pointed to the locations on the map. "It's only about a mile to go. I'm going to draw them off, whoever they are, and we'll meet at the car."

"But Charlie, don't leave us," pleaded Lucy.

"We'll manage Charlie. You go. We'll give you a couple of hours. OK."

"That's fine. Good girl. Now Lucy, brace up. Stick together at all costs. You take the packs. I'm going to have to run for it. Susan, here's the rotor. You know how to fit it. Get the food from the cache and the car engine going. I'll be along. Don't worry. Stay here until the coast is clear and don't move a muscle. Don't worry if you hear some shots. They won't get me," he said with confidence he didn't feel. "Bye."

Charlie crawled away in the general direction in which they had come until he was well clear, then walked towards the sound of men talking. He saw them. They were occupied by chatter and not keeping a look-out. He stood by a tree and waited, keeping absolutely still. The soldiers, Vopos, were in dark green uniforms, three of them. Charlie edged away from their position. They were sitting, smoking and joking, judging by the occasional laughter. They were between the twins and himself with about a hundred yards on either side. If they got moving soon he would need to know whether the twins would be in danger. He decided he would run. They would see him and either follow or shoot. He walked slowly backwards, keeping his eyes on the group, concentrating to see if they would notice him. Presently they got up, shouldered their automatic rifles and started to stroll towards the place where the twins were crouched. He decided that he would have to do something soon if they continued in that direction.

He put two fingers in his mouth and gave vent to a high pitched whistle. Then he ran pell-mell through the trees. After about half a mile he stopped and looked, peering through the sentinel trunks of the branchless pines. He waited. Then he saw them in line abreast, about fifty yards apart, walking steadily in his direction. He decided to change direction towards where he knew he would find the car and, with luck, work his way around the end of the line. Somewhat out of breath, he started to walk briskly in his chosen direction. There were no paths but nothing much in the way of undergrowth in this mature forest. Every so often he would stop and wait until he saw which direction the Vopos had taken. He decided that he could easily outrun them weighed down as they were with packs and arms but the sobering thought was that he couldn't outrun a bullet. This thought came as the first bullet struck a nearby tree, then a salvo from the rifle of the Vopo nearest to him. The others followed with a fusillade. He could hear the bullets rattling through the trees as they struck something solid. So far it wasn't him they struck. He was running down a steep bank toward a stream. At the bottom he had to leap across and then face the climb, equally formidable. This is where they'll catch me he thought with desperation. The Vopos could not run and shoot accurately at the same time. It seemed as though they were spraying the trees with bullets at random hoping that one at least would find its mark into his back. Now he was on all fours scrambling up the steep bank. A searing pain in his right hand told him he had been hit. A glance and he saw a vein gushing blood down his arm. The firing stopped. Perhaps they were just changing their magazines or perhaps they had given up the chase. If they wanted to catch him now they would have to climb the bank too. He threw himself over the brink, got onto his feet and ran on. He stopped to listen. Over to his right he could hear the car engine. By the time he got there he was totally out of breath and collapsed into the passenger seat.

"Get in and get going Susan. Move it," he gasped. "Don't worry about the cache."

"It's OK darling. It's all on board."

"Thank God. Gun it. They could cut us off."

"Darling, you're bleeding."

"So I am. Give me a hankie someone."

"You've been hit."

"Have we got the first aid kit?"

"We'll get covered. Charlie you're gushing."

"Carry on for the moment. Lucy where's the first aid kit."

"Patience Charlie. I'm just getting it aren't I? Here, gauze, plenty of it and an elastic bandage. Do it really tight."

"I can't on my own, here." He passed his injured hand behind him.

"It's going everywhere."

"Get the bloody thing on."

"I can't do a thing until we stop and now it's gone on my slacks."

The Beetle sped down the forest tack bumping and lurching as Susan tried to dodge the tree roots and rocks. A splinter hit a nearby tree. They couldn't hear the shots above the noise of the engine. She slowed slightly as they came to a bend and the car ran through a stream, the engine racing.

"Don't slow down now. For heavens sake step on it," Charlie shouted frantically. "One more bullet and we'll all be in jail." Soon they reached the smooth trail and sped along it leaving the Vopos far behind.

"The road's ahead. Which way?"

"Go right. We just want to get away for the moment. I'll navigate us to Bad Salzungen. Lucy, are you OK in the back?"

"Just about, thanks. I thought you'd forgotten me."

"No chance darling. You're the reason we're here. Next stop the Convent. You can take over the nav. once we get to Bad-whatever."

Susan drove on, crouched over the steering wheel in concentration. The engine spluttered and died. She pulled into the verge. She let her head fall forward until it touched the wheel.

"They'll get us Charlie," she cried. "Oh God, what next."

"Not if I have anything to do with it. We've got two spare jerry cans under the hood," He leapt out.

"Let me put the bandage on first," Lucy said.

"Later, I'll fill the tank."

"No, I must do it now. Blood's everywhere."

"Hurry, I can hear something coming," Susan shouted.

"OK. That'll do. I must get the fuel in." Moments later Charlie looked up and saw a large truck loaded with logs. He tossed the empty can aside, slammed down the hood and got into the passenger seat just as the truck passed them sounding its claxon. Now they were trapped behind it until they had the opportunity to overtake.

"We've got to get past," Susan cried.

"Look at it this way," said Charlie. "The Vopos didn't seem to have a radio. They would have to get back to their own vehicle, wherever that might be, and then they could easily mistake our route. Why should we be going away from the border? In any case we were almost out of the restricted area. Perhaps if I hadn't aroused their suspicions they would have let us go with a warning."

"And perhaps not."

"Well never mind. There's a turning off in less than a mile so we can get out from behind this load and have a clear run. The next village is Dermbach. Turn left. Lucy, you take over the nav. when we get to Bad-whatever. You'll recognise it."

"It's called Bad Salzungen. Zungen means tongues, so I suppose it's Salt-tongues. Bad means bath, so I think it means that if they take a bath in salt water they can taste it."

"Shut-up Lucy. Now is not the time for linguistics."

The Beetle ran well through the mixed terrain of forest and pasture for another thirteen kilometres. The only vehicle they met was another logging truck. After half an hour Charlie said,

"Here we are, at last, Route 62. Straight on here Susan and it's about half a mile to the centre."

"This is it. I recognise it. I think it's the second turning on the left past the church. It's not far now," from excited Lucy.

"Lucy, you've got to get us into this place."

"I know, I know. I'm not stupid. We should have written. They don't like people just turning up."

"Well if you won't try …."

"I will, I will try Susan…… Here, next one, it's here, quite narrow. This is the convent wall and then where it gets wider we come to the gate. We'll have to park here."

"Turn round, Susan. We may need to make a hasty exit," said Charlie. "We all need to come in Lucy, so I hope you can explain. Just tell them you didn't have enough warning about…."

"OK Charlie, I know what to say. You don't have to tell me everything. Right then, I'm off. Pity about the blood. I'll just have to tell them Charlie cut his finger if they ask."

"Here, don't forget the holdall and make sure you tell them about the clothes for them…."

"You two wait in the car. I'll be back."

Charlie got out and tipped his seat forward to let Lucy climb from the rear seat. She went up to the gate and rang the bell. She waited for what seemed like five minutes.

"Ring it again Lucy."

"Certainly not. We've just got to wait. They always come but in pairs."

After a few minutes a small door was opened at eye level in the heavy gate. Lucy could make out a face pressed close to the wood.

"Yes?"

"Please, I'm Lucy Wogart."

"Yes Frau Wogart. What do you want?"

"Please can I see my baby daughter?"

"Wait." The little door was shut. After another ten minutes which seemed like half an hour the door opened again.

"You may come into the waiting room." There was the sound of a bar being withdrawn from the heavy gate and bolts sliding. The gate swung open to admit the width of the human body, no more.

"Please may my sister accompany us?"

"This is not normal, Frau Wogart. There is no record of you having written. We are not expecting you."

"I'm so sorry to be a burden but my sister has arrived unexpectedly from England. She may not get the opportunity to come again for some considerable time."

"This is very unusual. I have no authority to admit anyone other than the parents. How do I know who is your sister?"

"That's easy, Lucy said with a laugh." She turned and raised her voice to the car. "Susan, come quickly." When the nun saw Susan and Lucy together she too laughed.

"Oh, I understand. You must be twins. Come in please."

"May my brother-in-law come also?" She beckoned to Charlie.

"I'm sorry," the nun replied. "Not into the convent, only into the ante-room. Men are not permitted."

"That's all right, sister. This is Susan my sister and this is Charlie."

Charlie kept his bandaged hand behind his back and greeted the nun with a little bow. She said,

"Please wait in there, all of you. I will go to see if your daughter is awake. What is in the bag? No bags are permitted."

"Just a few things for the convent. You can give them to people. Clothes." Lucy opened the bag and took out two bundles of clothes and placed them on a table in the anti-room. The nun said,

"That's kind of you. Wait here please. I will return in a few moments." When the nun was out of earshot Susan said,

"What happens now Lucy?"

"We'll just have to wait. Normally I go in and Charlene is either crawling about in the playroom or asleep in the dormitory. I expect the sister has gone to get permission for you also."

"What do you think our chances are? Will we get her out of here without a fuss, do you think?"

"I don't know what to think, Charlie."

"Well I don't know about you two but I think we'll have a struggle. If she's in some kind of care system the nun's won't let us take her out. If we try to do it by force, alarms will start ringing all over the place. The police will come and we shall be arrested. As things are, the Vopos we met this morning will have put out a general alarm for us by now. The car is standing in the street for anyone to see. I don't know about you but I'm getting nervous. We need a plan if things start to go wrong."

"What can we do? Have you an idea then?"

"I'm working on it," said Charlie.

Charlie borrows a tractor

20 The Convent

"Heino, I have two reports here from the Head of the Volkspolizei which need follow up. The first comes from a check point on the Route 87 at Taucha. Yesterday they inspected a black Volkswagen, Frankfurt Registered. They had no instructions to delay or arrest the occupants, a married couple by the name of Forbes. They are travelling legally with visas. The second comes from a patrol in the forest near Hüttenroda and was received this morning. A man was seen acting suspiciously in the restricted zone. When challenged he escaped in a black Volkswagen.

"It's my guess that he was heading for the Convent at Bad Salzungen. We've got him Heino. I want him arrested. He's probably heading back to Vacha or else to Berlin. I intend to be there when he is brought in. Get a patrol down to the Convent."

"Yes my Colonel."

****

"Listen you two. We've been here half an hour. I'm getting edgy."

"We can only wait Charlie. We can't hurry them up."

"When you get her, we'll make a dash for it. This building has fire-alarms. If necessary I'll set one off and in the disturbance you'll have to get out."

"Sounds a bit far fetched to me." said Susan.

"Look, you've got the doll and the bag. Surely you can work something out. If we don't get Charlene what are you going to do Lucy?"

"I'll go back to Carl I suppose."

"Won't he be angry? What will you say about us?"

"I won't tell him about you two, of course. What do you take me for?"

"Why don't you drop us near Dorndorf and then take the car with Carla to Helmstedt. We'll get back under the bridge like we planned to all along."

"I can't do that on my own," said Lucy.

"Of course you can," said Susan. "Shape yourself. You've got a choice. Either you take Charlene and the car or else you go for a swim with Charlie. Take your pick."

A minute later they heard the nun approaching. She entered the anteroom with another nun that Lucy immediately recognised as Sister Martfeld.

"Hello Sister," said Lucy.

"Guten Tag," Frau Wogart. "This is very irregular but the Mother has agreed to allow you fifteen minutes, just you and your sister. Come this way please."

The two nuns led the way down the corridors which Lucy remembered from her previous visits. Presently they entered the nursery where there was a long line of cots. Lucy picked out Carla, fast asleep, her tiny hands clenched on the coverlet and her rather ruddy face screwed up as if she had indigestion. Her head showed the first signs of dark auburn hair. Both the twins were overcome with emotion when they saw her. Lucy reached down and gently lifted her into Susan's arms. Carla gave a little whimper but did not wake. On her wrist Susan noticed a band with 'Carla Wogart' written on it.

"We must take her to her uncle." The nun hesitated and was about to refuse. "Please," said Lucy.

"Very well. I will accompany you," said Sister Martfeld. "He is in the anteroom."

Lucy led the way with Susan following close behind taking care not to awake the baby. Close behind came Sister Martfeld, her hard shoes making clacking noises on the tiled floor. As they reached the entrance foyer there was a shrill siren. They looked at the sister in alarm. She turned and without a word raced back down the passage towards the nursery. In a trice Charlie appeared from a lavatory. A gush of water appeared from under its door.

"What's happening Charlie?"

"Quick, get out, that's the fire alarm."

Charlie pounced on the main gate, opening the bolts and sliding back the locking bar. He swung back the heavy door. The way to the street was clear. Lucy put Carla into the hold-all. The baby was crying in response to the shrill noise whilst they could hear feet running down the corridor towards them. They ran out to the car, Susan got in the back with Charlene, Charlie at the wheel. They set off, engine racing, as the first of the nuns, some carrying the other babies, appeared. A stream of water from the sprinkler system followed them into the street. Charlie swung the car into the main road. In the rear view mirror he could see an army truck following, then to his relief it turned into the Convent Strasse. They could hear the bell of an approaching fire engine. Charlie paused to watch it clang past and turn as well.

"It's going to take them at least five minutes to sort that one out," he said. "With any luck, by the time they discover we've scarpered and that it's a false alarm, we'll be clean away. They'll have to get past the engine too. Now Lucy, make up your mind, what's it to be, me or Charlene?"

"I'll take Charlene," she said.

"OK then. Here's what to do. I'm going to double back via Rossdorf into the forest. Susan and I can get lost in there. We'll unload all our kit and then you'll be on your own. If you get stopped tell them that you are on your way to Hof. Forget about Helmstedt. Hof is nearer and they may not chase you going south. You've got to get onto the München Autobahn. Follow Route 19 going south from Bad-S., then pick up route 89 and then 281. This is a pre-war map so the numbers might be different but I doubt it. There's a torch in the glove pocket. The crossing point is over the river on the Autobahn. All your papers are in order. Just remember to call yourself Susan."

"Most of the signs have been taken down Charlie."

"So. It will be a good test of your map reading won't it. Don't stop anywhere except to look at the map. Just keep going through the night. It will be dark in an hour."

"All right, all right. I'm not a child. What about petrol?"

"It's roughly 200 kilos to Hof. This crate will do about 12 kilos on a litre and you've got 25 litres in the jerry can plus what's in the tank now. You'll do it easily to the border. I've got lots of Ostmarks. Here."   Lucy took the wallet.

"Give me a thousand for contingencies and keep the rest," said Charlie.

Nothing more was said until they reached a forest track which looked promising. Charlie drove with canny instinct into the thickest part as if he had been born there.

"OK. Now to unload. You sort out the stores Susan. I'll get out the diving kit. How's Charlene?"

She had slept all the way but woke as soon as the car stopped. Lucy quickly mixed up some powdered milk with some hot water from a thermos. In half an hour Lucy was ready for the road again. She had made an improvised bed for her baby behind the passenger seat. Charlene was very lively and wanted to crawl about.

"You can't wait here until she goes to sleep again. It could be hours."

"What can I do then? She'll just have to crawl. I expect she'll soon get tired. What are you two going to do?"

"Well, we've a long walk ahead of us and we need rest. It's about 30 kilometers. We'll stay the night here and make a move in the early morning."

"Give me some directions then to get started."

"I'll turn the car. Back along this track and turn left when you hit the tarmac. It's about a kilo to a right fork and then another one and a half to Eckardts. After some twists and turns you will get to Route 19 at Schwallungen where you must turn right, going south. Now be off with you and Godspeed. If you get stopped, turn on the charm. Tell them you're escaping from your husband in Berlin. You should be at the border in about six hours. Good luck."

"Good luck darling," said Susan as she embraced her sister for one more time. They stood and watched her drive away in the last of the daylight.

"Do you know where we are?"

"Of course I do. You keep on asking me that. Have you no confidence?" Charlie said somewhat brusquely.

"Well it's all gone wrong hasn't it?"

"Not really. True we've had to make fresh plans as we went along but all is not lost. All we have to do now is to get back across the Grenze."

"All? He's says that's all. Give me strength," said Susan mimicking someone at prayer.

"Don't be like that darling. We've got to work as a team."

"I saw the look on your face when you saw Charlene. Talk about the doting Dad."

"Well just let's hope they get through safely."

"Amen to that."

With that they settled down on the ground with sandwiches and water and tried to rest in their sleeping bags until daylight.

As dawn gradually filtered through the pines Charlie, who had slept barely at all, sat up and looked around. For the first time he was able to take stock of the surroundings. They were in some thick bushes on the edge of a clearing. He looked around amongst their possessions for some breakfast and then decided to light a fire to make tea. The crackle of small twigs and the drift of the smoke soon woke Susan, who sat up.

"Hello darling. Did you have a good rest?" he said.

"Not too bad. How about you?"

"Terrible. Hardly slept a wink."

"Charlie, is that a good idea?"

"What?"

"The smoke, we could be spotted."

"Well we're just innocent campers aren't we? We're well outside the restricted zone here."

"Dare I say 'where are we'," she asked teasingly.

"Here have a look at the map."

Charlie unfolded a large scale map of the area and spread it on the ground. He put his finger on a point about a kilometre north east of Rossdorf.

"We've got to cross the Hauptstrasse about a kilo south of here, and then we'll circle round to the south of Rossdorf. After about eight kilos we'll come to Glattbach where we cross our first road. Apart from the roads and tracks, we have five main roads to cross, the last one being about 300 meters from the river bank at Vacha. I want us to keep out of the villages in case Vopos have been told to look out for us. I hope to God Lucy gets to the border before they are put on alert but even if they question her I don't see how they can arrest her. To all intents and purposes she's just a British national going home. They'll probably be glad to get rid."

"That's being very optimistic."

"They'll never harm a baby, surely."

They ate their breakfast in thoughtful silence, stamped out the fire and packed up. They had two haversacks. Charlie had packed the heavy gear and the Walkie-Talkie radio in his and Susan took the food and sleeping bags. They soon discovered the rough going was slow and tiring work but after about an hour, just as Susan was tiring, they came to the road. It was free of traffic in both directions so without hesitating they crossed over and turned to head west. After another hour climbing, they stopped.

"Let's have a rest Charlie."

"OK but we'll have to do better than this to get there in two days."

****

"Mein Gott". Heino, who have we got working for us, men or apes? I've just had a report from the Volkspolizei in Bad Salzungen. They missed them. They bloody-well missed them. I can't believe that they came within two minutes of them leaving the Convent. Forbes was actually there and the nuns handed over the baby to her mother in spite of my orders to the contrary. I think there was another woman there also but that is not confirmed. So now we are looking for a black Volkswagon with a man, probably driving one, or possibly two, women and a baby. It's my guess that they will head back to West Berlin. Forbes is a member of M16 and so will have no difficulty getting on a military plane back to England. The RAF probably has a plane standing by. I don't care where he is, East or West, I want him shot on sight. Have a marksman at Tempelhof ".

"Excuse me Colonel. Have we actual confirmation that the man at the Convent was Forbes and not Wogart?"

"Good point Heino. In that case arrest Wogart for questioning. I want a full report about his movements yesterday. He will need an alibi otherwise we'll keep him locked up until this Forbes is caught."

"Comrade Colonel, have you given any consideration that Forbes and Wogart are one. There was a woman answering

212

Frau Wogart's description at the road check two days ago at Taucha."

"That's impossible. We know that a man, a doctor who we think is almost certainly Forbes, was working in the hospital at Magdeburg and that the Daimler he was using was the same car Forbes used to escape at Wahrenberg. No, discount that idea entirely. I'm going to ring the controls at Helmstedt and Hof, you deal with Berlin."

"Yes, my Colonel."

****

The forest was thicker and more hilly than Charles expected. It was quite unlike the part they were in the previous day. The pack on Susan's back was unwieldy and kept snagging on protruding branches. Even Charlie, for all his strength, found that the heavy diving bottle and the bolt shears were getting him down. After another hour they stopped to rest once more.

"Charlie, I'm not going to manage this. Can't we find a pathway? Just blindly following a compass course is no good."

"The paths are not marked on the map and following one could lead us hopelessly off course."

"Well then, let's follow the road, even if it means we have to walk by night. If a car comes along we can get off in good time."

"It's too risky."

"We shall run out of food and water by tomorrow night."

"All right then. When we hit the next road we'll walk into the village of Dermbach and try and buy some stores. We'll carry on along by the roadside and see how we get on but if we get stopped by the police we can't run for it with packs."

"OK then. You win. We'll have to stick to the forest, but let me dump you somewhere with the packs and I'll go to the village shop on my own. At least I don't speak the lingo with a Yorkshire accent."

"No, I've got a better idea. We'll get as far as we can to-day, sleep rough, and you can go shopping to-morrow."

"That's awful. Are you trying to get rid of me? By tomorrow the Vopos will be on the lookout in a big way. Let's just hope that they haven't posted wanted leaflets all over the place and in the news papers."

"Look, we don't need food. All we need is water and we can get that out of a stream. It looks pretty clean to me."

"Maybe we should go to the chalet and ask Carl to help us."

"Absolutely not. We've just abducted his wife, remember?"

Susan closed her eyes and rested her head on the pack.

"Just leave me alone Charlie. I want to think." Charlie got up to stretch his legs and look around. They were in a dense part of the forest, planted with young trees. Maybe in a few years the foresters would come and thin out this area but in the meanwhile the trees grew only two or three meters apart their branches interweaving. Pushing through them was exhausting them both. By nightfall they had only progressed about seven kilometres. As it got dark Charlie could see a light through the trees.

"There's a light," Susan said.

"Yes, I've been looking at it. I think it's about five hundred meters away. It must be the farm at Glattbach. Maybe they have a car we can steal or, I should say, borrow. I'm going on a recce."

"Be careful darling. If you get taken, I don't fancy my chances on my own."

Charlie took a compass bearing on the light and set off. He walked all round the homestead and decided that it was the home of a forester. The house was a simple wooden structure surrounded by open-sided barns under which was a collection of machinery and pens for animals. He dreaded coming across a guard dog. There was no car but parked nearby was a cabless tractor with a large trailer stacked with logs coupled behind. He sat on the ground at a convenient vantage point and took stock of the surroundings. He could see the road about two hundred metres away. A vehicle would pass along it from time to time. He could see lights in the house behind drawn curtains. Round about one o'clock the lights went out. He guessed that the occupants had gone to bed. He decided to make a move. He took a reverse compass bearing and walked back to Susan and told her about the tractor.

"Let's put on our boiler suits; we may not get a better chance. We'll leave all your gear here. I'll carry the heavy stuff. We're going for a ride," he said.

Back at the tractor, Charlie climbed on the footplate. He saw there was no key in the ignition switch.

"I'll hot wire it." he said. "And we need to cut their telephone off. The pole is over there by the road. Get out the W-T so we can talk to Bert. I hope he's awake."

Taking some pliers out of his tool bag he cut a piece of cable from the trailer's lights.

"Hide all the diving kit on the trailer, near the front."

He groped inside the guts of the engine and very soon made temporary contact between the battery and the starter motor. After a few alarming grinding noises from the diesel engine, it coughed and fired first on one cylinder and then on all four. They climbed aboard. Charlie engaged a gear and drove toward the road. He stopped by the telephone pole and, climbing on the load, gained the height to reach the cable and cut it.

"Here's the torch," he shouted above the noise of the engine. "You navigate. I expect we woke them up. Let's hope they don't have a car."

He rev'ed up and pulled out into the road turning right towards Vacha and changed into top gear. Susan shouted into his ear,

"If we fork left in Dermbach, it's more or less direct into Vacha from there. In a car we could manage it in half an hour."

Charlie shouted back,

"We don't want to go through the town if we can help it. I fancy turning off this road in Oechsen onto the minor road which goes to Stadlengsfeld. Turn left there and we shall see the Werra when we get to Domdorf. If we don't have to ditch this old crate we could probably drive right down to the river bank."

After a short distance he turned on the headlights.

"For heavens sake Charlie. Switch them off."

"We're safer with them on. For one thing I can see where we're going and if anyone sees us they'll think we're doing a late delivery or something."

"All the world can see us coming. They'll put up a road block. There's probably a curfew."

"You could be right about the road block. We've got to enter the restricted zone somewhere near Diedas. When I took the bus to Vacha from Eisenach I got stopped. The Vopo said I needed a special pass."

"Charlie, you terrify me. We can't go charging around the country with a load of logs in the middle of the night and without passes."

"Whose going to stop us? The quicker we are the less the chance of arrest and anyway the state you were in after only seven K's, it could have taken us three or four days. We could have met more Vopos in the forest like we did before."

"You're mad. How much longer?"

"The road and the river run side by side between Dorndorf and Unterzella. There's a power station serving the mines and it discharges warm water into the river so it won't be too cold.

We shall have about two or three K's to swim to the bridge. If we're spotted we just submerge. It's fast flowing, about five knots so we won't be in the water much more than half an hour."

After turning right in Oechsen the road became narrow and started to climb steeply. He put the tractor into a lower gear but the engine laboured to pull the heavy load over the pass. The forest closed in on either side. It was as though they were pushing the branches aside through a long tunnel. The black smoke from the chimney was choking.

"Will it make it?" Susan enquired anxiously

"Relax darling. I've got two more low gears yet."

The col was reached and then there was a steep descent into Stadlengsfeld. He kept in the low gear but the load pushed downhill relentlessly. Charlie wanted to engage a lower gear but was afraid the tractor would take charge while he was doing it. The brakes began to smoke as they gathered speed.

"Slow down. For heavens sake slow down," Susan shouted.

"I can't the brakes are fading."

"Get in a low gear Charlie. We're going to crash."

"Tractors don't have synchromesh. I can't change down without stopping and I can't stop."

"I don't care about your blasted synchro-whatever. We're going to crash. Run into the ditch or something," she shouted frantically. "Stop, stop, stop."

"There isn't a ditch here. I'm going into neutral to try to get into a low gear. Hold tight."

"Bugger you Charlie, I'm jumping off."

"Don't Susan. You'll be killed," he shouted frantically.

"We'll be killed anyway if you don't get into a lower gear. What happens when we get to the T-junction?"

"We turn left."

"You're mad. I knew I couldn't trust you. Not just mad but stupid. I'm sorry I ever."

"Don't say it. I love you. I really do."

"You've got a funny way of showing it. We're going to die."

"Hold on darling. Hold me round the waist and grip my belt. Here comes the corner."

The trailer with its ten tonne load of logs pushed the tractor relentlessly. Charlie's only control was the steering and even that was chancy since the trailer tugged from side to side as they plunged down the steep hill. The headlights picked out the first of the houses when they were a hundred meters away. They entered a narrow village street. The engine was screaming and drowning out all coherent talk. A small van was parked with two wheels on the pavement. With the shriek of tearing metal the trailer sliced into it. Lights started to appear in windows as they raced past. To Charlie's horror all he could see at the end of the street was a blank wall. Susan was squeezing him tightly, her face buried in his sweater, whimpering in terror.

Instinctively Charlie wrenched the steering wheel to the left. The speed of their onrush, the noise and the vibration paralysed his thinking. The trailer side-swiped the building on the corner. The shock caused it to jack-knife as it capsized. Above the roar of the engine, Charlie heard the logs cascade across the main street and the crash as they shattered the shop-front opposite. The tractor was wrenched side ways and as it came to rest it rocked onto two wheels and then with a crack like a pistol shot landed back on all four. He stamped on the clutch and disengaged the gear just before the engine stalled. Charlie wrenched Susan's arms away.

"Stay there."

He ran back to the trailer. There, amongst the fallen logs strewn across the road, he saw the corner of their haversack. With the superhuman strength only given to a man soaked in adrenaline he lifted aside several and grabbed the pack. He went to the trailer's drawbar. It was twisted almost in two pieces and the connecting pin was almost out of it.

"Here, hold this." He passed the pack up to Susan. Behind her he found the tractor's tool box. Conscious all the time that the village was now wide awake, he grabbed a heavy spanner and with three frantic blows on the pin, the trailer was unlinked. In a few more seconds he had mounted the machine and they drove away. Susan was crouched at his feet on the footplate, trembling and sobbing with fear.

"Darling, we're all right now. Relax."

"You beast. How can I relax? We're going to be arrested or killed. I know it."

"Well at least we can't be chased. The road is completely blocked."

"The Vopos will block the road ahead of us."

"I think you're right. I'll slow down a bit. It's getting light soon and we can try our luck across the fields before we get to the checkpoint."

"How do you know the way?"

"So long as we head north we'll be OK. Get the compass. It's in my shirt pocket.

****

"Good morning Heino," said Ivan.

"Good morning Colonel. I have two reports which came in over-night. This is the statement by the night staff. It was phoned in from the station in Vacha.

Ivan read,

'0330 Hrs   Stadlengsfeld
Trailer load of logs drawn by a tractor stolen from Glattbach
overturned in main street. Damage to adjacent buildings
to be assessed. Driver made escape towards checkpoint at Diedas.'

"That's very brief and nothing much to go on. However if that is Forbes at work he could be making his way to Vacha. What's the second?"

"It's also from Vacha, Colonel. The duty officer sent for Herr Wogart. He says that his wife has been missing since yesterday. When he returned to his home in the evening he found that the door had been broken and his wife away. He waited until this morning before contacting the Volkspolitzei. He's a very worried man."

"Heino, a pattern is beginning to emerge here. I guess Forbes went to the Convent with Frau Wogart and abducted the baby Carla. Are they making their way by tractor? But perhaps she made a break for Berlin, Hof or Helmstedt in the car and now Forbes is trying to cross the Grenze at Vacha. But why Vacha and why a tractor? We've got to get down there. I don't trust the Volkspolizei."

"We can be there in two hours, my Colonel."

"We shall leave in ten minutes and that gives you five minutes to phone the Eisenberg Volkspolizei. I want the bridge at Vacha manned twenty four hours until further notice."

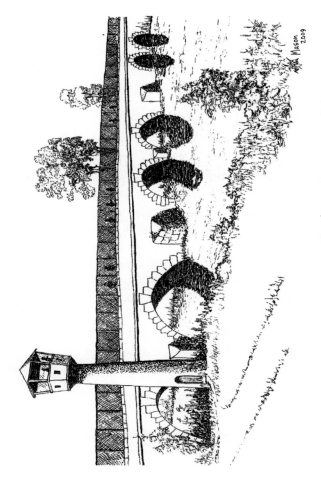

The Grenze crossed the Werra on the Bridge at Vacha

221

21 The Werra

The overcast sky presaged rain. Thunder rolled down from the Rhön hills. The first rain for over a month came in early morning. Great splashes hit the thirsty land and gushed knee high on river and road. The man on his bicycle ceased the uphill struggle and pushed it stolidly up the track to the Chalet. He stomped up the steps onto the veranda and rang the bell. Carl, pale and unshaven, came to the door. The long awaited rain drowned ordinary conversation.

"Hello Herr Gruber. Come in, come in. Have you any news? I've been worried sick."

"Good morning Herr Wogart. Yes I have news, good or bad, you must judge for yourself."

"Take off your coat. You're soaked. Hang it by the fire. Coffee or beer."

"Beer please. That would be nice."

"And the news?"

"It looks as though they have found your wife. At least they seem to have narrowed it down to a small area near Dorndorf."

"Go on."

"I was in the café, Maxi's, at five this morning and I overheard a conversation between three Volkspolizei."

"And?"

222

"It seems a tractor was stolen and crashed in Stadtlengsfeld very early. Its load of logs was tipped on the main street doing a lot of damage. My brother's shop was very badly hit. Unfortunately the tractor was left intact. The driver unhitched it before anyone could intervene and made off on the road to Dorndorf."

"That doesn't sound like my wife. What has she to do with it?"

"One of the local police recognised her as the woman who was accompanying the driver."

"Why didn't he arrest them?"

"He wasn't in uniform, going home after a party, and he was unarmed. He said the driver was a powerful looking man."

"I think I know who that could be. Possibly my brother-in-law, Charlie Forbes, but don't pass that on to the Polizei."

"I think the police will be coming for you, Carl. If your wife is involved in a plot of some sort they'll undoubtedly link you with it and they may link me with it too since I came here to warn you."

"Don't worry Herr Gruber. I'm not going anywhere. In fact I shall take the Trabant down there and try to find out what is going on. Put your bike in the back. Let's get moving."

By six o'clock the rain had eased. Sodden police lined the roads. Carl parked the Trabant near the bridge. He went to the nearest policeman who happened to be a sergeant.

"I'm Wogart," he said. "What's happening?"

"What is it to you Herr Wogart?"

"My wife's been missing since yesterday. I was hoping for some good news. I'm sick with worry."

"We are under orders to make an arrest. Your wife may be one of them. If you are in any way involved Herr Wogart or if you have any information which could help the police then you must go immediately to the police station and make a statement."

"I assure you I know nothing about this incident, but if I see my wife I will persuade her to report to the police in order to clear this matter. Meanwhile I prefer to stay here and observe any arrest."

"Suit yourself but don't get in the way."

****

The tractor, now free of its load, made quieter and easier progress. Charlie had dowsed the lights. In the east the twilight-dawn spread slowly across the horizon.

"We've got to get off this road. I think you're right about the checkpoint. It's probably at Dietlas.

"There's a turning Charlie, on the left. Why don't we try that?"

"OK, I will." As he turned into the track Charlie took stock of the surroundings. Since the crash and the hurried exit from the village the forest had receded leaving a level river-plain, cultivated on both sides of the road. Ahead and to their left he could see the great dark grey potash dumps The track led them in a straight line to a large farm. Charlie pulled on the decompression knob and the diesel died as he coasted into the yard and parked the machine between two other tractors.

"Let's not hang about Susan. Help me get the pack on my back." Susan did as she was bid and they walked away across the field towards some trees where they had a rest and ate the last of their rations, biscuits and chocolate bars. Charlie said,

"There's a stream across the next field which goes under the rail line and the road. It's our best chance but we'll have to get a move on. At the moment I think we're one jump ahead or maybe it's only half a jump. I'll just call up Bert. Once we're in the water the radio will be useless. He spoke into the microphone.

"Hello Bert, Bert, Bert." There was no answer. "I'll have to give him time to get his act together, I suppose."

"Try again in about five minutes."

"I will; meantime let's walk to the end of this copse."
Ahead they could see a shallow embankment.

"That must be the rail line. The stream's over on our right.
I'll try the radio once more."

"Hello Bert, Bert, Bert. Hello Bert, Bert, Bert."

"Hello Rover, this is Mike. Bert's sleeping."

"Hello Mike. Consignment e.t.a. due at A plus one or
plus two."

"OK, OK, OK. Roger, out."

"We've got two hundred meters of open before us but it's
early. Maybe there won't be anyone about yet," said Charlie
hopefully as they reached the edge of the trees.

Over the embankment, in the faint veil of mist, they could
see the loom from the lights of a vehicle on the road beyond.
There was a sudden crack of thunder followed by the onset of
the rain.

"We're getting wet."

"We'll be a lot wetter in the river. Come on Susan,
hurry."

"Don't nag me. I didn't bargain for all this."

Charlie put down the haversack and unpacked the oxygen
bottle, the valves, the croppers and a buoyancy vest for himself
to counteract the weight of the gear.

"What was that you said Charlie? There won't be anyone
about. The Vopos will be on patrol by now. It's almost two
hours since the crash and we haven't turned up at the control
point. We must be well inside the restricted zone here. They're
looking for us."

"We may need these sooner than we'd planned. Come on,
let's move. We'll walk, need all the puff we've got later."

They started to cross the open pasture.

"God Charlie. I'm frightened. It's all right for you. You've
done this sort of thing before."

"Yes, but so have you, remember that bastard Ellard, alias Fritz. when we were captured"

"How can I forget. That was down to you."

"It certainly was not. How was I to know that the Germans would cross into Switzerland to nail us?"

"It seems so long ago now. It is long ago. We were little more than teenagers then. If the Jerries could invade Switzerland when they were at war what's the betting that they won't hesitate to get us, this side of the Grenze or not."

"Don't forget we've got the British patrols. I hope Mike has laid something on, just in case. Walk a bit more to the right. I think I can see the top of the tunnel over there."

They reached the stream which was more like a small river, twenty meters wide.

"Let's see how much we've forgotten since we practised in the pool."

They slid down the muddy bank. Two steps in the water and they were up to their chests. The chill took Susan's breath away. Charlie dropped the radio and the metal probe.

"Thank God we've got this far without mines unless they've put booby traps under the bridge."

"I can hardly breath it's so cold. I can't stick this for an hour."

"You'll soon get used to it," Charlie replied. "Don't forget about the power station. The main river will be warmer. At least this water is fairly clean."

They waded along near the bank until near the tunnel the flow was faster and deeper. About half way through Charlie signalled to Susan to put on her mask and submerge. They linked arms and sank to the stream bed. In this way they passed under the road as well. The tributary had many twists and turns and, as they approached the Werra, the water became darker until, as they entered the mainstream, there was no underwater visibility at all.

Charlie swam with Susan underneath him as they had planned. She held tightly to his belt leaving him to do the swimming. They had rehearsed a series of taps on each other instead of the normal diver's hand signals. Near the bank Charlie came up to the surface and took his first look at the river which was about two hundred meters wide and flowing at a brisk six knots. They were soon swept along.

A Vopo standing on the bank near the road tunnel exit saw the disturbance of their underwater progress. He followed the faint ripple but failed to see any definitive outline of the submerged swimmers. Nevertheless he ran up the embankment onto the road to report what he had seen to his sergeant. If he had not done this he would have seen Charlie break the surface and look around to get his bearings. The Vopos on the bridge were told to be on the alert. Charlie guessed correctly that the banks would be mined but since they were already in the river they had nothing to fear from those. The mines would keep the Vopos off the banks. He tapped Susan on her shoulder to re-assure her that everything was all right. Charlie decided that if the oxygen supply got too low he would come to the surface and remove his mask. Susan would have the benefit of the Tadpole and stay out of harm's way under the surface. They swam together, Charlie paddling gently and relying on the current for their progress. He knew from the map that it was seven kilometres to the bridge and that it would be about fifty minutes from the time they entered the Werra. Already he could feel the extreme saltiness of the water, stinging his face and torso. He could only guess what Susan must be feeling. He surfaced again in mid-stream and was pleased to see that he was at least a hundred meters from either bank. He also checked the time.

He surfaced again after what he judged to be half an hour. He looked up and saw the multiple arches of the bridge about a hundred meters away. The silhouettes of numerous figures were only too plain to see on the parapets and the banks. One man was looking at him through binoculars. Blowing from his lungs he submerged once more. He felt the impact of a bullet which hit the steel bottle and bounced off. One more hit like that and he knew the bottle could explode. He paddled as quickly as possible towards the northern bank on his right hand.

****

"That's him, Heino. Did you see?"

"No, Comrade Colonel, I did not. Where about is he?"

"He was about a hundred meters, in a direct line for this arch. In five minutes drop a hand grenade where I say."

Heino went to the sergeant.

"We need hand grenades. The spy will be under the bridge in about five minutes."

"Yes, comrade. We only have a few. Where do you want them placed?"

"Take your orders from Colonel Rostovski."

Four grenades were duly primed and dropped over the parapet to Ivan's instructions. Fortunately for Charlie and Susan they had chosen to navigate under the extreme northern arch. Here the current was slack and the river was shallow. The shock was excruciatingly painful. Susan let go of Charlie to cover her ears. Charlie covered his ears and stopped paddling but by this time they were under the northern arch and the piers did much to break the impact. Great jets of water shot up into the air and soaked the watchers above. With the last of the explosions the Vopos, Ivan and Heino looked over both parapets but the high fence of the Grenze obstructed their inspection on the western side.

"There, I see them," shouted one of the Vopos, pointing at Susan who had just broken the surface. He let go a volley from his machine pistol. Susan felt the impact as one bullet scored her shoulder. Carl ran across the bridge and grabbed the Vopo by his neck and wrestled him to the ground. Another Vopo calmly took aim and shot Carl in the back of his head.

22 Rescue

Charlie pulled Susan under the surface as he kicked for the protection of the arch. He forced her below him and once again paddled down and back the way they had come to get into deeper water. He could only guess at what lay under the bridge. Once more invisible in the black river to the Vopos above, he felt for the wall of the pier and turned round to face upstream. He groped along the wall, dragging a hand in the silt of the river-bed to slow their backward progress in the fierce current. His feet made contact with an obstruction. He tapped Susan three times which was the signal for her to let go. He transferred her grip to his feet as he turned again. He quickly discerned that the obstruction was metal mesh. He used it to reach the surface in order to have a brief look at the oxygen gauge. It told him that he had ten minutes left in the bottle. They descended to the river bed once again and he used five of those precious minutes to crop a hole large enough for them to swim through.

Relieved of the weight of the croppers, which he dropped on the river bed, he let out some air from the buoyancy vest. Susan followed holding tightly on to his ankles and once through the hole she regained her position underneath him. He paddled furiously away from the bridge in the fastest part of the current. Well clear, he took out his mouthpiece and clamped his teeth round the snorkel. He surfaced just enough to be able to breathe whilst Susan below had the benefit of the remaining gas. Again he took one more deep breath and sank down. His lungs felt as though they would burst after he had swum underwater for about ninety seconds so he came up to the surface once again. By now they were well into the American Zone so Charlie looked for the Jeep, Bert and Mike. To his everlasting relief he saw them parked on the right hand bank road. He signalled to Susan to come to the surface. Susan helped him shed the weight of the diving gear, which they abandoned and they struck out for the river bank. Suddenly there was a burst of fire from the south bank. It was the Vopos with machine pistols. The bullets struck the water all around them. Charlie was hit, first in the shoulder and then in the crotch. The pain was excruciating. He cried out. A stream of blood came to the surface as they thrashed out for the shore. Still there was another fifty meters and they were exhausted. Bert and Mike waded in to help them with arms outstretched, but Charlie could swim no more.

Suddenly there was a burst of fire from a heavy machine gun overhead. They looked round. A Daimler armoured scout car was returning fire to the Vopos on the other bank. After a couple of salvoes from both sides, all firing ceased. They saw the enemy retreating rapidly. Mike entered the water and helped the swimmers climb out. A Royal Engineer Captain climbed out of the car.

"A close call that," he said. Lucky we were here. Let's get everyone under cover in case those buggers come back with some proper guns."

Charlie lay on the grass and fainted. Blood was pumping from between his legs. Susan cried out in despair. She sunk to the ground next to him, her good arm around him.

She said,

"Where's Bert?" They looked around and saw him lying by the water's edge. His left leg was shattered. Another soldier appeared, a Sapper, from the armoured car. He brought bandages and other first aid. He said he knew what to do and stooping down they stripped Charlie, bound up his terrible wound to staunch the blood, wrapped him in blankets and placed him in the jeep. Susan, throwing modesty aside, also stripped. Bert had provided several jerry cans of water to wash away the saline solution of the river and dry clothes. The officer tended Susan's shoulder. Bert was placed in the Scout car and the two vehicles set off to Osnabruck.

****

Herr Gruber, watching the events on the bridge from a building nearby, saw Carl gunned down. He went to the post office and reported to the postmaster. Later that day a letter was sent to Berlin.

Frau Werner,   *20 June*
Cicero Strasse 57a
Berlin

Dear Aunt Gerda,
    I am sorry to say that Uncle Silas died very suddenly this morning. I am assured that he did not suffer. I would like to say how sorry we all are. He will be sorely missed not only by me but all his friends and relations. His wife was away visiting friends in the Federal Republic at the time. I am not sure how we will deal with his personal effects. Perhaps you are in a position to give me some guidance.
Your true friend and nephew,
Albert

****

At BAOR. HQ. on the day following Brigadier Morris rang the Matron.

"Where is he now?"

"He's still unconscious in Ward 3, Sir."

"I see. Let me know when there is an improvement please."

Turning to Captain Lewis, he said,

"Who authorised those vehicles to go into the American Zone?"

"Frankfurt gave written permission for the journeys. They were asked to assist in helping three British nationals leave the DDR. The Americans said they had no resources available to help in a private matter but that we should go ahead and deal with the problem in the best possible way in order not to disturb relations between the Federal Republic and the DDR."

Brigadier Morris sat in deep thought for a full minute. Then,

"I agree that you acted correctly. To deploy a whole section of Sappers to Vacha may have been an unnecessary expense nevertheless they did find a booby trap on the bridge and they disarmed it. I am full of admiration for their expertise and bravery."

"Two traps actually. SM70's, deadly."

"Anyway we can put down the episode as a valuable training exercise. I hope Forbes will come to realise what danger he placed those men in. I'm sorry to hear about Mr Higgins, very unfortunate. They should have realised that the north bank of the river was exposed to firing from within the DDR. The Commander will be sending a letter of protest to the relevant authorities via the Foreign Office. We have enough incidents on the border as it is but we must, under no circumstances, concede that soldiers of the DDR may fire weapons into our zone. Has anyone anything more to say on this event? Yes Mr Brown?"

"Brigadier, whilst we are all here I would just like to say a few words about Lieutenant Forbes."

"Very well. Commander, have you the time to listen to this?"

"Indeed I have. I need to know more and I shall be asking for a written report from each of the parties involved. Incidentally, I understand that Miss Robinson, Miss Lucy Robinson or should I address her as Frau Wogart has turned up here, safe and sound, along with her baby girl Charlene. Is that correct?"

"Quite correct Sir. She crossed at Hof into the American Zone. A brave girl, that one."

"In that case I shall be interviewing her myself. She has probably obtained a lot of interesting intelligence and we must not lose the opportunity to glean what we can. Berlin, via a letter from Albert, has informed us of the death of your man Wogart, Brigadier, a sad loss. How do you intend to fill the gap?"

"I have no plans yet Commander. Perhaps we can discuss the problem at some future time. I do have some ideas however. Now David, what is it you wanted to say."

"Yes, Sir, Brigadier, Commander, I have known Forbes since 1941. It has been a long association and I still hope to employ him in some intelligence role within MI6. I know your feelings, Brigadier, about his competence but I believe he has acted in good faith, making the best use of resources available to him at the time. His bravery has never been in doubt. He is recovering slowly from his injuries. He has received about eight units of blood, a rare group I may say, much of which was ferried out from England. Sadly, he is now a eunuch, having lost his testicles and some of his penis in the fire fight. But apart from the loss of blood, his injury was not life threatening. Knowing Charlie as I do, his loss will be a great blow to him, more so than to many men. I fear that unless he is given more work to do that he will become very depressed."

"Yes Mr Brown, I hear what you say but, frankly, I have to tell you that in my estimation, Forbes is a maverick, a liability to the service. I have no further use for him in MISU. Whatever the Foreign Office decides, that's their affair. He went directly against my orders and used his leave to invade, yes invade the DDR. It is only due to you David that he has not been court marshalled."

"Is that your final word?"

"Yes. You should consider that he has been relegated to his Regiment. I intend that he should be given a home posting. His National Service only has three months to run. After that he is free to resign and apply to a hospital to finish his training or he could possibly stay in the service by signing on for another seven years. What you decide is up to you and your superiors."

"I shall be sorry to lose the service of such a competent and resourceful man. I'm going to see what I can do about it. Can I take it that this meeting is now finished?"

"All right Commander?"

"Yes indeed I must get about my business. Good day to you both."

The Commander, David and Captain Lewis left the office as Brigadier Morris picked up the phone.

"Get me the sister on Ward 3 please and ring back."   Ten minutes later the phone rang.

"Yes, good evening sister, thank you for returning my call. Morris speaking. I need to know how Lieutenant Forbes is progressing. Is he fit to receive a visit from me? As soon as possible I wish to interview him, perhaps tomorrow.... Not advisable.... I see.... Who is his doctor? Ah, yes. Perhaps you could ask him to call me when convenient. I shall be in my office tomorrow from nine o'clock...... You will? Thank you. Good bye."

A week later Charlie was sitting up in bed. The pain had subsided, under the influence of powerful drugs, but he was still in a state of emotional shock, bordering on depression. He would only talk to Lucy, no one else. His main wound was healing due to lavish use of antibiotics but his shoulder had become infected and was causing him more anguish than the loss of his private parts. The surgeon said he would try to reconstruct a penis if Charlie agreed.

"Plastic surgeons have had more horrific cases than your's Charlie. Some of the burns which came out of the Battle of Britain were far worse." He got no response.

Day after day Lucy sat by his bedside, hoping for a break through. Susan was in the womens' ward recovering from her shoulder wound. The nurse said that it was touch and go whether her right arm was infected. Everyone wondered how she had managed to continue with the underwater swim. Susan said,

"It was easy. Charlie did all the work. I hope the salty water prevented infection. Apart from us, I don't think anything could survive in that river, not even bacteria!"

Lucy came as usual at the evening visiting time.

"Now you're able to get up Susan, why not come down to Charlie's ward. He's devastated and blames himself for what happened to you and Bert. An old man like Bert should never have been involved in such a dangerous venture. Eliza is distraught."

"Where is Bert? I must pay him a visit."

"Too late I'm afraid," said Lucy. "They sent him back to Hull Infirmary. They are going to patch his leg with a plate. He'll be in hospital for quite a while."

"Poor Bert. I do hope he gets better properly."

"We all do. You didn't bargain for so many Vopos, did you?"

"No. Bert did so much to make it a success. We couldn't have done what we did without his help and advice."

"Advice yes, but he shouldn't have been allowed to participate. Oh well what's done is done. By the way, Brigadier Morris came to see me. He told me that Carl was shot dead. He pushed the Vopo down. The one who wounded you and then he was shot in the head by another. But for Carl, you would have been killed by the bridge."

"How did Jim get that? He might have told me first."

"Oh, he has his ways and means. He asked me to break it to you, gently. Now he's got to work out what happens to the chalet in the forest. I expect he'll cut his losses and get an agent to sell it to the Forestry."

"So Carl was faithful to the end," said Susan pensively.

"Poor Carl, I really could have loved him you know," said Lucy as she wiped away a tear. She felt overwhelmed. She had to get away. The hot air in the ward suddenly became insufferable and she started to sweat.

"Sorry Sue. I've got to get some fresh air." Outside the building she panicked. Where could she go? It was time to collect Charlene from the crèche. They would be closing and wondering where she was. A terrible load of guilt bore down on her. She felt faint as she sank to the ground. Carl gave his life thinking that it was her in the water and all because she had written that fateful letter.

****

The following day Susan was discharged from the ward. She was told to report back in two weeks for a check-up. The sisters spent hours each day talking to Charlie or talking across Charlie because he still steadfastly refused to say anything. A few days later Lucy brought Charlene up to the ward but the visit made no impression. Charlie smiled at his daughter and held her in his good arm on the bed but beyond that he had nothing to say to anyone. Back at the apartment, Lucy and Susan received a consignment of empty boxes and slowly started to pack their belongings.

"So much ingratitude Susan, I can't believe they are doing this."

"I can believe anything of the Brigadier," replied Susan. "It's true though. We're all going home. David says that he can retain his commission if he signs on for another seven years. He wants to keep Charlie on the books but Jim Morris says there are no assignments for him in MISU."

"It's all very well but who's going to take care of Charlie if we go. Why can't we stay on until he's fit to travel?"

"He will be fit next week. He's due to have the stitches out tomorrow. They'll give us time. Don't worry."

"It won't be like the homecoming we had in 1945. Will it?"

"No it won't. Father's dead. Charlie and Bert are in hospital. Carl is dead and Eliza's distraught."

"And all because of me. What's to become of us, Sue?"

"We'll get jobs of course. Uncle Frank will probably come up with some ideas. Perhaps we can be nurses in the new National Health Service. At least, with Dad in his grave, Charlie might apply for a position in the Manchester Royal when he's better," Susan replied.

"I can't get a job. What about Charlene and what about your Charles?

"I'm going to go to Cleethorpes when we land. I've got to see Bert   He's going to be in plaster for two months at least. It's going to take a while to get him back on his feet. When Eliza's in a happier state of mind I'll bring Charles back home. Until jobs come along we'll look after the children and later on perhaps Aunt Edna will help out."

Two weeks later Charlie, still on a stretcher, with his family, Susan and Charles, Lucy and Charlene left Osnabruck to return home to an uncertain future.

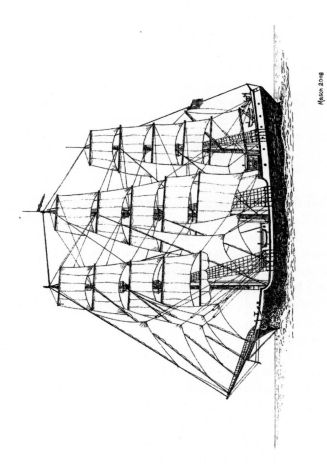

The Lenin

Mason 2008

23 The Lenin

Commodore Vladimer Maikovitch felt that he had reached the top of his profession. He had made the sea his career, putting ambition before his wife and children. Not that they were children any longer. His son was a lieutenant in a nuclear submarine and his two daughters were both married to wealthy Soviet apparatchiks. His wife was a long stay patient in a home for the mentally ill. Magyar Maikovitch, after years of loneliness and neglect, had sunk into deep melancholy from which there seemed to be no escape. The Commodore seemed a kindly man to all who met him but his devotion to a navy, intent on the worldwide promotion of the Soviet system, was uncompromising.

Now in his early fifties he had a choice of active service at sea or a post in the Naval Department of Government. He chose the former. At first he resented the sideways promotion which command of 'The Lenin' entailed but with the dawn of the atomic era it was obvious that the age of great battleships was over. He soon took charge of all naval training. He found stepping back into the age of sail exciting. As well as the mandatory skills of ship operation, management and navigation, Vladimer arranged classes in physical education, languages and marine biology. There was always a long waiting list of potential officers hoping to join the ship for a year.

Although he believed that nuclear submarines would be the invincible dreadnoughts of the modern age, he knew that the skills and demands of a three-masted-full-rigged ship would drill and toughen cadets for a life on and under the waves.

The Lenin lay alongside the quay in the Leningrad River. She had been built in St Petersburg in 1904, as a passenger and cargo ship for trade with South America. Her original name was The Tsaritsa Catherine. When in port she attracted crowds of tourists all anxious for a guided tour. Every sightseer was impressed by the size of her and the height of her three masts capable of carrying 24 sails with a total area of about 2900 square meters. The Lenin presented a challenge to all who sailed in her, not least her Captain who insisted on high standards of maintenance and seamanship in all departments.

Colonel Ivan Rostovski had decided the ship would be ideal for his purpose. He confided as much to Heino,

"How else can I get a trained band of assassins into Britain. Not only will the British Government waive all the normal rules of entry, they will positively welcome my party. Our goodwill mission has already been planned for visits to London, Hull, Liverpool and Southampton as well as Brest, Rotterdam and Copenhagen. I shall enjoy the cruise as Fourth Officer. Ideally we should have liked to capture Forbes and interrogate him about his confederates in the DDR but I am reconciled that he will avoid that. I shall be content if we merely neutralise his activities."

"How will you achieve that?" Comrade Colonel.

"Various alternatives are under investigation. The simplest methods are often the best."

He held a meeting with his security staff at the Harz Missile Factory.

"Comrades, the spy Forbes was admitted to the military hospital in Osnabruck on the day after the shooting. He was rescued on the river bank by a small group of three or four, armed with a scout car fitted with a heavy machine gun and a jeep. Their operation was carefully planned and designed to cause maximum confusion. A woman called Susan Forbes passed the Hof checkpoint at 0635 hours last Saturday. She had her baby daughter with her. Forbes and a woman, whom we now believe to be Frau Wogart, found a way of penetrating the Grenze at Vacha by swimming under the bridge. Such a venture had not been thought possible, partly because the bridge was protected with mesh and SM 70 guns and partly due to the pollution of the water. However Forbes was well prepared and the guns failed to operate. Already steps have been taken to ensure that such a breakthrough cannot happen again. One man in the rescue party was seen to fall as a result of our men firing from the south bank. The British have sent a strong letter of protest to our Minister about that, but needless to say it will be ignored since they were shooting at my men with a much heavier and more accurate weapon. Two of our men were hit, one killed. Also one of our men on the bridge shot Herr Wogart dead at the scene. I have now been advised that Wogart and Forbes were only a small part of a spy network.

"So much for the background. I need hardly stress that this Forbes is a dangerous man. He has eluded capture on two occasions where we thought we had him trapped. Our next operation will, of necessity, take place in Britain. I intend that this man will be hunted until neutralised."

"Comrade Colonel."

"Yes, Comrade Minister."

"Colonel Rostovski. Forbes has been wounded. We don't know how serious his injuries are but you have been told, have you not, that he has been sent back to Britain to recover?"

"Yes Minister that is the case."

"Well so long as he remains there, surely we cannot afford to waste more time and resources tracking him down."

"With respect Minister, I do not intend that we should leave matters there. Firstly he can return at any time and secondly we cannot allow our security services, The Stasi and the KGB, to be defeated in this way. Already plans are in place, Minister, to rectify this wrong. All I need is your sanction to proceed."

"Very well Rostovski. I will give this matter priority. You will hear from me next week about time and cost limits, which, need I say, must be strictly observed."

"Thank you Minister. I shall be taking personal responsibility for the success of the operation. My assistant, Captain Hermann Klein, will take care of this base while I will work in the field. We already know Forbes' home address in Manchester which he gave to the Direktor of the Magdeburg Hospital. Also we know, from correspondence mailed out of Osnabruck, an address in the town of Cleethorpes, near the port of Hull, where he resides from time to time. I am taking four security comrades with me on The Lenin. This will leave you short handed here on the base but Klein will be arranging temporary replacements. When we return we shall have ensured that Forbes is no longer a threat. I hope we'll be bringing him with us."

Vladimer and Ivan had hated each other almost from the moment they first met. Vladimer had been born of an aristocratic family of Viking blood. Down the generations the Maikovitch men had been tall with striking manes of blond hair which turned white in later life. Vladimer was no exception. He had a neat white beard, striking blue eyes between which was a prominent aquiline nose, a wide mouth which could produce a pronounced sneer when called upon to disapprove of ill discipline. He had been brought up in the family's mansion on the edge of St Petersburg. The Maikovitch family once owned a great estate and a fleet of sailing ships. All this came to an abrupt end in 1917 when his parents and his close family were annihilated in the year of the revolution. He escaped to spend his youth in Minsk where he attended the university. Vladimer, as ship's captain, was always concerned for his men. He knew his crew and their families well. He showed concern for every detail of their health, diet and welfare.

Ivan, by contrast, came from peasant stock. He was a fighting man. He had been ruthless in obtaining his rank and position, willing to sacrifice any career, any life, provided it enhanced his own. For him, his subordinates were chosen to be mere robots, devoid of any humanity.

Vladimer was under orders to accept Ivan as the Fourth Officer. When he discovered that this supernumery position had been awarded to an army colonel, with no experience of ships and whose sole duty would be the security of the ship, his dislike turned to contempt. He ordered his officers to be on their guard at all times against political opinions which could place them and possibly the whole ship in jeopardy. Vladimer had also been told that four additional ratings were under the direct control of the colonel and not expected to stand watches like the ordinary sea cadets.

"I have been asked by my superiors to provide your men with berths alongside my cadets Comrade Colonel. May I suggest that they bunk in the fo'c'sle. They will not be disturbed there and they can have it to themselves."

"Certainly Captain, I will see to it myself," Ivan agreed, not realising that this was the most uncomfortable cabin in the ship.

In 1925 the Captain of that day had persuaded the government to fit a diesel auxiliary engine to enable berthing to be undertaken without necessarily using tugs. The old steam winches had been replaced by electric, consequently The Lenin was able to motor against the gentle westerly breeze until sea-room was obtained to allow all plain sail to be hoisted. The cadets were sent aloft, to climb the ratlines into the crow's nest and then to use the footropes to spread out along the yards. This required some courage. The greenhorns were reluctant at first but soon took the lead from their peers.

"On a day like to-day, Comrade Colonel, it's easy. You should see them fight the canvas in a gale." Ivan thought that he would rather not.

The westerly breeze was unrelenting and set in for the whole week during which The Lenin shouldered into mounting seas, first on one tack and then the other. Off the city of Tallin they were able to bear away on a starboard tack and sail southwards. By nightfall the light on the isle of Gotland was plainly visible off the starboard bow. On the following day the citizens of Copenhagen and towns along the Sound turned out in small boats to enjoy the spectacle of a ship with three masts, under all plain sail with a 'bone in her teeth', making twelve knots as she entered the Kattegat. Three days later The Lenin entered the Thames estuary and anchored off Tilbury. The socialist Prime Minister, Clement Attlee, came with a welcoming party. The officers were lined up to pipe them aboard. Ivan managed to leave his bunk for the first time in two days, having been sick for most of the voyage.

After the shore party had departed, Ivan asked for the jolly boat to be lowered so that he could take his own party ashore. The cadet crew was overtly angry and jealous but Vladimer was reluctant to let them go also for fear of desertions. The first officer, Georgi, said,

"Let them go Sir. There's nothing for them ashore. They don't even speak the language."

"Perhaps when we get to Hull I will consider it," Vladimer replied.

Late in the afternoon Ivan ushered two members of his party, Nowak and Braun, into the jolly boat. Once on shore he ordered a taxi to take them, under cover of darkness, to a safe house in Ruislip. The following morning they went to Euston station where Ivan made sure that they caught the early morning train to Manchester with instructions to report to the East German Consulate. Ivan returned to the ship.

"Where are Nowak and Braun?" queried Vladimer.

"I have sent them to Manchester."

"I shall enter in the ship's log that two of the crew did not return to the ship at Tilbury. I can only reiterate that I strongly disapprove of your operation which will discredit the reputation of the Soviet Navy."

"I would advise you not to obstruct my orders, Comrade," Ivan retorted. "You are not in any way responsible for them. Your ship, as you choose to call it, is merely being used as a conveyance. Anything that happens ashore is my problem not yours. Do we understand each other, Comrade?"

"Perfectly, I only wish that I had received instructions direct from a higher authority."

"Take it from me Comrade Captain; my orders come from the Politburo itself."

24 Revenge

As Susan came out of the bathroom, she heard the doorbell echoing up the wide stair of the family home in Barlow Moor Road. Farmleigh was almost fully restored to its pre-war glory but sadly lacked adequate staff to look after it. Since the death of Hugo, his brother, Frank Robinson and Edna, his wife, had gone to live there.

Susan hurriedly donned a bathrobe and went to answer the impatient bell. On opening the door she saw two youngish men smartly dressed in dark blue business suits.

"Yes," she said.

One smiled a greeting at the lovely lady standing in front of him. He could easily have forced an entry into the house but that was not Rupert Braun's style.

"We would like to interview Mr Forbes, Mam. Is he in residence?"

"Where are you from?"

"We are from a magazine telling authentic stories of the last war for general readers. We think that Mr Forbes might like to enter a contribution. He would be well rewarded."

"Oh, I see. Well this is not a good time for us. What is your magazine called?"

"We represent 'True Stories of the War' and I am in charge of collecting war incidents."

"And your colleague?"

"He is not yet fluent in English. He is Polish but intends to settle here."

"Well, my husband is still in hospital. I suggest you try again in about two weeks. He may be home by then."

"I see. How unfortunate. I hope he is soon better and restored to full health. May we visit him in hospital?"

"I'm afraid that will not be possible. All the time is taken by family. Please call again but I will tell my husband about your visit. He may decide to write something while he is in bed. You know what it's like. Having something to do could be good for him. Now if you don't mind, I must go."

Smiling broadly at the two men Susan gently shut the door. She watched them from the lounge window. They didn't seem to have a car and, as they slowly walked away, they kept turning to look back. Then one of them crossed over and took a few photographs of the house and the road. Wearing a puzzled frown she went to see Lucy who had been listening on the upstairs landing.

"Did you hear any of that?"

"Not really Sue. I saw them talking to you. I didn't like them much. What did they want? It's a bit early in the day to be calling. Did they make an appointment?"

"No they didn't. Is Uncle up yet?"

"He'll be down soon. I took them some tea about half an hour ago."

Before the war Susan and Lucy had been banned from the basement kitchen which had been the domain of 'Cook' and a housemaid. Now the family always assembled there for breakfast, prepared by Edna and Lucy. Round the breakfast table Susan explained the morning call.

"Have you ever heard of a mag. called 'True Stories of the War', Frank?"

"I can't say that I have."

"Two men called and said they wanted to interview Charlie."

"About?"

"They wanted him to write an article about the war, his experiences," said Susan. "I made a mistake opening the door in my bathrobe. I thought it was Mrs Calaghan come to clean. The second man never said anything. He just leered at me. I didn't like the look of them. They gave me the creeps."

"You should be careful, Susan. You never know who's about. There's quite a lot of homeless living in temporary places, even garden sheds, these days. In any case Cally always comes to the back door."

"They didn't look homeless; I must say. They reminded me of small time business spivs on the make. My idea of journalists is sweaters and corduroys."

"I think I'll try to follow it up," said Frank.

"How can we?"

"When I get to the office I'll comb the directories and try to find the mag. What puzzles me is how they got something on Charlie. Of all the men who went through the war in one capacity or another, why pick on him and why now? I suppose they expected him to be here at this time in the morning. I think I might have a word with Barker, the police super and while I'm about it I'll phone the hospital."

"What, about Charlie? said Lucy.

"What about him then? said Susan. "Do you think he'll take it in? What shall we tell him?"

Frank intervened,

"Certainly we must tell Charlie. Tell him all about it. Maybe it will wake him up. Something to think about. This could be very serious for all of us."

"I'll tell him at evening visiting," said Lucy.

"Aren't we making too much of this?" Edna said. "They were just two men trying to get copy for their magazine."

Susan said,

"No, I don't believe that for a moment. They were foreigners. Not the type. They are up to something, I'm sure and what's more I told them to come back in two weeks. I told them Charlie would be out of hospital by then. So they know that this is his home. I told them too much, didn't I?"

"We can't blame you for that Susan," said Frank. "You weren't to know. Anyway, I must be going. I'll be home for tea, about five."

"It's time to get Charles up and off to school. He'll be late."

"And I must see to Charlene. She'll be awake by now. Bye Uncle Frank."

Frank took the tram to Albert Square and walked to his office in King Street. The imposing stone and marble façade of the National Bank in the wide thoroughfare blended well with other leading banks and the headquarters of the Ship Canal Company. This financial centre had, by some chance of the 'Nazi Blitz' escaped almost unscathed, unlike the docks and the main rail stations. His office on the top floor could only be reached via a reception room occupied by his secretary. After the usual morning greetings had been exchanged he asked her to track down a publication called 'True Stories of the War'. By lunch time she had failed. He put through a call to the Central Police Station.

"Barker here."

"Cyril, it's Frank, Frank Robinson."

"Frank, dear fellow, how are you? We haven't seen you at Rotary for weeks."

"No, I've been away a lot. Since my brother died I've had a lot to do, seeing to his affairs. He left all his finances in a terrible mess and for his daughters' sakes I've been sorting it all out. They haven't much idea about what goes on in the real world."

"I see. Well, to what do I owe the pleasure of this call?"

"Cyril, I can't talk over the phone but I must come and see you."

"When?"

"To-day, now, it's a police matter."

"Well, I have a meeting in half an hour which should finish at twelve. I'll meet you in the Reform Club. Wait for me there. I won't be long."

"Thanks Cyril. A thousand thanks. See you then."

Over lunch Frank explained the incident of the morning. The Superintendent's reaction was urbane.

"Don't you think your somewhat impressionable nieces might be over-reacting?"

"I'll have to explain the circumstances. My niece's husband, Charlie, has been working for the army intelligence. He was shot in an incident on the East German border, The Iron Curtain. The Soviets know Charlie was trying to smuggle their rocket scientists to the west. My niece, Susan, thinks the KGB is out to get him. At the moment he's recovering in hospital. His wound has healed but he has been recovering from some plastic surgery. I seriously think that the East Germans may have agents over here intending some mischief, if not to him then my family."

"Well in that case Frank, I can put a man into the hospital and another in Farmleigh but that's all I can do. We're fully committed in other directions and it can only be for a week. I honestly think that this is a matter for the Home Office and MI5."

"I think so too and I'm going to London to-morrow. I want to see Charlie's boss."

"You've nothing much to go on, have you? Why not wait for a day or two and see if anything develops?"

"That makes sense. I'll speak to London by phone this afternoon."

Cleethorpes Evening Advertiser   4ᵗʰ July 1953

SHOCKING MURDER ON THE PROMENADE
A well known and popular member of the local
community was murdered in her own home early
yesterday morning. Miss Peggy Petrie was stabbed to
death after an intruder had forcibly gained entrance.
The police were called to the scene when the tragedy
was discovered by her sister later in the day. The house
was ransacked but nothing apparently stolen. Police
are searching the house and the area for clues to this
motiveless crime.

"Susan, Susan. Where are you? Answer me, Susan please."

"Heavens Lucy, whatever's the matter? I was only upstairs.
Stop crying and calm down."

"It was Eliza on the phone. It took her half an hour to get
through."

"Tell me then. What's happened?"

"Charlie's aunt Peggy has been stabbed to death in her
home. What has she done?"

"Lucy, calm yourself and stop blubbing. I can't tell a
word."

"She's dead. Dead I tell you. She's done nothing. It's on
the front page of the Cleethorpes Advertiser. Eliza wants to
speak to Charlie. I gave her the number."

"Who discovered her?"

"Eliza did. She always goes to see Peggy on a Tuesday
morning. Poor Peggy must have been stabbed yesterday evening
and bled to death. We must tell Frank. He's already talked to
the police about yesterday. Eliza's in a terrible state. First Bert
and now this. She's convinced someone's after Charlie."

"She's probably right."

****

With a sigh of impatient resignation the Superintendent picked up his phone for the twentieth time that morning.

"Barker".

"Cyril. It did develop. There's been a murder."

"Has there indeed. Where, not in Manchester?"

"In Cleethorpes."

"Cleethorpes. What has......? Who told you?

"We had a call early from the sister, Mrs Forbes, Charlie's mother. The murdered woman was Charlie's Aunt."

"This has got to be a joke, Frank. Who would murder Charlie's Aunt for heaven's sake?"

"This is not a joke Cyril. Peggy Petrie was my niece's husband's aunt. The coincidence is too striking to be one. I am going to London to-morrow and I am going to see Charlie's boss and I am going to claim police protection for Charlie and my family as from now."

"I see. Are you sure that in your book two and two don't make five?"

"You may like to know that there is a Russian sail-training ship tied up alongside in the King George's Dock, Kingston upon Hull. It is only a twenty minute trip by ferry across the Humber to Grimsby and from there a short tram ride to Cleethorpes."

"All right, all right. I don't need a lesson in geography."

"If you want to know more then get a copy of the Cleethorpes Advertiser. The sailing vessel 'Lenin' was in London two days ago and the Prime Minister was a member of the welcoming party from the Ministry of Culture. There may of course be absolutely no connection but I think it should be looked at very seriously."

"You seem to have done some work on it Frank. You should be in my outfit. You're wasted in the bank. I'll have a twenty four hour watch on your house and I'll put Charlie in a private ward and no visitors will be allowed."

"Thanks Cyril. I knew I could rely on you. Bye."

****

The Inspector from Hull CID was at Eliza's home.

"Mrs Forbes. I'm so very sorry. First your husband and son are shot and now this."

"It's my Charlie's fault. If he'd got a proper job like his Dad, instead of messing about with spying and things, none of this would have 'appened. I told him it would end up in tears. He said he had to 'ave a job and ......" Eliza dissolved in tears as she held a soggy handkerchief to her eyes.

"Your son is a very gallant man and he works for the Secret Service doesn't he? Would you prefer me to come back tomorrow? I can see you are not in a fit state to talk about your sister's death."

"No, it's all right. What do you want to know?"

"You always come round to see her on Tuesdays and you found the front door unlatched. Is that right?"

"Yes. She was lying just inside. There was a lot of blood on the lino. The man must have trod in it and taken it upstairs on his shoe. He was looking for something. I think he may have been looking for Charlie. Whoever it was, I bet he went off with a lot of blood on him. Somebody must know something."

"I can't say I can hold out much hope unless someone comes forward, Mrs Forbes. As you correctly say, someone somewhere must know something. If you'll excuse me I'll leave my team at Miss Petrie's home to complete their examinations. Rest assured if we find a suspect we should be able to prove his guilt fairly easily. He has left bloody prints all over the place. Please ring us if you need any help or if you find any leads which might help us."

After the Inspector left, Eliza sat quietly, musing on the misfortunes which had overtaken her life, about Peggy whose life had been blighted by her fiancé's death in the Great War and about her Jack's death at Dunkirk. For nearly five years the sisters had been a comfort to each other but now she thought, with dread, that her whole family might be in peril. The joy Charlie and his two children had brought them could be wiped out by this cruel stroke. She consoled herself with the knowledge that Bert's leg had healed well and that he would be back home in a few more days.

"He's the luckiest man alive," she said to herself.

****

It was mid-day. Vladimer viewed the boarding party with anxiety as they came up the gangway. There were ten of them headed up by a man whom he took to be the Chief of Police, judging by his uniform and the silver insignia on his shoulders. The others were the typical 'Bobbies' of legend. If the Captain had feelings of anxiety then these were only mild compared to the queasy uneasiness in the mind of Chief Constable Myles-Johnson. The town of Kingston upon Hull had been fortunate in its choice of a Chief. Myles-Johnson, 'Jonny' to his friends, had a commanding presence, an air of authority which almost oozed from his saturnine features. He had an uncanny knack of discovering the truth behind every situation. Never taking anything at face value, he could read people's true feelings like an open book but this situation was something completely new in his extensive experience. How would he acquit himself?

Vladimer thought to himself that here was a man to be reckoned with. Should he hide behind a feigned partial knowledge of the English language or should he be completely open in his dealings? He decided that the latter course was the only honourable one. The Lenin was penned behind the gates of the King George Dock. Escape by sea was impossible. The whole police force of the town was busily engaged in returning every man of his 200 crew to the ship. Every pub, hotel, boarding house and brothel was being searched. When the formalities and introductions had been completed, the Chief and several inspectors accompanied the Captain to the ship's wardroom. There they met the three officers of the watch. The fourth, Colonel Ivan Rostovski was missing. Added to this assembly was The Emeritus Professor of Russian of Hull University.

"May I see your manifest please?"   A leather bound volume was produced.

"We shall organise a role call, if you please Captain and then every man will be confined to the ship until you sail. Any crew member not on board by nine o'clock will be arrested and taken to the central police station."

The ship's company was complete by six o'clock except for Ivan, Nowak and Braun. They were delivered by taxi from the railway station at eight, having travelled from Manchester. Vladimer asked Ivan to come to his cabin.

"What took you to Manchester, Colonel?" said Vladimer.

"Both my men had relatives living there. I thought I should go and make sure they caught a train back here in safety."

"We have visitors Colonel. The chief of the city police and others. There was a murder."

"I see…. and where was this murder?"

"In Cleethorpes, a town across the bay, not fifteen kilometers from here."

"And why should the police come here? Do they think we are involved?"

"Do you think so? Are you surprised, Colonel?"

"Yes, I am and I'm all the more surprised that you should think otherwise."

"Well, think again Colonel. There are two pieces of compelling evidence that point in our direction."

"What might they be?"

"First, a bloody footprint in the victim's house (she was an elderly spinster by the way), which matches the pattern on our sea cadets' uniform footwear. Second, two men from this vessel were seen returning on the Grimsby ferry on that morning."

"So?"

"They were reported as behaving suspiciously."

"How so?"

"They were discussing something intensely, whispering together. One was seen to throw something over the side. It could have been a knife and then he took off his jacket and threw that over too."

"Who saw all this?"

"The Chief of Police was not prepared to tell us that."

"We should sail on the next tide."

"That's not possible. We are trapped here until the gate is opened. The continental ferry had to moor in the river and the passengers have been brought ashore in motor boats. Every man is being carefully examined and that includes your men Colonel."

"This is outrageous. Has our embassy been informed?"

"Everything is being done that can be done. A terrible crime has been committed and by ill-chance we are at the centre of it."

Myles-Johnson interrupted this conversation as he entered the captain's cabin.

"Gentlemen, I have to report that we have discovered one of your regulation plimsolls in a bowl in the wash room. My men have it here, in an oil skin bag and we shall be taking it with us for examination. We think there were traces of blood in the water under the sink.

"This is outrageous Mr Chief Constable," said Vladimer. "Our Ambassador is due here to-morrow. I hope that he will successfully put a stop to this time wasting work."

"Let me assure you Captain, that as soon as we have completed our investigations, you and your ship will be free to sail, with the exception of any member of your crew who is suspected of perpetrating this vile and seemingly motiveless crime."

"I protest. This arbitrary arrest will provoke severe retaliation at the highest level."

"Your ship will be guarded day and night Captain. We are satisfied that all the crew and officers are aboard. I will see that you are fully provisioned, water and electricity are already available. To assure you of our goodwill to you, your officers and crew, anything we supply for your comfort and sustenance will be free of any charge."

"Very well, you will have our list of requirements early tomorrow."

"Thank you Captain and now I will say good evening. I hope that you will do all in your power to help us with our enquiries."

****

"Am I speaking to Myles-Johnson?"

"You are indeed. Is that David Brown?"

"Speaking."

"Your courier arrived here half an hour go. Very unexpected. I can see this investigation has ramifications far beyond my experience Brown. To answer your query, the answer is 'Yes'. The fourth officer on the Lenin is indeed Ivan Rostovski and what's more he is supernumery."

"Yes."

"The Captain has been quite forthcoming. I'm not sure that he realises any London connection."

"I'm sure he doesn't unless Rostovski has confided in him."

"Do you need anything more?"

"Not for the moment Chief but on no account let the ship sail and confine the whole crew aboard. I'm arranging for your men to be relieved by a company from the Yorkshire Light Infantry."

"That will be welcome I'm sure. My men are not armed and hard pressed with other duties."

"I want my courier back here post-haste with a full report. Someone on that ship has caught us on the back foot. The crime has international implications Mr Johnson."

"Call me Jonny."

"Carry on with your forensics Jonny. I need answers and quickly. Bye now."

"Bye Brown."

****

Charlie had been lying in the Royal too long. In the ward in the early hours it was still dark. He had been brooding over his misfortune for a month. In his heart he knew he was capable of getting up but a dreadful torpor held his limbs in a grip as strong as steel. There was nothing to get up for. After the operation he was barely conscious but he remembered the crushing indignity, the wry giggles of the nurses as they changed his dressings. He remembered the whispered remarks Susan made to the Doctor and the humiliation of his reply. Silently, he cried like a baby. Then a slow and burning anger grew within like a canker. It took hold of him and ruled his mind and then his body. His marriage was dead. How could he remain married to a wife who was without pity, who found his wounds a source of wit and release. What was the use of pity anyway? He didn't want pity. Release, release from what exactly? He was consumed with self pity because of the realisation that Susan had rejected him. All the joy and love that he had found in his marriage and fatherhood had been destroyed by one indiscrete word heard through a ward curtain. 'Funny, funny, funny.' His tortured mind screamed the word out loud during the night.

But then, as he wrestled with his self-pity and restless with his sores, he became aware of a shadow. Turning he saw his

258

wife, but not his wife. Through his tears he focussed. She was sitting looking and holding his hand. His was warm and hers was icy.

"Lucy, Lucy. How long have you been here?" he whispered.

"No matter dear," she answered.

"You're trembling."

"I'm frightened."

"Why?"

"Read this and then you'll know why."

Charlie was aware of a gentle pressure on his hand. She lifted it and placed it on the bed-cover. Under his fingers he felt the envelope. She took her hand away and then she was gone. He slept once more and then in the early hours his fingers tightened on the paper as he pushed it secretly under the mattress. Presently he swung his legs round and on to the mat beside the bed. He sat up and stayed that way staring into a void of unfocussed and shapeless curtain. He pressed the bell. A nurse hurried in. Still sightless he stretched out a hand. A quiet but firm voice spoke.

"Now then Mr Forbes, where do you think you are going?" Without replying he tried to stand. The nurse used all her strength to support him as he groped forward. He stumbled and fell on to one knee. The nurse left him but returned seconds later with another. Together they raised Charlie to his feet and spent the twilight hour walking him up and down the corridor, helping him regain his balance and his strength.

Later that morning, sitting beside a window, he found he could open the envelope and read Lucy's letter.

Darling, may I call you that?

You will wonder why I should write a letter when I see you every day. There are some things which I find too difficult for speech. It is better this way and then I won't be in fear of stumbling. Do you remember the first letter I ever wrote to you? That stupid letter has changed the course of all our lives, your family, my family. It was an evil letter, a silly juvenile prank for which I should be ashamed. But I'm not sorry because through that I came to love you.

Please read on. I desperately want you to read and reread this because it is the only way I can abase myself and plead for myself. Charlie, I love you, deeply, truly, wholly, trustingly, humbly, beautifully, committedly, for ever, resignedly, with complete surrender of all that I have and all that I am.

I wanted to say this many months – years ago. I very nearly did when we made love that one and only time but then I saw that I had betrayed my sister. I couldn't compound my felony by revealing my inner self as well as my outer. I can only do it now in the knowledge that Susan has rejected you. Please don't be angry with me. We are here on this earth for a brief span and in our lives we are allowed one, and only one selfish act, and that is to declare our love, an honest love, devoid of guile, born of lust (maybe) but love, true love nevertheless.

Charlie. I know what hell can be like. I've been there. I was bridesmaid to my lovely,

*talented sister with whom I have always shared
my secrets, except this one. Charlie, marry me.
I couldn't betray her, not without creating for
myself a heavy burden of guilt. But now I find
that has slipped away and I am free at last.
I don't hate Susan. She is what she is and I
love (Sisterly love) her too. I have been in her
shadow for too long and she has needed me. I
know that too. But does she need me any more?
I don't think so and I say this because there is
another who loves her too. Please Charlie. Don't
retreat. Don't let bitterness rule you. Come back
to us, to me.*

*I never really loved Carl. He tried, poor
dear, to love me (He did love me for a time)
but how could he when I refused to consummate
our wedlock willingly? I killed his budding
love. But he was true to me and he gave his life
for me. (Yes of course he gave it for Susan but
he thought she was me). I was desperate and
homesick. I had locked myself in a dangerous
cage by my own stupidity. Can you ever forgive
me? You and Susan together risked everything
to get me home (Also Bert of course and all the
soldiers). But your love Charlie could release me
yet again from even more guilt. Please, please,
let us build new lives together with Charlene,
away somewhere when present dangers are past.
Marry me my dearest.
Your loving Lucy.*

He sat in the sun for the remainder of the day. The nurses
looked in the ward from time to time and thought he was

asleep. Instead his mind was working overtime. In a strange way he came to think that this was the happiness he had always wanted. Now he knew that to be wanted was the most important thing in his life. David had always wanted him for the dirty and dangerous work. Susan wanted him to gratify her own desires. His mother had wanted a child as a token, a badge. His father had wanted him to succeed in an important career. Perhaps the only true friend of his childhood had been his aunt and it was in this frame of mind that he opened the pages of the Daily Telegraph which the nurse had placed on his table.

The shock hit him like a thunderbolt as he read about her murder. He shook with a fierce anger. He vomited and soiled his pyjamas and gown. He cried in despair. The nurse ran to him in concern. He thrust the paper at her pointing to the lines.

Early the following morning, unshaven and in his casual clothes, he caught a train to London. At Euston he phoned David, who came to meet him in a company car.

****

Back at the hospital the ward sister rang Susan to inform her that Mr Forbes had discharged himself. Stunned, she picked up the phone.

"Uncle Frank. Is that you uncle?"

"Yes it's me. Is that Lucy or Susan?"

"It's me uncle, Susan. Uncle, something awful has happened."

"I know. I've known since yesterday."

"No you haven't. This is new. Charlie's checked out of the hospital and we don't know where he is.

"Since when?"

"Since this morning."

"Where are you speaking from?"

"I'm at home. I think he called David. He might be on a train to London. I'm beginning to see Rostovski's hand at the bottom of this."

"Rost-who?"

"Colonel Rostovski. He's high up in the Red Army intelligence. He's the one who cross-questioned Lucy when she was arrested in Vacha. I don't think Charlie's in a fit state to travel. For one thing he's still depressed and for another his shoulder still hurts him like hell."

"Maybe if this is the crisis that you think it is then it will shake him out of it. Charlie's an action-man. Being on his back all that time did him no good at all."

****

David was shocked by Charlie's appearance. He took him to his own flat to clean up and shave.

"Hell Charlie. You're a mess. You look dead on your feet."

"I'll be OK, just need a good bath. If you can get through maybe you could send a wire to Susan. Tell her I'm here."

"Will do."

"What next?"

"You're right Charlie. Rostovski is on the Lenin, but he didn't murder your Aunt. We might suspect that he pulls the strings but we'll have a devil of a job proving it. Jonny, that's the Chief at Hull, sent me a report. Frankly I don't know the best way of dealing with this."

"I know precisely how to deal with it."

"How?"

"Murder him or should I use a more respectful word and call it assassination."

"Steady on old chap. I know you feel vindictive but."

"Too right I am. This has got personal. He threatens not just me but the whole family, both families. The bastard kidnapped Charlene for heavens sake. God, I need sleep."

"OK. Old chap. We'll plan our next move to-morrow.

The following day they entered the imposing portal of the Foreign Office on King Charles Street. They eschewed the lift and climbed the marble stairs to the attic, to David's domain under the rafters. From there they had a clear view down Whitehall. David stood with his back to the odd shaped window.

"You managed that all right."

"Managed what?"

"The stairs. You're not even out of breath."

"Ha. A test. Is that it. You're a bugger David."

"Look at it this way. You're my only weapon now. I need you. That's the long and short of it. By the way, I'm not surprised MISU gave you the push."

"Neither am I," said Charlie.

"You acted without authority and out of personal interest. That's not what we pay you for."

"All right then. Pay me for something else."

"The 'else' is quite simple. We want Rostovski eliminated too."

"And that's official?"

"We've had a letter from Rita."

"Good God. I never thought we would hear from her again."

"She sent it to Auntie in Berlin. It was written in jargonese but I deciphered it. Since then I have delivered an acknowledgement via the BBC and she sent the OK, so we know it was genuine. She confirms that it was Rostovski who scuppered the Schultz operation. You were bloody lucky to get away with your life. As for Jim Morris, he got a lot of egg on his face and he blames you for much of it."

"Well, if we hadn't invested in a barge I would be dead wouldn't I?"

"I think Rita's in danger. If Jim has a heart he'll get her out before it's too late."

"Oh God."

"Rostovski's been playing a waiting game. He's probably bugged their flat and he intercepts their mail. If he manages to decipher her letter, which I doubt, it will be curtains for her. It's dynamite.

"Can I see it?"

"'Fraid not. Not a lot of point really. It's history now. It just confirms things we already know or nearly know, but it lets him know we know and that's not a good idea."

"I see."

"One thing for sure, Eric was a plant but we've shipped him off to the States with a user-caution. He could be a good conduit for misinformation though. Now what about you? Are you fit again?"

"As fit as I ever will be once this scratch has healed."

"They told me you were depressed."

"I was, am. Well wouldn't you be. I'm a eunuch."

"I don't know, old chap. I wouldn't be in your shoes."

"You don't know it all. My marriage is finished."

"Gosh really? I'm sorry to hear that.......Divorce then?"

"Her family wouldn't allow it. That's a no-go. In any case, I've no grounds and neither has she."

"A weekend in a hotel with her sister would fix it."

"Out of the question. Lucy's too good to go down that road, well, not too good exactly but frightened and considerate. She has too much respect for her sister to humiliate her in that way."

"But frightened?"

"You London types are you all the same. We're not cosmo. in Manchester. Her family would cut her off. I wouldn't stand for that."

"Well then, just carry on."

"In loveless wedded bliss; no thank you."

"What about Charles?"

"I might go for a separation and ask for Charles. She might go for that. She's not maternal. Never has been. Can't stand being tied down. She's not domestic. She could have been a man."

"What's that supposed to mean?"

"Don't you know Susan? She's a society girl and likes to be calling the shots, a natural gang-leader."

"You don't like her do you?"

"Like her? I worshipped her. She was the light of my life until ...."

"What?"

"Until now...... I've had a love letter from Lucy."

"Wow. Really?"

"She says she wants to marry me."

"So you *could* go away together."

"I don't know, I really don't know. David, I'm the most knotted, mixed-up, tempestuous agent you have. Frankly I was contemplating suicide when I was in the Royal. I think Lucy's letter just saved my life."

"Anything else?"

"Enough of me. Let's get down to business."

"I've got one or two ideas. The Lenin's going to move to Liverpool. You're the only person who can get Rostovski off that damned boat."

"I'll need lots of help."

"Leave the details to me, Charlie. As soon as his feet touch our shore he'll be as good as dead."

"He's going to have another try. Those goons who did a recce' on Farmleigh will have reported back. All you have to do David is to shadow him and his gang every step of the way. Once I make contact it will be over to you.

The conversation continued until David phoned JD on the internal. He joined them a few minutes later. After more discussion, David said,

"OK. It's just lunch-time. Let's go to the Red Lion."

25 Retribution

Chief Constable Myles-Johnson sat at his desk in deep thought. He had the reports in front of him. The plimsoll retrieved from The Lenin had yielded enough blood for the group to be identified. It was the same as the blood of the late Miss Petrie. While this did not constitute proof, it would probably be enough to convince a jury. By a big stroke of luck the sailor's jacket had been recovered from the Humber by a pleasure fishing boat. He came to his decision and rang the bell on his desk.

"Sir, you rang?"

"Miss Wrag. Please will you send a message to the sergeant on the quay, the duty-sergeant. He's usually in the wireless truck."

Twenty minutes later Jonny heard the military tramp of the sergeant on the stairs.

"G'morning Chief," uttered Sergeant Sprat as he snapped to attention and gave the Chief a salute to end all salutes.

"Sergeant. Good morning." Jonny smiled, rose and shook him by the hand.

"How are the men?"

"Morning detail just came on duty Sir. The victuals van arrived. They're helping to unload. They're fine. This business has delayed their posting to BAOR so they're pretty pleased."

"I want you to do something a trifle tricky. Something that will take a lot of tact. Are you good at that sergeant?"

"Tell me what it is, Sir, and then I'll tell you."

"I've got a pretty good grip of how things are in their ward room. The skipper is a loner and if my instincts serve me correctly, he's a cut above the other officers and a thoroughly decent chap. Now I want you to go on board and request a meeting. Ask him, very politely, if he will accompany you here. He may be very reluctant to leave his ship without an escort. If that should be the case then by all means agree but try to avoid another officer coming over too. Do I make myself clear?"

"Yes Sir, perfectly."

"Another thing. You may as well know. The fourth officer is not a sailor. He's a member of the KGB. My information, from London, is that he's a dangerous man. Furthermore, we think we have identified his reason for making this voyage and, believe me, it's far from a 'goodwill' mission in his eyes."

"In other words, you don't want him."

"No, indeed not. Try to get the captain on his own on deck and then the two of you can just walk off, hopefully reach the gangway without interruption. It's all a matter of trust. Be friendly and make sure that he knows he's not under arrest. I know; tell him I've invited him to dinner...... No, on second thoughts he might think that's a trap."

"Wouldn't it be better if an officer went aboard, Sir?"

"You're the senior officer here at the moment. Am I right?"

"Yes Sir. Or you Sir. Go yourself in person."

"No, I have a reason for not going. If he turns you down then I can always follow it up but if he was to turn me down then it becomes difficult. See what I mean?"

"I've got the picture Sir. Leave it to me."

"Thanks sergeant. See what you can do."

"Oh ... and in case you didn't know Sir, I've got a telephone link to the signals truck. Hull, having it's own exchange, is not part of the GPO so it was easy. Just ask the exchange to put you through. You don't need to know the number."

"Very useful, thanks."

The sergeant saluted again and stamped out of the Chief's office. Jonny, standing by the window, saw him striding off down the road to the quay.

"Salt of the earth, that man," he thought.

****

"Commodore Vladimer Maikovich. I am very pleased to meet you."

"And I you." Vladimer strode across the spacious office and extended a hand to Jonny.

"We meet again Mr Chief of Police. Who do I have the pleasure?" he said.

"I'm John Myles-Johnson. It's a mouthful … call me Jonny."

Vladimer smiled. Jonny thought that they had got off to a good start but how to continue? That was the crunch. There were two easy chairs to one side of the desk.

"Have a seat, please. No need for formalities. Coffee?"

"That would be pleasant. Thank you."

Jonny reached to the desk and pressed the bell. Coffee arrived.

"May I call you Vladimer?"

"Please do."

The secretary placed the cups on a low table with separate milk and sugar. There was a short pause in the conversation which Jonny welcomed as he marshalled his thoughts. He said,

"First let me say Captain, Vladimer, how sorry I am that this state of affairs, this tragedy, has occurred which has spoiled your voyage and delayed your programme. I have never encountered anything like these terrible circumstances in my career."

"Neither have I and, what is more, I find myself in a situation which will probably end my career. Officially I find the delay unreasonable and my embassy in London has guaranteed that the culprit, the perpetrator of that terrible murder, will be brought before a court in our homeland and if found guilty, punished according to our laws."

"Very good Vladimer, but unofficially?"

"Unofficially, how do you say it, off the record? I have to admit to knowing the man. He is Bruno Lang, a German, who is a member of a security arm from the Harz Missile Base. He is under the direct command of the fourth officer on my ship, Colonel Ivan Rostovski. I have no jurisdiction over him. The Colonel is a member of the KGB. Frankly, I feel somewhat sorry for Bruno. This may seem strange to you. I can best explain my attitude by saying that Bruno is not in control of himself. He is a vicious killer by instinct, a psychopath. He should be in a secure hospital. Ivan knows this and exploits his mind. On Ivan's instructions two men, Bruno and his companion, Oskar Krause, went to the home of Miss Petrie in order to assassinate a man known to us as a spy, an employee of your MI6. Oscar says that Miss Petrie denied them an entry into her house and, before he could prevent it, Bruno had lunged forward and killed her. He then went on a fruitless search of the house leaving traces of blood and fingerprints everywhere. In truth the other two men that Rostovski has on board are almost as dangerous as Bruno. They are thugs of the worst kind."

Jonny was completely disarmed and amazed by Vladimer's frank and open confession. He sat in silence, nonplussed. Eventually he said,

"You have told me a lot more than I knew. I know that there is a killer on your vessel, Captain but without identification I was undecided how to act. It would have been necessary to fingerprint every man aboard. On the other hand if you can identify this Bruno, we can limit our enquiries to him alone and also his accomplice, Oskar. The man we really want is your fourth officer."

"Agreed but he is out of our reach, mine and yours. Unless he steps ashore he is safe and he will be able to justify his actions to his superiors. I have no doubt of that."

"Very well Captain, you have been absolutely straight forward with me. Now let me be the same with you. You have no love for the man, Ivan. If I read matters correctly, and I am rarely wrong, he is not of your class and you dislike him intensely. From our side we regard him as a threat not only to our 'spy', as you call him, we call him a courier, but we know he is a threat to the families involved, the wife, children and other relatives. We are, at this moment, planning to have him arrested. What we cannot do within the law we shall leave to our own security services, MI5 and MI6. I'm sorry not to be able to disclose anything further. I am, even at this stage, in the dark, so to speak. Our plan will be to neutralise the illegal activities of those men but I don't see how we can do much if they remain on the Lenin."

"I concur and I will do what I can, within my own constraints, to help you."

"With the evidence we have, fingerprints etc. we could arrest Bruno now and charge him with the murder but that will compromise you. Whatever we do, it will not restore Miss Petrie and you can prevent any further incidents by keeping the culprits on board. Can I have your assurance that they will be arrested on your return to Leningrad?"

"You can indeed Jonny. However I cannot be sure of the outcome. Rostovski is a powerful man and Bruno will merely enter as his defence that he was under orders."

"If I do arrest Bruno and Oskar it will open a can of worms, I am sure. The case could drag on for years and sour relations between our countries for a long time."

"That is the sad truth of *Real Politic,* Jonny."

"I will have to report to London. I assume that you will continue with your planned voyage. To go back now would not look good in the world press."

"Indeed, I shall continue if I am permitted."

"With that decision, Vladimer, you can return to your ship and claim to have negotiated a way forward. You can say that due to your ministrations, The Lenin will be allowed to proceed on the next tide, destination Liverpool. In case you are unaware, Manchester, the other address of Ivan's quarry, is close to that port. He should be content with that."

"I think so too. We are in complete accord. I should like to thank you for this interview. Maybe, if there is a trial, we shall meet again."

"It's been a pleasure to meet you Vladimer, even though it is under these unfortunate circumstances."

They shook hands once more and parted. Jonny saw the Captain, escorted by Sergeant Sprat, striding back toward the dock.

At 1800 hours the Lenin slipped her lines, the gates were opened as she was warped about and gently motored through the narrow entrance into the tideway. The cadet crew were piped aloft to spread the main topsail and the spanker. Watchers on the quay saw her melt into the dusk and breathed a collective sigh of relief.

Jonny was on the phone to his opposite number in Liverpool.

"Hello Chief. You will have been reading about our troubles in the dailies I guess."

"Too right Jonny but thanks for phoning. I take it they're continuing with their planned itinerary."

"I'm sorry to have to confirm that to you. If they get a fair wind she should be with you the day after tomorrow. They are going via Pentland and may stop over in Orkney but that's unlikely."

"I see. We'll put them in Queens and I have asked the Mayor to be on standby."

"Be prepared for trouble."

"What sort of trouble?"

"There's a courier on the way to you. He has a full report. You will be assisted by the Special Branch, that's all. Best of luck."

"Thanks for the warning."

"Sorry I can't be of more help. Bye now."

"Good bye Jonny. Thank you so much for sending them to me," the Chief responded with heavy sarcasm.

****

Charlie returned to Manchester. He took a taxi to Farmleigh and arrived just before lunch.

He rang the bell which was answered by Susan.

"Charlie, why didn't you tell us where you were going. We've been worried sick?"

"David said he would send a telegram or ring you."

"Well as a matter of fact he did, this morning, but that doesn't exonerate you. We've been worried. Where did you stay?"

"David put me up at his flat."

"Did he tell you he was coming here?"

"No, indeed not. When you say here, do?"

"I mean here. I made up the spare," said Susan. "Charles will have to move into our bedroom for a night or two."

"Oh. Was that necessary?"

"He wants to talk. Talk without fear of being bugged or overheard."

"When?"

"Probably the day after tomorrow. He said that they've identified Peggy's killer. He's a sailor on the Lenin apparently."

"I know that."

273

"Well David's got lots of things to talk over with us. He seems to be a very worried man. I told him about the 'weirdoes' who called here. That got him rattled. I told him we have police protection at the moment and he just remarked that that might not be enough."

****

The Lenin made the best of the windward shore, having crossed the Firth of Moray during the daylight hours on a northerly course. The light on Duncansby Head was clearly visible over the bow. As she tightened the sheets close hauled on a port tack she felt the full blast of a westerly gale in the Pentland Firth. In the early hours of the following day she pitched into the steep seas, first on one tack and then the other. It was apparent that she was making no progress with wind and tide against her. The four men in the f'c'sle were prostrate. They lay in their swinging hammocks unable to rise and clear the cabin sole of vomit and worse. Vladimer relented and ordered the master to give up the struggle and put into Scapa Flow until the weather improved. As soon as they lay in the quiet waters he ordered the bosun to get the forecabin cleaned up.

"Make them do it. They messed it," he said with relish.

It was to be another five days before the Lenin entered the Queens Dock on the north bank of the Mersey. Two of her sails had been torn to shreds by the unexpected gale. The delay gave David and the Chief Constable ample time to prepare a reception in Liverpool.

****

"David, David, David. I'm over here," Susan shouted as the throng leaving the train filled the platform. She ran towards him, arms outstretched. David placed his bag on a nearby seat.

She came to him and he held her. He planted a brotherly kiss on each of her cheeks, continental fashion.

"Oh dear, David, we're so glad you came. I'm so glad you came." A tear rolled down her cheek.

"Here." David proffered his handkerchief. "What's the matter?"

"Take no notice of me. I'm just a bit overcome that's all. We're all in a terrible state at home. You've no idea. We've got two police on duty. Uncle Frank's friend changes them over every two hours and even through the night."

"Especially through the night I expect."

"Our neighbours wonder what's gone wrong. They seem to think we're all under arrest. Charlie's completely changed since he came out of hospital. I can't make him out. He's so moody and quiet. Do you remember how smiley he used to be?"

David picked up his overnight bag and they wandered to the ticket barrier.

"Let's walk, shall we?" she said. "It's a long way but it will give us time for a chat."

Her arm through his, they walked across the city and along Wilmslow Road, past the Hospital and the University, past the Platt Fields and Withington. At the crossing they came to a café.

"Phew, I'm whacked. Let's have a cuppa."

They talked about their lives. For the first time David opened up to her and Susan told him about their schooldays, how her close love for Lucy grew out of parental rejection and how their meeting with Charlie had sowed the seeds of discord. They recounted their first meeting when David came to the mansion in Breiten. The many nights of fear, as Charlie braved the minefields on the French border, the terrifying journeys across Switzerland that she and Lucy had made, and the embarrassing moment when David witnessed their invitation to Charlie for a night of pleasure.

For his part, David told her of his unhappy marriage, how his wife, Mary, had flung out of the house one morning with their four year old son. They had had a fierce quarrel over money, yet again. She had met a tanker head-on, just as she reached the school, killing both herself and the boy. Susan recollected the brief notice in the paper she'd read in the previous July. Overcome with grief for him, she gripped his hand in sympathy. To her surprise David placed his other hand on hers under the table and smiled. As they strolled on towards the turning into Barlow Moor Road he placed his free arm around her shoulder.

"I decided then that I would never marry again," he volunteered. She paused in mid-stride.

"Why ever not?"

"I'm a bad chooser. I'm one of those starchy public school boys who never had any early contact with girls of my own age. Now I'm just too set in my ways."

"How old are you David?"

"Forty."

"There's ten years between us. Oh well."

"Dear Susan, what's that supposed to mean?"

"Nothing, just an observation."

They walked on but David pondered her remark and inwardly smiled to himself. "Maybe things are not so stable in the Robinson/Forbes household after all."

****

The Lenin looked majestic as she sailed up the buoyed channel into Liverpool. Just off New Brighton three of the harbour tugs came out to meet her. Close in, past the lighthouse, the coast was lined with sightseers. Ivan stood rigidly to attention on the poop deck while Vladimer and the master shouted instructions to the other three officers, stationed at the foot of each of the three masts. Instructions were relayed to the leading seamen on the yards who in turn ordered the furling and stowage of the acres of canvas. The tugs took charge and guided her to the dock entrance on the high tide.

"Why can't they moor us in the river? We don't need to be in this Queens Dock. We'll be trapped in there, just like we were in Hull."

"It's traditional Colonel. We are to have a Civic Reception by the Mayor and Council and we shall have to welcome the public on board. We are expected to charge one pound to view us and we shall have school children to entertain. All the money we get we shall donate to their charities. We can control our own crew at the dock gates but I shall take responsibility for allowing them to explore and admire the city in organised parties."

The Lenin slowly edged into the tidal lock and after the inner gate opened she was warped alongside.

Vladimer and Ivan were deep in conversation in the captain's cabin.

"Captain, I've got to have a line ashore."

"Their post office engineers tell me it will be connected today. I have a number, Chapel 2346. Feel free to go ahead Colonel."

"It's probably tapped."

"So you'd better be careful Rostovski. I don't want a brush with their security forces in here."

"Don't worry Captain. I know how to manage. I have a scrambler."

"So you came prepared?"

"Naturally. Shooting is our last resort. I want him here. On board."

"And bring their whole security police about our ears?"

"It's planned already. It can't fail."

"Would you mind telling me what your plan is?"

"Certainly, but not now. There are still a few things I have to arrange."

The following morning Ivan Rostovski, Nowak and Braun set off to walk to Lime Street Station and catch a train to Manchester. A policeman on the dock gate telephoned Superintendent Cyril Barker. An hour later he received a call from one of his own force on duty at Exchange Station in Manchester.

"Nobody answering their description got off the Liverpool train, Super."

The Super turned to one of his subordinates,

"Ian, double the watch on the Robinson home. The Ruskies got off along the line. We've lost them for the moment. Anyway they won't get far. If they're up to mischief it will be at Farmleigh. I'll phone them."

"Get me Jenkins please Claire." After a delay,

"Constable Jenkins here Sir. I'm on their dining room extension."

"Good, Jenkins, Listen, The Lenin docked at 1800 hours yesterday. Three of the crew, one of whom I take to be the Colonel, Colonel Rostovski, and two others walked off the vessel at 0900 this morning and boarded the 0930 for Exchange. They didn't arrive so they must have got off along the line, probably Eccles. There was no one on duty there. It wouldn't surprise me if they had a car waiting, so for the moment we've lost contact. I have the registered numbers of their Consulate cars in the hands of the Flying Squad but that might not be of any use. There are three more chaps coming down to you."

"How long will The Lenin be in Liverpool, Sir"

"She sails on the tide the day after tomorrow and in the meantime we must keep Farmleigh under constant watch. Do I make this clear?"

"Yes Sir."

Ivan and his two subordinates, had been picked up by a Consulate car at Eccles and driven to a safe house in Cheetham Hill, Manchester.

****

Wednesday morning in the Robinson household seemed to be like any other. Frank said he would give Charlie a lift. He drove to his office two mornings every week. He dropped him at the city hall where he had an appointment with the Head in the War Damages department. He was having a futile argument with him over the restoration of the old stables. Frank had told him it was a waste of time to persist with his claim for reparations but Charlie was slow to take 'no' for an answer.

"Will you be all right Charlie?" queried Lucy.

"I'll be fine. You're in more danger staying here but then you have the police guard outside and David inside. No one's going to take a pot shot at me in broad daylight. Anyway, it'll be good to stretch my legs in the shops. Cooped up here, it's not real. I've got to get out sometime."

"Why don't you wait till The Lenin sails?

"That won't make any difference. If they've got men on the ground here, in Manchester, then we'll have to wait until David gives us the all clear."

"When will that be?"

"It could be months."

"Let's just do our best to lead normal lives. Frank's friend promised us that we would have adequate cover. We've got to get out too you know. Susan and I want to take the children for a walk in the park."

"You'll be fine. Frank says that a 'cop' will be with you all the time. Anyway it's not you they want."   At the town hall, Charlie waited. The lady behind the desk told him that Mr Smithers would be free to see him soon. After an hour of waiting his interview was short.

"I'm sorry, Mr Forbes. Your application was considered by the Committee last month. You should have been notified. We are only authorised to aid the restoration of living accommodation. The stables at Farmleigh do not qualify."

"Oh well it was worth a try."

"However, your companion said he couldn't wait but he will be in touch with you later. I'm sorry."

"I didn't know that I had a companion."

"Oh. Well, well, I quite thought that the gentleman who came in with you was a colleague of yours. Never mind. He seemed to be in a hurry. Good day to you."

"Good morning," replied Charlie as he took his leave. He had forgotten the incident by the time he reached the pavement in the Square. He decided to pay his uncle a visit, besides which he needed to cash a cheque. He set off on the short walk to King Street.

"Excuse me Sir," a voice spoke at his elbow. "It's Mr Forbes, isn't it?"

Charlie stopped in mid-stride and looked at the man who had addressed him. He saw a tall broad shouldered man, wearing a light grey raincoat under which he noticed a dark blue blazer or suit. It was hard to tell which. Still smarting from the unsuccessful interview in the City Hall he took a moment to gather his thoughts. Should he admit to being Charlie or not? His accuser stood his ground, eye to eye with Charlie. Then he smiled and Charlie could not help himself. He smiled in return.

"And what if I am?" he said.

"Sorry if I alarmed you, Mr Forbes. I'm not the police. I am employed by the Manchester Evening Clarion. I watched you leave your home and followed you here. I'm also sorry that my boss asked me, instructed me rather, to approach you in this way."

Charlie wiped his smile away. He wondered how this man could possibly have trailed him from home. He was lying. He was sure of it. He retorted.

"So you damn well should be. We have nothing to say to each other."

"Why is there a police guard on your home, Mr Forbes?"

"Mind your own bloody business."

"It is a matter of public interest, Sir. If there is danger to you and your family then the danger could spread. Our readers have a right to know what is going on."

"And what do you intend to do about it?"

"We are in touch with the police Sir. There are rumours. We think it best to ask the man at the centre, the one who knows precisely what is happening at Farmleigh, Barlow Moor Road."

"How much does your paper know already?" Charlie asked.

"I can get you to see my editor within ten minutes of here, Sir. He will answer all your questions and we hope that you will answer all ours but we will print nothing without your permission. In a matter, which could be of importance to national security, my newspaper would be guided by you."

"All right then," said Charlie. "It's no use standing here arguing. Give me your editor's number and I will ring him from the call box over there." Pointing.

"What's your editor name?"

"Newman, Sir."

"And the number?"

"Ancoats 4367, Sir"

"All right then." Charlie pulled the door and shut it quickly behind him. He lifted the receiver and asked the operator for directory enquiries. He asked for the Manchester Evening Clarion." After a delay the operator said,

"I've got News and Standard but no Clarion."

"Give me News please," said Charlie.

"That will be tuppence." After he loaded the box Charlie heard the phone ring out and a voice answered almost immediately." He pressed button 'A'.

"Evening News."

"Excuse me for asking," said Charlie "But is there an Evening Clarion in Manchester?"

"Just a minute." There was silence for a minute. The voice came back.

"Hold the line please I am putting you through." Another voice.

"Yes?"

"I have been told to contact the Evening Clarion in Manchester. Please can you help me? Do you have their number by any chance?"

"There is no Clarion Newspaper in Manchester."

"Thank you." Charlie rang off and then rattled the receiver rest a few times to attract the operator again. He smiled through the glass of the call box to the man waiting outside. He placed two more pennies in the box and asked for Ancoats 4367. Another voice answered.

"Newman."

"Mr Newman, this is Charlie Forbes speaking. Are you the Editor of the Manchester Evening Clarion?"

"Sub-editor actually," a cultured voice replied.

"I think we should meet, Mr Newman."

"What is this about?"

"I have been approached by a member of your staff who wants to know answers to personal questions, Mr Newman. I am not prepared to be questioned by a so called member of your staff in the street. I don't know him or you or your paper. I will meet you later if you want to interview me.

"I'm a newspaper man Mr Forbes. My job is to ask questions and employ reporters to do just that. Yes, I will be glad to meet you."

"The foyer of the Midland Hotel," Charlie interrupted before Newman had a chance to say anywhere else. "Let's say four o'clock this afternoon." Charlie wanted this interview to be on neutral ground.

"Why not have lunch with me, Mr Forbes?"

"No thanks, four o'clock." Charlie rang off abruptly. Outside the kiosk he said,

"I've arranged to meet your boss later today. Now leave me please because I have business to attend to at the bank."

"Very good Sir but in order to make sure you are able to keep the appointment my boss insists that I maintain contact."

"Do what you bloody well like," said Charlie as he walked off smartly towards his uncle's office.

Some minutes later Charlie reached the bank. He informed the teller that he had an appointment with Mr Frank Robinson. After finding the long stairs he got past his uncle's secretary.

"You look a bit flushed." His uncle greeted him.

"Those stairs."

"You should have taken the lift."

"Maybe. Just a precaution that's all."

"What's going on Charlie?"

"We are being threatened, that's all."

"Charlie, I think the time has come for you to move out of our house. You've brought some pretty nasty characters to our home and I'm not happy about it. Do you think we're enjoying having a police guard? Hugo knew that you would bring trouble. He had more perception than I. If anything should happen to my nieces ……"

"I've just fixed up to meet a sub-editor of a Manchester newspaper which doesn't exist." Charlie interrupted. Frank paused to think for a moment.

"Charlie, you must be out of your mind. Bravado is one thing but stupidity is another."

"OK Uncle, I know what you think of me…much the same as the late Doctor Hugo. All I want is a hot line to your friend the Super. My bogus reporter is conning your empire at this moment just waiting for me to emerge. Also I want to speak to David. He should be at Farmleigh. I think he's planning to go back to London tomorrow."

"All right Charlie, you can use this phone after I've spoken to Cyril." When Frank had relayed the situation to the Super he put through a call to their home. A few minutes later the secretary said she had Mr Brown on the line. Charlie took the receiver.

"Hello David."

"Just a minute Sir, I'm putting you through now."

"David. Is that David?"

"Yes Charlie. What is it?"

"Contact, we've got contact. I've arranged to meet in the foyer of the Midland at four o'clock. Can you get support? Uncle Frank's already told the Super but he won't do anything without a call from you. Don't let him flood the place with 'cops' and frighten the enemy off."

"You'll be met by two armed plain clothes. Be at the memorial on Peter's Square at a quarter to. I'll fix that. Are you armed?"

"Of course not."

"I'll send you a shooter as well."

"No need for that, thanks all the same, not my style."

"No, nor mine Charlie. We can't effect an arrest unless."

"I know that. I was picked up outside the City Hall by a well spoken guy claiming to be a reporter for a non-existent Manchester newspaper. I'm supposed to be meeting his boss. It could be Rostovski in person."

"No way. They've got men on the ground here. Rostovski's not the man to get his hands dirty."

"So what's the game then?"

"The game is to shoot you Charlie."

"In the Midland?"

"Anywhere they can pin you down."

"So where do we go from here?"

"Your contacts will be arrested, have no fear. Once you've identified your man we'll move in. You keep out of the way and let the Special Branch handle it. I'll get the foyer cleared of the public before four."

"That will be a bit obvious, won't it?"

"Just leave the stage management to me Charlie. I'll be in the Central Library at five. You'll find me on the mezzanine."

Promptly at four o'clock Charlie walked up the steps and into the Midland. The spacious foyer appeared calm with several people standing near the reception desk commanding attention from the cashier and his colleague. Three couples were seated at coffee tables chatting idly. Charlie thought to himself,

"If this is stage management I'll take my hat off to David." There was no one remotely resembling his contact of the morning or the mysterious Mr Newman. He sat at one of the tables and picked up a magazine. He realised that he was a sitting duck for anyone in the gallery above or near the main entrance. He began to sweat. A waiter came and he ordered a coffee. Charlie could stand the tension no longer. He got up and started to move to the main exit doors. The janitor held one open for him. A taxi drew up to the rank. They had arrived. The man of the morning held the door for his companion. Then he turned and focused on Charlie who was standing on the top step just outside the door. Charlie froze. There was a third man in the taxi. He was holding a rifle and pointing it straight at him. He was trapped. His mind raced back over the last few moments. "How had they timed their arrival so perfectly? There must be an accomplice in the building or somewhere. Flight was useless." The bogus reporter of the morning walked up to him and said,

"Please be good enough to come with me Mr Forbes. He held a short pistol palmed in his hand, pointing at Charlie's stomach. He smiled. Charlie looked around in panic. "Where is the S.B. that David promised?"

He had no alternative. He walked toward the taxi. "Where is the bloody S.B.?"

"My God," he thought. "David's let me walk into the trap, the bastard." He felt the pistol prodding his kidney." His assailant whispered in his ear.

"You're a dead man Mr Forbes. Now do as I say. Answer our questions and then we'll take you home otherwise......." He left the sentence unfinished. Charlie thought, "Well, sod this. David must know what's going on. He said this was to be a stake out by the Special Branch. They'll be following for sure." He entered the taxi. As he did so he felt the needle stab through his trouser into his buttock.

****

The pier master at Glasson Dock on the estuary of the river Lune opened the tall gates to let the consulate's car enter. It had covered the distance in two hours. At that time of the night the A6 was clear of traffic. Once out of the city the driver had put on speed. He was anxious to make up for the time which had been lost in transferring the unconscious man into his car. The man calling himself Newman explained that the Police had been tracking them through the city. They shook them off using the oldest trick in the book. By placing the consulate's car at the top of the narrow alley, Nowak and Braun had brought Charlie from the taxi in a wheelchair. Confident that they were no longer followed through Preston the car turned into the narrow lane.

Sleepy Glasson Village had once been a noisy commercial centre. The dock had been built to receive the blockade runners from the Southern States during the American Civil War. The war over, it lay abandoned for a century until pleasure craft once more brought it to life.

Ivan alighted. The pier master handed him the keys of a large motor cruiser, 'Albatross' floating in the deep lock.

"Cutting it fine Sir," he said. "Fifteen minutes from now and you wouldn't get over the sill. I should've closed the gate by now."

"Thanks for your trouble, Pier Master. Here's my cheque for the owner and here's something extra for your good service. It's a calm night for a crossing we expect to be in Dublin by dawn."

Bidding them 'Good Night' and wishing them a fine crossing he left them to unload the car and transfer the unconscious Charlie. At mid-day following, with a brass band playing on the quay of Queens Dock and crowds cheering the crew, who manned the yards, The Lenin was warped out into the river. The tugs took charge and two hours later, under all plain sail, she set a course for Holyhead and then Land's End.

****

The Albatross and The Lenin made a rendez-vous ten miles north of the Skerries light off the north coast of Anglesey. The companionway was lowered and Ivan climbed up to the deck of the ship, a smug smile on his face.

"We've got him at last," he said to Vladimer.

"Can you be sure?"

"We're sure alright. He answered to his name when our man accosted him in Manchester."

"How is he?"

"Drugged. I'm going to give him a bucket of sea water to wake him up."

"You know the rules. I won't have them broken on my ship."

Charlie was still unconscious as he was hauled up the ship's side from the Albatross. Very few were on deck to witness the tight bundle, wrapped in an old piece of tarpaulin, which was lowered with little ceremony through the forward hatch. They stripped him and tied him back to front to an upright chair in the forward cabin.

Now Ivan stood in front of him stroking a bundle of leather thongs secured to a wooden handle. Bruno stepped forward and dashed the bucket of cold water in Charlie's face. With a smile of triumph Ivan said,

"So, Mr Charlie Forbes, we meet for the first time. I almost gave you up. Now if you want to get back to your lovely wife in one piece I strongly recommend you answer my questions. Oh, by the way, I see that someone has already deprived you of your manhood. Pity. I was looking forward to seeing that done. Never mind. I have other ideas."

Charlie shook the water out of his hair and eyes. With his hands secured behind his back and his ankles tied to the chair-legs he was helpless. Ivan passed the whip to Bruno.

"Give him ten across his back for a start." Bruno complied. Charlie convulsed and groaned with the agony. He felt warm blood trickling down his back. He knew he could not stand much of that treatment. Now he had another fear. Would these devils capture the twins or even the children and what would happen to them if they did? "Were the hell is David?" he asked himself.

Ivan interrupted these thoughts a few seconds later.

"You should know that I specialise in persuasion, Mr Forbes. We shall have you screaming soon. Tell me, was Carl Wogart working for you? Answer." Before Charlie could open his mouth Bruno applied five more lashes.

"Yes." He saw no reason to deny it since Ivan could not inflict any more harm on a dead man.

"And who is your control?" Charlie said,

"I work as a courier for Brigadier Morris. I'm not a spy."

Bruno stepped forward and raised his arm once more.

"No more," shouted Charlie. "What more do you want with me?"

"Do you know Rita Smidt?"

Charlie groaned but before he could answer the stillness of the day was shattered by a loud explosion. The ship heeled as the helmsman brought her up into the wind. The sails were taken aback. The yards shook and thundered, beating against the masts. The Lenin vibrated with the shocks. Shouts of alarm echoed down the open hatch. Ivan ran for the companionway but he was too late. Vladimer was descending. He said,

"The British are here. They're putting a boarding party on us."

Ivan turned and drew a pistol. He aimed at Charlie and fired. At the same instant Vladimer fired too. Colonel Ivan Rostovski fell dead. Bruno ran forward and grabbed the pistol which fell from Ivan's hand but before he could raise it Vladimer shot him also. Charlie lay in a pool of blood. Krause raised his hands and grasped the open hatch above his head. With the superhuman strength of a desperate man he heaved himself up and over the edge of the coaming. He gained the deck above. Vladimer looked up through the open hatch.

"Bosun," he shouted. "Get that man and put him in irons and then get down here with the doctor."

"Are you all right Sir?"

"I'm all right. Just do as I say and quickly. I've just shot those scum. Get help for that young man. He'll bleed to death in ten minutes. Get some clothes on him and ship him over to the Brits. Hurry man. I don't want him to die on my ship."

On the deck of the destroyer, HMS Bangor, David looked up and watched as a stretcher was slung across the gap between the two vessels and lowered to the deck. Charlie was taken below to the 'Bangor's' sick bay. David climbed up onto the destroyer's bridge. He spoke to the captain.

"I want that motorboat blown out of the water. The men aboard are both criminals."

At a range of two cables the Bangor's main armour opened up. In a most spectacular ball of flame the Albatross disappeared. David looked across the widening gap between the two vessels. He saw the tall figure of the skipper, easily identifiable on the poop of the Lenin, his arm raised in an exaggerated salute. In the Lenin's signal room, Vladimer ordered the officer of the watch to ask the Holyhead Coastguards for a telephone link to the Chief Constable of Kingston on Hull, John Myles-Johnson.

****

Back at Farmleigh on the following day the twins and David recounted the whole story. Charlie was returned to his ward in the Royal Hospital.

"You're getting to be a regular client of ours," the ward sister remarked. Charlie forced a smile of recognition. The surgeon said,

"You are the luckiest man alive, young Charlie. You absorbed every ounce of our blood stock. The bullet went clean through your arm, broke your humerus, grazed your lung and lodged behind your breast bone. It missed your heart by an inch." Charlie forced a weak smile and sunk into unconsciousness once more.

26 The Final Reckoning

David and Susan were walking in Withington Park a week after Charlie had been rescued from the Lenin. Lucy was visiting Charlie in hospital. Susan asked,

"So why did you let them take Charlie?"

"It was unavoidable. They had laid their plans well in advance even though the meeting at the Midland was arranged only two hours before."

"I don't see it. You had a dozen SB's around the place. You could have shot the man in the taxi."

"You've got to be joking. It was a real taxi. Imagine the fuss in the newspapers. Charlie didn't stick to my instructions. They had a gun on him from the moment he stepped outside. We gave chase but we lost them in Pendlebury. The launch they had was capable of twenty five knots."

"And how did you come to be on board the 'Bangor'?"

"HMS Bangor was our standbye, shadowing The Lenin. I had myself helicoptered out from Ringway. Luckily I got the flight straight away."

"Lucky for Charlie. Did you see his back? It's in ribbons. He's got to stay on his tummy for two weeks."

"I know. He held out as long as he could and any information he gave to Rostovski died with him. The gang, all bar one, are dead, thanks to Vladimer."

"Poor Charlie."

"You show a lot of concern for him. He thinks that you don't love him anymore."

"Oh dear. David, I'm not sure I ever really did love him."

"Then why on earth did you marry him?"

"You know why. Charlie loved me and I was having his baby. I thought I would grow to love him but Charlie never grew up. In some ways he never has grown up. He kept on saying that he loved both of us, equally. He was unfaithful. I still don't know the rights and wrongs of it, whether he was seduced by Lucy or whether he took unfair advantage of her. The only thing I am sure of is that I don't love him anymore. How can I love a man who's not a man?"

"That's a cruel thing to say."

"I know that but I can say it to you David. I'm being honest, with myself and with you. I'm not a very nice person."

"I suppose that makes two of us. We're two of a kind, you and me."

"How can you say that? I don't believe it anyway. I like you. Everybody likes you."

"That's my job, to be liked. It's the way I operate. Let's face it. I have used your husband. I trained him and I've used him. He suited my purpose, right from the start, strong, fearless, craving excitement, clever. He was ideal."

"Will he be ideal any more?"

"Hard to say. At the moment he seems to be depressed. He's convinced that I deserted him in his hour of need."

"And I."

"Why, what did you do?"

"Charlie overheard a joke I was sharing with his surgeon."

"Tell me."

"I'd rather not. Anyway it was a bad joke."

They walked round the rose garden for another half hour. They held hands. Then Susan broke the long silence.

"David."

"Yes Susan."

"You use people; don't you? Do you think you could use me?"

"In what capacity?"

"As your wife."

He received this in stunned silence for a moment. Then,

"Is that a proposal? Is that a joke?"

He stopped and turned to face her. Susan barely reached his shoulder. They looked into each other's eyes. He was the first to look away.

"Don't be silly," he said. "You're married already. You once said that divorce is not permitted in your family. Not without the gravest repercussions. I couldn't go through with that."

"Would you like to be married to me, David?"

"Don't try to seduce me Susan. I might say yes."

"You do like me a little bit, even though I'm wicked?"

"Susan I like you a lot. You know that. I dream about you."

"Trust me David. Let's make your dream a reality."

"How?"

"Trust me."

No more was said but David smiled secretly to himself. So he was right he thought; things are not so stable in her home after all. David decided there and then that nothing would stand in his way. Susan had proposed. He would dispose.

****

A week later Susan and Lucy were having coffee in the Kardomah Café in St Anne's Square.

Susan said,

"Lucy, we need to chat."

"Susan, how can you say that? We've been chatting for the last half hour."

"This is serious Lucy. Really serious."

"About Charlie?"

"Yes about him."

"About the children?"

"Them too."

"About David?"

"Yes, about David."

"I thought so. He's more than just a friend isn't he?"

"Well......."

"The way you kissed him when we saw him on to the London train."

"Can you keep a secret?"

"Depends."

"Please."

"Well what is it? I may not want to know."

"It's David. He proposed marriage."

"To you? That's terrible. I suppose you told him where to go. What about Charlie?"

Susan reached across the table and placed her hand on Lucy's.

"Yes, it's not so much terrible as terrifying. Lucy, dear Lucy, if Charlie proposed to you what would you say?"

"I would tell him it was impossible."

"But if I ran away with David, what would happen then?"

"I don't know, do I? I suppose that Charlie would want a divorce."

"Exactly, and then you'd be free to marry him. Would you?"

Lucy started to cry.

"You know I would. Why are you talking like this? It's all nonsense. I want to go home."

"All right, let's go home. You've told me what I wanted to know."

"Oh, and what was that then?"

"You'd like to be married to Charlie, wouldn't you?"

Lucy buried her face in her handkerchief. She sobbed all the more.

"Why torment me Susan? Can't I keep anything secret, especially from you?"

"Does Charlie know that you love him?"

"Yes. Yes he does. I told him. He was in hospital, the first time. He was suicidal. I couldn't stand by and do nothing. I told him I loved him, that I couldn't live without him, that his death would be the death of me."

"Oh Lucy, you're torturing yourself. I want you to find happiness. You can't, mustn't live your life out with the knowledge that your true love could be your's, but isn't. Don't you see? Between us, you and me, we can each have what we really want. It's not selfish to love."

"No, you are right Sue. I know that, but we can't do anything about it"

"We can and we will."

"How?"

"Not now. I've got to talk to David first."

"What about Charlie?"

"We can't talk to Charlie until he's better and you must be the one to do it." The twins caught the next tram homewards.

Three weeks later Charlie was discharged from The Royal. His arm was still in plaster. Susan said,

"David's coming down. He'll be here this evening. Let's all go to meet him."

"What's he coming for this time?" said Charlie.

"He has a letter from Moscow, from Commodore Vladimer Maikovitch."

"The Captain of The Lenin. Why doesn't he just send us a copy?"

"He told me the gist of it. Oskar Krause, the sole survivor of Ivan's hit men was put on trial and sentenced to ten years hard labour in Siberia but that's not all."

"Another assignment for me perhaps? It'd better pay well. No, I'm not coming to the station. My arm's giving me hell."

"Nor me," said Lucy. "You go Susan and don't come back here until you two have decided what you'd like to do."

"This sounds all very mysterious," said Charlie.

With Susan out of the way, Lucy said,

"I've not gone back on my word, my letter. I meant every word of it dearest and what's more Susan and I and, I think, David too are all in agreement."

"Tell me then. What is this about?"

"This is about us, the four of us. It's about the future," said Lucy.

"What future? I'm not sure that I have a future."

"Oh Charlie. Don't be like that. You've everything to live for. You're rich. Who do you want to spend the rest of your life with? What do you want to be, to do?"

"I don't know, do I? It's the scrap heap for me."

"Before I start this has to be a secret between us four. Frank and Edna must never know, nor Eliza, nor Bert, in fact nobody. Most of all the children."

****

Susan flung her arms round David as he alighted from the London train.

"Hey, steady on girl."

"I love you, I love you, I love you."

"Nonsense. You know you don't love me but you will, I promise."

"Don't be so pedantic darling."

"Is it all sorted out now? Do we know what's happening? Do Charlie and Lucy know the plan and are they in agreement?"

"Lucy's telling Charlie at this minute. We have to go and have dinner somewhere. Let's try the Grand in Aytoun Street." We'll get home about tennish."

"And tomorrow?"

"The BIG DAY, in capital letters. We're all going to the Registry Office."

"And after?"

"After is the BIG NIGHT, also in Capitals and then we go our various ways. Do you know where you're going darling?"

"Indeed I do."

"Dare I ask where?"

"You can dare but I'm not telling you until it's all over."

"Now we are getting mysterious, aren't we"

David just smiled as the doorman of the Grand Hotel made way for them.

27 The Big Night

On the stroke of midnight Susan and Lucy stood on the ornate landing between their two bedrooms. They stood facing each other about a yard apart. They were naked. Watched by Charlie and David, who stood in the open doorways of the two rooms, they each held a 'parchment' from which they read out in low tones in case they should wake Frank or Edna. First Lucy:-

> *"To my dear sister Susan,*
> *I solemnly promise to give up everything I possess to her, to take her life and make it mine, to be like her in every way within my power, to love her, to be true to my new husband, Charlie, and to guard this secret with my life until the end of my days."*

Then Susan read:-

> *"To my dear sister Lucy,*
> *I solemnly promise to give up everything I possess to her, to take her life and make it mine, to be like her in every way within my power, to love her, to be true to my new husband, David, and to guard this secret with my life until the end of my days."*

Susan said,

"Lucy dear, your ring."

"Not that surely, Carl gave it to me."

"Everything, that includes your ring."

"Not even to remember him by? He gave his life for me"

"Especially that." Lucy removed her one last possession and handed it to Susan.

"You can't give me your scar, Susan."

"It will fade. The surgeon said it will be invisible in less than two years. Meanwhile I'll keep it covered."

As a symbol of finality, Lucy, who had married David that morning, handed her marriage certificate to Susan and Susan gave her own in return. Each declaration was signed, duly dated and exchanged. Then they embraced and walked past each other, toward their new husbands and into their new lives.

The short ceremony over, David and Charlie stepped forward. David picked up his new bride and carried her over their threshold. Charlie, whose arm was still in plaster, had to content himself with putting his good arm around his love and guiding her into their bedroom.

****

Within two months David and Lucy took up residence in Copenhagen. David was appointed His Majesty's Second Secretary at the Embassy. Charlie and Susan bought a house in Bolton. He became a general practitioner. Susan enjoyed bringing up Charles and Charlene with doting help from Eliza and Bert who came to live near them.

Uncle Frank, Aunt Edna, Bert and Eliza Higgins never knew what had taken place on that fateful night when the twins swapped their identities. The mimicry which they had perfected in childhood came in useful at last.

Read "The Imperfect Circle" to discover what fate has in store for Charlie, Susan, David and Lucy, Charles and Charlene

Author's Note on 'The Black Diamond' and "The Isosceles Triangle'

The three main characters in my novels came into my head by chance when we were asked to write a short story, in our Creative Writing Group, based on pictures. The one I chose depicted a boy and two older girls dressed in clothes worn in the early decades of the last century. I became so intrigued with my own story that I decided to develop it.

The stories have unfolded as I wrote them. There was no cut and dried plan at the outset, although I knew where I was heading and how the story would end. The stories are fiction although historical characters do help to create the backcloth on which I have painted.

I have had more than a passing acquaintance with most of the places and events that I have used, although the details are my creation. I have had many holidays in Blackpool and Cleveleys as a child, but St Hilda's School is my invention. Similarly I have sailed in the Humber Estuary and kept a yacht in the Grimsby Fishing Harbour, although if there is a Dock Street in Grimsby I have never been to it, neither have I been to Cleethorpes. I have been to Zeebruger but not Dunkirk. Although there was a vessel called the Melrose Abbey, the ship of the same name in my story is fictitious. I know the lower reaches of the Rhine and the Scheldt through cruising there, also the Rhine upstream as far as Mainz. I have been to the Rhineland and the Ruhr whilst serving in the Royal Engineers from 1950 to 1952.

The small town of Breiten and the Lescault Mansion are my inventions. The details of Charley's exploits lifting mines and the minefields on the Swiss/French border are drawn from my limited knowledge gained as a result of army training. I have never sailed on Lake Constance/Bodensee but have motored along its banks. Paris I know quite well and Manchester very well, having been born and bred in Bolton.

I am also familiar with the docks at both Liverpool and the little port of Glasson, having kept a sailing boat at the latter for a season.

All the characters in my stories are inventions of my own imagination, although in a few instances I have borrowed names of friends and acquaintances I have met. I apologise to any who are offended by this. The descriptions of my villains are fantasy. I have never been to the Headquarters of the British Army of the Rhine and I have no reason to suppose that there ever was an organisation remotely resembling the Ministry of Intelligence, Special Unit.

I have been to Berlin and passed through Hannover but I have never been to Magdeburg, Brandenburg, Helmstedt or any of the places on the river Elbe. The town of Bad Salzungen is real but I have no knowledge of any convent there.

Vacha and the surrounding area are well described in the very informative books by David Shears and Anthony Bailey. There is also a good photograph of the bridge at Vacha in the book by Brain Rose so, although I have never been there, I feel as if I have. The maps I culled from the Google Maps.

The Russian Government has fostered knowledge of the sea and seamanship for many years in wonderful tall ships but the sailing ship 'Lenin' is, once again, my invention.

****

Acknowledgments

1   Doctors Geoff and Pat Newton and Dr Fiona Haslam for editorial and technical advice

2   Joy Mawby, Alexa Sturrock, Ian Hazelhurst, Myrrah Stanford-Smith and other members of the Amlwch Writing Group for editorial advice and corrections.

3   Bettina Frances for help with the German language.

4   The staff of the Llangefni Public Library.

5   My son, Pip, and my wife, Mary, for their encouragement criticism and corrections.

Bibliography

Along the Edge of the Forest   Anthony Bailey
The Ugly Frontier   David Shears
The Lost Border   Brian Rose
Hamburgs Hafen in der Stunde Null.   Jan Heitmann
Google Maps, Polyglot Maps and Euromap
Wikipedia

Author's profile

Born (1931) and brought up in Bolton, Lancashire.

Educated at Oundle and Cambridge, Hons Degree in Engineering.

Two years National Service, commissioned with the Royal Engineers mainly in Germany.

Graduate Apprentice with the English Electric Company, (Now British Aerospace).

Main Career, director of family Builders' Merchants, Haulage and Storage Company.

Married, Mary and had four children, two of each.

On retirement built a 40 ton Ketch and went sailing with wife and younger son for four years.

Now overseeing a family farm on the Isle of Anglesey.